DEAD RINGER

In old age Edwin James looks back over his scandalous life in law and the theatre: he recalls his rise to fame and fortune which begins as a debt-ridden counsel in the case arising from the Running Rein scandal of the 1844 Derby. He begins his hunt for the missing witness and the Derby winner which has been spirited away. Aided by ex-convict Ben Gully, he probes in the dark belly of the London underworld while at the same time trying to avoid his creditors.

DEAD RINGER

Prologue

I married your mother, so I suppose you have every right to know about me.

I've no doubt you'll have heard bad things about my life, for I've made many enemies in my day, and though I note that you look askance at this dwelling – and the single, miserable maid we have – you should be made aware that we have seen better days. In my heyday I moved among giants. There was a time when that old shyster lawyer Abe Lincoln sought my advice – though, admittedly, he failed to take it. Honest Abe! How he could be called that, with that light-fingered, shop-obsessed wife of his, I've never fathomed. And before I went to America I was on the point of being knighted, as Solicitor General, before that pompous prig Prince Albert poked his proboscis into my affairs. I think he was annoyed by the sparkle in little Vicky's eyes when she spoke to me that day in the Blue Room at Windsor. Because I always did have a way with the women, I admit. Even if, as it's been rightly said, I have the features of a battered bare-knuckled prizefighter.

But there you are: I took after my mother,

you see.

And though you'll be aware I eke out a meagre living now, giving legal advice here and there in London, I'll have you know there was a time when I was the highest paid Queen's Counsel in the land. One of my jealous enemies remarked maliciously that I made my name only in cases involving the reputation of actresses or horses, but that wasn't so. Name a big case, and I was retained as counsel. Palmer the Poisoner? I was briefed by the Treasury but they hanged the saintly Billy in spite of his weeping mother's protestations, but that was old Campbell's doing. A hanging judge if ever there was one. The Duke of Gloucester, when he was caught exhibiting his erection in the window of his house in Horse Guards Parade? I was on hand to collapse his construction in court. I was the one who proved that the rumours regarding the Bishop of Birmingham – that he shagged young girls while confirmin' 'em – were untrue. And then there was that scandalous matter of the rocking gondola in Venice: I got Admiral Codrington's errant wife way out of her depth over that little fling of hers. And we won't even talk about Lord Cardigan's creaking britches and cracking boots when I told the court about the private detective who was hiding under the sofa on which the hero of the charge of the Light Brigade was cavorting with someone else's wife.

No, the indisputable fact is that I was once sought by all, lionized by Society, £5,000 a year was the remuneration I earned at the Old Bailey and I was made welcome at the greatest of houses: Disraeli's, Earl Combermere's, Lord Lucan's, Lady Holland's. Never Gladstone's, of course – we had a spat when I suggested in court that he'd acted like a pimp after Lord Lincoln had eloped with the Duke of Newcastle's wife and put her in the pudding club. Gladstone took the comment personally, got into a huff, demanded an apology, but dammit, it was just *advocacy,* you know? And I obtained substantial damages for the grocer I was representing, so...

But there were hundreds of other hearings: you can read them for yourself in back copies of *The Times.* So it wasn't all just a matter of actresses and horses, though ironically enough, that's how it all started. Over a horse, I mean. The beginning of my rise; and in a sense, the commencement of my fall.

It was in 1844. The horse was called *Running Rein.*

Chapter One

1

Now I'm not going to pretend I was not getting a little desperate that day in June 1844.

You're probably well aware that the ruling pleasures of England in those days were gambling, whoring and bare-knuckled boxing. I never indulged personally in the last of these ... though I went along to enjoy the spectacle, of course. But I was certainly conversant with the others (I mean, few men at some period of their lives have not dealt in mercenary sex and the Temple was conveniently close to the West End for a man to take a young whore back to his chambers late at night) while the gambling clubs were a popular entertainment among young men of affluence and distinction, real or imagined.

During the previous week I'd had a bad run playing at *rouge et noir*, roly poly (roulette you'd call it nowadays) and chicken hazard at White's Club. I could have gone to my father but I knew he would be unsympathetic if I asked him to help clear the gathering cloud of my debts: he'd just become Secondary of the City of London and was getting all high, mighty, moral and parsimonious. My maternal grandfather *could* have helped: he'd made a great deal of money in the brewery trade, and he was always fond of me, but I'd tapped the spigot on that cask a little too much lately. So when I met Lester Grenwood that evening in the dandy hell at Bennet Street corner in St James's ... you know, the gambling house that was run by a former clergyman who used ruined gamblers captained by the Black Dwarf as recruiting officers ... I knew I had to be firm with him.

The Honourable Lester Grenwood was all smiles, standing there among a crowd of gamblers, with his black velvet collar and white corduroy breeches. He always did cut a handsome figure with his tall, athletic build, grey eyes sparkling affably. And when he caught sight of me he was affability itself.

'James! It's good to see you!' But he must have seen the combative light in my own eye immediately because he forestalled me in my determination to have things out with him. He drew me apart from his companions who were gathered under the glittering chandelier that lit the green baize tables. He laid a hand on my arm, squeezed gently. 'Now you know I'm demmed grateful for your signature on that paper ... what was it? Two hundred?'

'At three months, and it's fallen due,' I growled, 'and I'm being dunned for it. Look, Grenwood, things are a bit tight at the moment and–'

'It's not a problem, James,' he interrupted breezily, and flashing me a confident smile. 'You shall have it from me the moment the old man stumps up with my allowance. And in the meanwhile, why don't you do what I'm going to do? I'm in a tight corner like you, and in such situations it pays to be bold!'

It was then that he gave me the sure fire tip for the Derby. But no money.

'Grenwood,' I said firmly, 'I need *tin*, not tips. And the money you owe me–'

He interrupted me immediately. 'Short of the ready? That's no problem!' He put his arm about my shoulders and guided me across the room to introduce me to a lean, ancient, Dundreary-whiskered, shuffle-footed, dead-eyed moneylender of his acquaintance, persuaded me that my short-term debts could be resolved by a flutter on the nags and pressed me to finish a bottle of claret with him. By the end of the evening I concluded that it would not be Lester Grenwood, but Epsom, and *Running Rein,* that would be the solution to my financial embarrassment.

Epsom. I am aware that you've spent most of your young life at sea off the Americas so you probably don't know what Derby Day was like half a century ago. It was a great national holiday. London emptied early: by mid-morning the dust would be rising high along the Downs as the hansom cabs swarmed out of town. There'd be crowded omnibuses, fast drags bustling along with elegant dandies and their lolling ladies, costermongers' carts and post-chaises, barouches and phaetons, gigs, donkey carts and vans packed with raucous drunks and casks of beer.

On the course that day, as usual, blue-coated, top-hatted policemen were trying valiantly to control the gangs beyond the gypsy encampment, and the turf was crowded with spreading picnics while the Hill, the Stand and the Corner were already black with people when I arrived – among a mass of peers and pickpockets, tradesmen and turnkeys, parliamentarians, petermen and prostitutes.

I had placed my wagers on the nag Grenwood had recommended, but before I entered the Grand Stand to visit the parlours, or take refreshment in the Jockey Club I wandered around enjoying the scene: the betting ring, the groups of plush carriages laden with languid ladies, the 'glove repetitions' of the recent pugilistic encounter between Tom Sayers and Sam Martin – I'd lost a bundle on that sanguinary epic at Hampstead Heath too, believe me. There were Punch and Judy shows, performing monkeys, cartwheeling children, and foot-sore dogs prancing on hot tin cans, as they'd been trained to do by their spangle-dressed owners. In the overall hubbub Italian peasants, albeit with Whitechapel accents, mingled with German bands, painted clowns, red-haired villains playing the three-card trick and hunt the pea stalls that scattered as soon as a constable approached. It was all there: colour, noise, bustle, excitement. I loved it!

But I was waiting for the moment when the horses and their jockeys came dandling and cantering along the course. I make no pretence: my heart began to beat faster when the last odds were declared at the betting ring, and I had placed a few more wagers on *Running Rein,* and then I watched the churning and the shunting as the sweating animals twisted under tight reins. The jockeys shouted the usual obscenities at each other as they struggled for advantageous position – you seamen before the mast have no monopoly of choice language there, believe me; there was a plunging and shouldering as the crowd on the Hill bayed – and then the moment came, a rush, a trampling of excited hoofs and the great, ululating sound that burst from thousands of throats as the horses surged into motion.

The Sport of Kings, they call it, my boy, and so it is. You'll not appreciate the roar, the kicking turf, the thunder of hoofs, the colours blurring into a vast swirl against the massed background of surging spectators unless you've actually experienced it...

I recall well that the favourite that day was *Ugly Buck*, who'd already won the Two Thousand Guineas. He got caught in the mêlée coming out of Tattenham, there seemed to be a certain amount of deliberate boring, and he veered wide, perhaps knocked out of the rhythm of his stride. The manoeuvre immediately cost him his chance and he faded against the rails, caught in the trailing bunch. It was *Orlando* who then took up the running, but he was pressed close: glistening flanks of horseflesh straining close together, whips rising and falling, until the *Lysander* colt was interfered with and came limping to a stop. Thereafter it was a group of five in close contention, with two other colts pressing hard, and men waved hats and gold-topped sticks and cheered lustily, ladies stood up in dangerously swaying carriages, and the thunder of the drumming hoofs was almost drowned by the roaring of the crowd.

You can guess that the criminal classes were quickly employed: pickpockets were active as usual, scurrying like marauding rats among the excited, heedless throng. The horses swept into the final straight: the favourite was now out of contention, and it was clear that the second favourite, *Rattan,* was also going to finish way down in the pack. *Orlando* still held the lead but *Ionian* was at his shoulder, and two lengths behind them, moving up with a powerful late run, was the colt Lester Grenwood had recommended to me.

Running Rein, trained at Malton in Yorkshire.

Two hundred yards to go and *Orlando's* jockey was crouched low, his whip flailing metronomically; *Ionian* was fading and my throat was becoming hoarse as the unfancied *Running Rein* came edging inexorably to the shoulder of the straining leader. My financial salvation! If he came home I'd have a fistful of tin by the end of the day! For fifty yards they were neck and neck but *Orlando* was losing his rhythm, the Malton colt began to edge ahead and suddenly the crossing line was past, the race was all over, arms were raised, hats thrown wildly into the air, and pink-faced ladies sank back in their carriages, fanning themselves rapidly. As the last in the field cantered in disconsolately men and women were already turning away, back to the jugglers, the drink tents, the pies and the entertainment. Winners were seeking out the wooden signs

16

and soapboxes where bookmakers had cried the odds. Champagne was uncorked – there was the odd shout of "Gone away!" as infuriated punters discovered a bookmaker had decamped into the crowd – and I made my triumphant way towards the leaden-roofed Grand Stand.

For the moment, once I was back in the City and got to see my bookmaker, I would be able to pay the moneylender, satisfy my other creditors and my financial problems would be eased.

I bypassed the first floor refreshment room and the police court where two magistrates were dealing out summary justice to the thimble-riggers and pickpockets the police officers had managed to collar. I made my way to the Jockey Club, where I knew I'd find Lester Grenwood: I had it in mind to toast him with a glass of fizz for his assistance.

The room was packed when I entered and there was a buzz of excited conversation in the throng: Ernest Wood, the Epsom corn merchant who owned *Running Rein* was there, surrounded by members clapping his back, seizing his hand to offer congratulations. I watched him as he stood there in his brown coat with gilt buttons, red-faced, perspiring with happiness, accepting the plaudits of the members. In a little while, after he had enjoyed the congratulatory comments he began to make his portly way down the steps into the luncheon room. It was at this point, as the crowd thinned, that I caught sight of Lester Grenwood. I waved, he responded and I made my way towards him. He was beaming, his lean, handsome features alight with pleasure.

Lester was always the dandy. On this occasion he was wearing a coat with a black velvet collar, yellow waistcoat and white cravat in which was tastefully displayed a diamond pin. When I came up to his side he waved his champagne glass, his broad grin extended, white teeth flashing under his muttonchop whiskers. He clapped me on the shoulder. 'Didn't I tell you the nag was a cert? Wood's owned that colt for three months only,' he enthused. 'He's made the bargain of his life!'

'A happy man,' I agreed, glancing across the room to the owner of the losing horse. 'Like you and me. Unlike Colonel Peel, I'd wager.'

The colonel, you should know, was brother to the Prime Minister. He was a cold fish: tall, angular-featured, pale, haughty of eye and always soberly dressed. At this moment he was displaying his unhappiness in the iciness of his glance. He'd entered two well-fancied horses in the Derby, *Orlando* and *Ionian,* but he had failed to gain the prize he had lusted for. Both nags had lost out in the final furlongs to the outsider backed by Grenwood and myself. Colonel Peel was clearly not enjoying the glass of champagne he held in his left hand, as others gathered around him in commiseration: that inveterate gossip Charles Greville was in the group, along with Lord George Bentinck, and other members of the Jockey Club committee.

'Hullo,' I heard Lester Grenwood murmur as I swilled my celebratory champagne. 'Something's up!'

The Chief Steward at Epsom in those days was Baron le Tissier. The baron was a thick-necked, stocky man in his late fifties. I followed the direction of Grenwood's gesture and saw le Tissier shouldering his way across the room towards Colonel Peel. Lord George Bentinck met him and engaged him in lively conversation. In moments some kind of argument seemed to be developing, as they circled each other like snapping, disputatious mongrels. Le Tissier was shaking his heavy head in violent disagreement, and his jowl had reddened; Lord George was wagging his finger aggressively, and standing at the edge of the dispute Colonel Peel had raised his narrow, finely chiselled nose and was scowling about him in a patrician manner.

It was quite the wrong moment for Ernest Wood to swagger forward to present his compliments and indulge in a little peacock preening. But then he was only a provincial corn merchant and I suppose knew no better. Greville saw him coming and muttered something to his companions, Lord George Bentinck shot a cold, hostile glance towards the puffed-up, swaggering, triumphant merchant and, as Wood reached the group, Bentinck pointedly turned his back, stepped aside.

I made my excuses and left Lester Grenwood to edge forward on the trail of the corn merchant. I was impelled by curiosity, of course, but there was something else: a nervous coldness in my stomach, a forewarning of trouble. I always had an instinct about such things. I could always sniff out trouble. Not that I often acted upon such instincts, I must admit.

As Bentinck moved away, stiff-backed and stiff-legged, the group broke up, with Greville, then le Tissier and the others following him, leaving Wood to converse with Colonel Peel alone. Wood glanced after the retreating men and frowned: it was common gossip at Brooks's that Bentinck had wagered a large sum on *Orlando*, but Bentinck – the self-proclaimed 'dictator of the Turf' – was not normally noted for being a bad loser. And he was a rich man who could afford to pay up if he had backed a loser. Unlike me. With growing anxiety, I edged even closer as the corn merchant turned towards the owner of *Orlando*.

Colonel Peel's lidded eyes were cold, grey and expressionless. He was a taciturn, stiff-backed, lean sort of fellow at the best of times, normally controlled in his manner but known for occasional short-tempered out-bursts in the House of Commons. Now his mouth was set in a grim line and he seemed to be holding back a simmering rage.

In his excited confidence Ernest Wood was grinning, fatly innocent in his lack of social niceties. *Orlando* had not been the favourite: the sporting newspapers had all reckoned *Ugly Buck* would win in a canter. The betting world had reacted accordingly, and the corn merchant's horse had been a rank outsider – which meant a considerable windfall for Wood, the owner of the triumphant *Running Rein*. And more importantly, for me, when wagers came to be settled.

'Well, Colonel,' Wood said in an affable tone, puffing out his cheeks, tapping his hand lightly on Peel's shoulder and smiling broadly, 'a close run thing, as the Duke of Wellington might say! What was it, three-quarters of a length?'

Colonel Peel made a visible effort to reply in a civil tone. He inclined his narrow head, raised a supercilious eyebrow, brushed a hand across the shoulder of his sober, dark frock coat as though removing an irritating insect. 'So I am informed, sir.'

'Well, we can't all be winners, hey?' Wood

asserted gaily. 'And your *Orlando* put up a gallant fight, a gallant fight.' He glanced around triumphantly and caught up in the triumph of the moment could not resist the jibe. 'So will you be putting your nag out to stud, now?'

Someone nearby laughed, a ripple of amusement spread among the bustling crowd, and Colonel Peel's sallow features began to flush. Lord George Bentinck was now near the steps leading from the room, his hand on Baron le Tissier's arm. He turned back, gestured to Colonel Peel. His voice rang clearly above the general hubbub. 'We should be moving off,' he called out, 'if we're to get back to Coombe Hall in good time.'

Peel's cold, baleful glance slipped past Ernest Wood. 'You'll excuse me – I must be leaving.'

The corn merchant waved a careless, happy hand. 'Of course, Colonel. It's not a problem. I can call on you later in the week.'

Peel hesitated. It seemed to me that something dark moved in his narrowing eyes, and his lean, saturnine features were tense. He raised his chin in distant contempt. 'Settling up ... I'm afraid it will take me a little time, Wood.'

The owner of the Derby winner was grandiosely unconcerned. After all, he was dealing with the Prime Minister's brother, and they were all gentlemen together here. There was no cause for anxiety. He smiled, waved his hand in a gesture of generous acceptance. 'Of course, Colonel. Take your time. It's of no consequence. I'll call in a few days and we can discuss matters.'

There was a great deal of money at stake but for the moment Ernest Wood was in no hurry: he was enjoying his triumph. But the cold feeling in my stomach grew as I watched the figure of Colonel Peel cross the room, rejoining the sour-featured Bentinck, the Chief Steward and the committee members of the Jockey Club. Bentinck looked back from the tight little group, glared at the exultant Ernest Wood and said something to Colonel Peel. The owner of *Orlando* smiled grimly. Then they were gone.

A half-inebriated young buck at the edge of the crowd called out a toast.

'To Running Rein!'

Champagne glasses were raised, renewed cheering broke out, but as I watched the Jockey Club committee members leave in a surly group I had an icy foreboding of disaster. I hesitated, then gave way to my anxieties. I stepped forward, reached the corn merchant, touched his elbow. He turned, grinned at me. He did not know me: in those days I was merely a struggling, impecunious almost unknown barrister in his late twenties. Well, early thirties, anyway.

And if I then went and broke the rules that day, well, you must understand it was because of the coldness in my gut. And the money I still hoped to collect.

You see, the rules of the Temple were clear: barristers should not directly approach members of the public, touting for business. But, well, there you are...

'Mr Wood ... may I present my card, sir?'

2

In parts of the city on a Sunday, London could be likened to a sponge; it sucked in straggling droves of sheep, oxen and pigs, cackling geese and hens, while wagons crammed with calves and lambs were followed into the Uxbridge Road by cattle-jobbers, graziers and pig-fatteners, a swelling of life animal and human all heading for the holding pound at Paddington. Knackers' drags and insistent beggars mingled with a tide of Bible-thumpers distributing un-wanted religious tracts, ragged sellers of journals, purveyors of scandal sheets, and producers of hastily printed pamphlets containing explicit bloody accounts of the latest scaffold confession, while rabble-rousers surged about, noisily yelling among the boisterous, thrusting crowd of low humanity.

But elsewhere in the city it was different. In social terms, I tell you, my boy, a wet Sunday in London has nothing less than the aspect of a vast, ordered graveyard; in Mayfair and Belgravia nothing seemed to move in those days in the damp, drizzling streets. That particular Sunday in 1844, I kept close in my chambers most of the day and surveyed my prospects, suddenly gloomy again. The fact is, it's well said that there is not a harder life than that of a barrister in large practice – except, I emphasize, that of a barrister in small practice.

Particularly if he's been living well beyond his means by frequenting the clubs and night houses. And that was my situation at that time. Moreover, the bad news I'd been half expecting had just broken and was the talk of the Town: Colonel Peel was refusing to honour his wagers and, with the backing of influential members of the Jockey Committee, was claiming that *Running Rein* was a ringer. That meant all bets were off, and the money I'd borrowed to lay on *Running Rein* would have to be repaid along with everything else I owed.

I was distraught. You see, expecting the windfall from the Derby win, well, what I'd borrowed, I'd already spent on the tables at Almack's.

So there it was. I sat in my dreary chambers in front of a meagre coal fire and considered my situation. It was not a promising one. In 1844 I was already turned thirty years of age but making little by way of practice fees at the Thatched House Tavern and the Marylebone Police Court. I was under considerable financial obligations to various rascally, hard-hearted moneylenders and now I'd learned that, as I had feared, Colonel Peel was disputing the running of the Derby, with the consequence that bets were off. It was clear to me that I'd be hard put to it to dun my creditors, and keep the importunate villains at bay.

The result of the Derby was like a sore boil in my armpit. It was Lester Grenwood who had led me to his moneylender acquaintance, helped me lay on some of the borrowed money I'd put on *Running Rein,* his so-called sure-fire tip, and there was also the question of the £200 he'd borrowed from me previously, and never paid back. It was urgent I saw him, if only to recover that money.

And perhaps a little bit more to help me in clearing at least some of my debts. I mean, if you can't borrow from friends, who should you borrow from?

So, now that the news of Colonel Peel's default had been confirmed, miserable, and never averse to avoiding late hours poring over Blackstone's Commentaries, that gloomy evening I finished my brandy and water, slung an old *roquelaire* cloak over my shoulders and made my way out of my chambers.

There were various options open to me: Evans's (also known as the Caves of Harmony), the Albert Saloon, and other night houses available for carousing and song-singing but I decided against them. The Cider Cellars, I thought to myself: the Cider Cellars, that's where I'll find some congenial company tonight. And with luck, Lester Grenwood among them.

I hailed a hansom cab in Fleet Street; we rattled along the damp, foggy cobbled streets until the driver deposited me near the stage door of the Adelphi in Maiden Lane. The gaslights were still blazing outside the main entrance to the theatre, holding at bay the thin, yellow, whispery mist that scraped at your lungs, and there was the usual scattering of weary whores wandering up and down the road, footsore and limping, in various degrees of faded finery. That's the worst thing about their profession, I've often heard them claim: it's hard on the feet.

I'd always thought it'd be the bedsores.

'Hey, chuck, you want a quick one?'

I've no doubt that, as a sea-going lad, you'll know the alley-cats who throng the bordellos of the seaports well: it's a damned sight worse in Maiden Lane than Marseilles,

I assure you, my boy. They emerged with the fading of the afternoon light: gaudy and exhausted, gay and weary, painted, faded, and brazen, thronging the street, offering their wares to all.

I ignored the lascivious ladies of the night on this occasion, of course. I was on a mission.

The house next door to the Adelphi, the Cider Cellars, was well known in those days, throughout the city and beyond: it drew a considerable number of tradesmen and farmers up from the country who would be seen there, involving themselves in the singing and consuming large quantities of made dishes – a roast, a bird, a plate of cheese all washed down with numerous pints of beer or porter, or glasses of gin or brandy. But it was not their exclusive preserve: the clientele was wide-ranging. It included rakish young medical students and braying heirs to family fortunes, young university layabouts, guardsmen, hussars, and florid bucks from the clubs of St James's. I'd seen Thackeray there often enough, and young Tony Trollope was sometimes ambling about, while Dickens occasionally poked his inquisitive nose in. I must tell you about Charlie Dickens some time, and the way he lampooned me so unfairly in *A Tale of Two Cities*...

Anyway, the Cider Cellars was also a haunt of lawyers as well as literary men, along with politicians and judges and smartly attired members of the swell mob. When I shouldered my way into the crowded room that evening I was met with the familiar gusty rush of warm, fetid air, the smell of beer and wine and cigar smoke, and my ears were assailed by a roaring chorus of the favourite bawdy ballad of the day. You might have heard it yourself, along the waterfronts...

Oh, my name is Samuel Small, Samuel Small,
And I've only got one ball, just one ball,
Yes, my name is Samuel Small
And I've only got one ball,
But it's better than none at all,
Damn your eyes, blast your soul...

I had hardly entered the crowded room when a heavy hand clamped on my shoulder and a beery breath engulfed me. 'Edwin James, my friend, is it not a matter for public amazement that they should all still be singing about a murderous chimney sweep whom we rightly sent to the gallows from the Old Bailey last year?'

I turned in the crush of cheering, singing bodies to see a face I knew: Charlie Wilkins, stocky, pot-bellied, with muscular arms, wild staring eyes and generous mutton-chop whiskers. His waistcoat bulged uncomfortably under his dark coat, showing an expanse of sweat-stained shirt, and I suspected he had come straight to the Cider Cellars from a late sitting of the court. His pudgy fingers dug into my neck. 'Come on, James, I've got a table in the corner – been out to relieve myself and the buggers had better have kept me seat till my return.'

Reluctantly, I allowed himself to be dragged by Serjeant Wilkins through the crowd, half-deafened by the Sam Small chorus. I glanced back to see the man leading the singing: he was dressed in a loose, dirty smock and seated across a rickety chair, his face made up to a ghastly prison pallor with white chalk and rouged lips, and dark-ringed eyes.

He was waving his arms violently as he shouted out the refrain, an empty pint pot in his hand, but I felt there was something familiar about him. Then he was lost to sight as I was pulled across to a table near the stairs and room was made for me and Wilkins by the three men seated there.

I knew them vaguely: they were undistinguished members of the Bar, middle-aged, relatively unsuccessful but regular denizens of the West End entertainment palaces. They were laughing loudly, howling with drunken laughter, beating the table with their fists as the final words of Sam Small crashed out in a last triumphant chorus. There was a bout of wild cheering and the crowd began to break up, some fighting over tables, others starting to drift towards the doors, many calling for more service. In the milling pandemonium several chairs were overturned and one of the waiters stood on a table and appealed in a loud voice for order.

The cry was taken up in mockery by the drunken revellers: *'Or-dar! Or-dar!'* until it took on a rhythmic, thunderous beat. The barristers whom I had joined began to thump their pint pots on the table in unison, and the noise was deafening. Wilkins caught my still sober, disapproving eye. He winked, nodded towards another table that had just been vacated, located near the stairs which led to above-stairs accommodation occasionally frequented by clients and their companions. He led me away from his erstwhile company. 'I'm not as young as I used to be,' Wilkins remarked, panting and shaking his head as he lowered himself onto the bench seat.

'You never were,' I replied.

You wouldn't know about Charlie Wilkins, my boy. He was reckoned to be the illegitimate son of that holier-than-thou, do-gooding hypocrite Lord Shaftesbury. In his youth Charlie'd earned a living for a while as a commercial traveller, sang and told bawdy jokes in alehouses, was once a member of a group of strolling players, even did a stint in a circus as a clown – in other words had just the right training for a successful career at the Bar.

The judges liked him for his dramatic gestures and declamations. Clients liked him for his enthusiastic championing of their causes, successful or not. They felt they got a handsome return for their money. I'd learned a lot from watching his histrionics in the courtroom.

Charlie and I were good companions in those days. He died of drink, some years ago, while I was still struggling to make a new career for myself in New York, as a lawyer and a newspaperman. I regretted his passing. But there you are... I hear he had a proper send off, in one of Mr Shillibear's patent hearses drawn by black-plumed horses, decked out in the appropriate grim paraphernalia of woe...

'Aaaargh!' The apparition that suddenly appeared in front of me, I tell you, it made my heart leap in panic. The hollow, blackened eyes, the ghastly white, chalky face of the man who had performed Sam Small was thrust before me, grimacing and mouthing wildly. For a moment I was taken aback, half rising to my feet, and then I realized who it was. 'Grenwood! That was *you* leading the singing?'

'None other!' the Honourable Lester Grenwood said cheerfully. He mopped his brow: he was sweating freely and the chalk on his handsome features was streaked and dirty. 'What did you think of it?'

'Loud enough for sure,' I replied.

Charlie Wilkins leaned forward, grinning. 'But don't try to make a living at it, my friend. The money's not good enough.'

Grenwood laughed. 'I've no such intention. I just wanted to see how I could handle a mob – and I wanted to collect a wager.'

'Talking of which–' I began, seeing my opportunity, and always quick to jump in where money was concerned.

'Keep a place for me at the table,' Grenwood interrupted. 'And I need a pint of porter. Just give me time to wash this lot off.'

He thrust his way through the milling crowd, enduring much backslapping and catcalling congratulations. Wilkins watched him go. He pulled a face. 'Friend of yours?'

'An acquaintance,' I admitted.

'Wealthy?'

'His father is. Lord Havermere.'

'That bloody skinflint.' Wilkins shrugged and inserted a probing finger into one hairy ear. 'I acted for Havermere some years back. Had more than a little difficulty prising my fees out of the old bugger. I warn you, your friend will hardly be kept in the ready money by that tight-clawed old buzzard.'

He paused, eyed me reflectively with his sad, wise eyes, and shook his head. 'Talking of which, I hear you've been facing some difficulties recently.'

I sniffed carelessly. 'Let's just say I'm keeping close to the Temple these days.'

Wilkins caressed his muttonchop whiskers with thoughtful fingers. He nodded. 'Right. Sensible behaviour. Can't get you there, damned tradesmen.' He hiccupped loudly and took a long swig at his porter. 'Though it's said about the Inn that most of your debts are due to your activity at the gaming tables.'

I could tell from the tone of his voice that Charlie was about to give me sound advice. I'd had more than enough of that from my penny-pinching father. It was cash I needed, not homilies. Another song had started up. *There were three whores from Mexico and they went out to dine...'* I turned away from Charlie, and beat my hand on the table to the rhythm. Charlie took the hint, and devoted his full attention to his pot before joining in with the roaring chorus.

By the end of the numerous, sometimes repeatedly bawled verses, Lester Grenwood had returned. He had washed his face, removed the dirty smock, and looked reasonably presentable again in his well-cut, high-collared coat and somewhat wine-stained satin shirt. His face was still flushed with excitement and drink, however, as he took his seat and gestured to the pint pot.

34

'This mine?'

I nodded, and watched as Grenwood drained it. He turned in his seat and bawled at the waiter, who came hurrying across. Wilkins accepted the offer of another pint pot with alacrity; I settled for a brandy and water. When I heard Grenwood order three more drinks I raised my eyebrows.

Grenwood winked at me. 'Some people joining us. Crosier Hilliard's due here – with some company he's collecting for us.'

I stared at him. I knew Hilliard slightly: a moneyed man-about-town who had purchased a commission in the Hussars ... not that he'd ever stir himself to fight for Queen and Country... He was an assiduous frequenter of low night haunts. I didn't much care for him: he was little more than a loud-mouthed bully who enjoyed swaggering around town in his uniform, in my view. And while I was never a saint myself, there was one thing about Hilliard that disgusted me: it was his incontinent pursuit of pleasure. It marked him out as an appropriate companion if you were roaring drunk yourself and inclined to disregard flea-bitten hovels and penny a pinch whores. But on no other occasions. Even so, I needed to talk to Grenwood, so it seemed I would have to put up with Hilliard's company. A few moments later I caught sight of the moustachioed military man swaying his way through the milling crowd, with a young woman clutching each arm. He was drunk. Inevitably. And the women were free souls.

'Grenwood,' I began urgently, 'if we could have a word before–'

'Dollymops,' Grenwood chuckled amorously, eyeing the girls on Hilliard's arm. 'Out for a night on the town with the *gennlemen*. Lieutenant Hilliard ... ladies ... we would be delighted that you are able to join us.'

He stood up, attempting a low, exaggerated bow but staggered, laughed loudly and then pushed me along the bench to make way for the two gaudily dressed women. They were young, I observed, not yet twenty: they wore pork-pie hats with waving feathers, silk *paletots*, wide skirts. They had Irish accents, were giggly, foolish, and slightly drunk. They would not be Haymarket professionals, they'd have no pimps, probably be milliners, I surmized, or seamstresses, picked up outside the Adelphi, and out for a good time. There had been occasions, I admit, when I had taken some such back to the security of my chambers late at night, but of recent months I had become bored with that game. Couldn't afford it, either. Even dollymops came at a price.

Charlie Wilkins was not averse to the additional company: he'd already slipped his arm around one of the young girls and was whispering in her ear: she giggled and leaned provocatively against him so that the scarf she was wearing fell forward loosely and we were all treated to the sight of a half-exposed bosom of generous proportions. Hilliard sat down on the other side of the girl, across the table from me and looked a little angry. He had clearly been drinking heavily, and his plum-coloured roll-collared waistcoat was stained, marked with porter and chalk. I guessed he had helped prepare Grenwood for the Sam Small chorus, before going out into the Lane to pick up the dollymops.

'Right, Crosier, we made a wager, so pay up.' Grenwood stuck his open hand under Hilliard's nose. Reluctantly Hilliard slipped some notes into Grenwood's hand.

I eyed them acquisitively as Grenwood crowed, 'Never thought I'd do it, did you?'

'Never thought you'd be fool enough, that's for sure.' Crosier Hilliard scowled behind his flamboyant moustaches.

'Aw, go on,' the second girl disagreed, stroking Grenwood's face. 'I heard him as we came in. He's got a *beeyewtiful* voice. Good enough for the hopera, says I.'

But Hilliard barely paid attention to her. He was out of temper, glaring at the elderly lawyer seated opposite and the young woman girl placed beside him, clearly incensed by the manner in which Charlie Wilkins was fumbling drunkenly at the girl's bosom. His blue eyes were cold with fury and there was a line of perspiration in his thinning fair hair. He tugged at his side whiskers and leaned forward to remonstrate with Wilkins.

Things could get ugly very quickly in such circumstances as you'll be aware: you'll have seen more than a few bar-room brawls in American waterfronts, no doubt. I've never been one for settling business with fists so to create a diversion I tugged at Grenwood's sleeve. 'So, about this *Running Rein* business—'

Grenwood gave me an owlish look. 'Colonel Peel is welshing, I hear, but if you ask me it'll be that bugger Bentinck behind him, flicking his flanks with the whip.'

'That's as may be, but there's also the matter of the money you borrowed against that paper I signed—'

But Grenwood was turning away, guffawing, amused at Hilliard's discomfiture at the sight of his projected conquest being enjoyed by Wilkins. He himself had his own prey firmly embraced, and he leered at her, taunting Hilliard. 'And what did you say your name was, my pretty chick?'

His left hand was gripping the girl's chin while his right pawed at her half exposed bosom. The tightness of his grip had caused her heavily-rouged cheeks to puff out, and she was unable to reply. Hilliard, drunk as he was, frowned and put out a restraining hand. 'Go easy, Grenwood, that's not the way–'

'To hell with you, Hilliard,' Grenwood flashed in a quick burst of temper. He was always a bit that way, quick to take offence. 'The arrangement was that you were taking the other one.'

'There's not much chance of that, with this old lecher mauling her!'

'Lecher?' Charlie Wilkins was fuddled, but had enough wit left to pretend to resent the term. 'Now I could show you lechers, if you desire, but *my* intentions...' He hiccupped, and leered at the young dollymop, while he squeezed her knee and fumbled with her skirt. 'I assure you my intentions are entirely dis ... dishonourable...'

'Then I'll trouble you to find your own company,' Hilliard snarled. He stood up, reached across the table, grabbed old Charlie's wrist and twisted it, pulling his hand from the girl's thigh and shouldering Wilkins away from her. The push was a violent one and Charlie Wilkins was sitting on the end of the bench. I put out a restraining hand but was too late: my fat friend lost his balance and lurched sideways: his ungainly, portly body was too heavy for his drunken legs and he went down in a heap beside the table, his head under the stairs. He let out a shout of indignation, and struggled for a moment, but then looked up at the sneering Hilliard, seemed to have second thoughts about getting to his feet: he wriggled a little, sighed and gave up the fight. He put his head back, began breathing with a deep snoring sound, smiling at the stairs above his head. After a little while his eyes began to close.

'He'll be all right there, and out of harm's way,' Crosier Hilliard said roughly, and sniggered in a high, nasal tone. He slipped into Wilkins's place and put his arm around the girl he had selected for his own conquest. 'Now then, Cissie – that's your pretty name, isn't it? Drink up, and we'll have a good time here before we take you to one of the supper houses.'

'I'll drink to that,' Lester Grenwood agreed. He drained his pint pot, thumped it on the table, and roared for the waiter. He glanced at me. 'James, you'll be joining us?'

Suddenly, I was bored with the whole scene. It was clear to me that Grenwood was in no state to listen to my pleas for a little financial assistance to tide me over. I was flogging a horse that'd already expired. I shook my head, and gestured towards the man lying below the stairs. 'No, four's company – five gives a problem. Besides, I'd better get Charlie back to Serjeants Inn. He's due on his feet in the Old Bailey tomorrow morning.'

'Get the fat lecher home,' Hilliard said, his mouth vicious beneath his flamboyant cavalry moustaches. 'That'll teach him to interfere in another man's pleasures and handle what he's not paying for. For a penny on a drum I'd just as well–'

'Leave it, Hilliard,' Grenwood interrupted. 'He's beyond it, anyway, rumbling away down there like a flatulent horse. So, James, if you're leaving–'

I was rising to my feet but Grenwood suddenly stopped speaking. His glance had slid past me and was fixed on someone standing behind me. I turned, looked over my shoulder.

It's more than thirty years ago, you know, but the odd thing is I can still see her in my mind's eye, even after all these years. She was no more than eighteen, I guessed. She had soft brown hair that lay curling about her face, and she was dressed carefully in a becoming fashion, a white silk bonnet trimmed with ribbon, light cotton gown and a grey cloak. Her eyes were wide, dark in colour, and her complexion was fair, but she had applied a little too much rouge to her cheeks, and there were dark rings under her eyes. She was dressed for a night out in the West End, showing a fine bosom, but her mouth was edged with unhappiness, and in her eyes there was a mingling of anxiety, anger and sadness. She stood there silently, eyeing Grenwood and the dollymop in his arms, clearly distressed.

'Harriet,' Grenwood said after a moment, with an unpleasant sneer. 'Sweet Harriet ... come and join us! Here you are, James, here's company.'

The young woman's glance slid away from the girl Grenwood was caressing, to look briefly at me. She shook her head, almost helplessly, turned back to Grenwood. 'No, not tonight. I came ... I would like a word with you, Lester.'

Crosier Hilliard snorted, glanced at Grenwood and giggled in a high falsetto. '*Lester,* hey?'

'Come and join us,' Grenwood insisted roughly, nettled at Hilliard's jibe. 'You can take your pick of the company. I'm already engaged of course, but there's James here – or there's the old ruffian on the floor, if you can wake him up before morning.' He laughed uproariously. 'Get him into a hansom cab and you could turn out his pockets and he wouldn't know a thing about it. Or take him back to his chambers in Serjeants Inn and you could dun him for all he's got!' He eyed her with an insulting calculation. 'Now that could bring you a far better fee than you'd be accustomed to.'

She started as though slapped. 'Lester, please.'

The girl's voice was low and urgent. I watched her. Her hands clutched at the handkerchief at her waist, and her eyes were pleading with Grenwood.

'Please what? You want a word? Have as many as you desire! We're all friends together. Come and join us. James here, by the way, is an up-and-coming man of the law and you'd be well advised–'

I was sober enough to feel irritated. 'I'm leaving, Grenwood,' I snapped curtly. I was uneasy about the girl and disliked Grenwood's tone with her.

'Lester, please, I'd like a word in private.' The girl was near to tears.

Grenwood shook his head. 'Harriet, sweet Harriet, I'm having a good time. I'm not inclined to be interrupted at my leisure. You can't come in here with a mournful look and expect me to walk outside with you, when I've other arrangements in hand.' He grinned at the bold-eyed dollymop beside him and plunged his hand into the top of her dress, jiggled her breasts roughly while she squealed and wriggled in mock distress. He looked back challengingly at the woman in front of him. 'So, if you don't want to join us and look after James here, or the old sot on the floor, well, then get out of here!'

She blinked and there was the glistening of tears on her cheeks. 'Lester, I–'

'Lester, Lester, Lester ... who gave you permission to use my name freely in public?' Grenwood snarled. His eyes were suddenly filled with a cold fury and his tone was contemptuous. 'How clearly do I have to give you the message? I'm busy; I'm having a good time with friends. *New* friends,' he added emphatically, as he pulled at the girl beside him, hugged her to him fiercely, until she gasped in open-mouthed protest. 'You've had your time with me, Harriet, and for a while it was a good time, but it's over. You begin to bore me with your whining, you hear? So I'm not going to have a word with you – in public or private – so get out of my sight.'

A vein throbbed angrily in his temple. As he glared at her, I could almost feel the rage building up inside him. His tone suddenly became even more vicious. 'And another thing – that sporting brother of yours had the temerity to accost me in the street! You tell him if he approaches me again I'll horsewhip him within an inch of his life! Now, get out, unless you've got some other fancy young buck you can turn to here. Back to the street, before I get the waiters to turn you out. They don't care for unaccompanied sluts in here!'

It was as though he had punched her in the stomach. Her face paled. She took a step backward. For a long moment she stood there staring at him, as though she was unable to comprehend. Then her paleness was replaced by a slow, staining crimson as she became aware that curious faces were turned towards her from nearby tables, hearing Grenwood's upraised voice. She hesitated, trembling, helpless fingers twisting together. She seemed to be about to say something but the passionate words died on her lips. There was desperation in her eyes as she turned away, pushing through the crowd. A few moments later she was lost to view.

I had watched her go in silence. I turned back to Grenwood. I no longer wanted to borrow money from him or talk to him about maybe taking on my paper at a discount. I felt that badly about his vicious behaviour. 'That was ill-done, Grenwood, and harsh.'

'Harsh?' Grenwood snorted in contempt. 'If you're so concerned about her, go after her. No one's going to make a fool of me.' He pushed the dollymop aside in a sudden movement, stood up and leaned forward drunkenly, a vicious anger twisting his mouth. He faced me, knuckles on the table. 'Are you criticizing me? Over a slut like that? Because let me tell you about our sweet little Harriet. Have no illusions. I've given her a good time for three months now, which is longer than I'd give most of her kind, but she was fun, she could hold her liquor better than most, and she was good in bed. But if she thinks she can come in here to touch me for money, she can think again.

45

I've told her it's over, and that's enough. I won't be embarrassed by a whore in front of my friends.'

'She was distressed–'

'Distressed be damned. It was an act. I know what it's all about. She reckons she's pregnant.' He sneered at me. 'And we've all heard that story before, haven't we? She says she was a virgin when we met, and now she's with child–'

'The Immaculate Deception,' Hilliard sniggered.

Grenwood whooped with laughter. 'I can hardly claim that's the case, the way I've been rogering her these last months! But when she came up with that old story, I gave her five pounds and told her to seek some other fool to dun. And then her thug of a brother comes complaining to me! I told him he could go to the devil! Pregnant be damned!'

He snorted indignantly. 'It could be any-one's. She'll not convince me I'm the only man who's been mounting her at night. She's nothing but an amateur whore trying to step up market. But not with me, she won't – not on my back!'

'Nor on your front, either, hey, Gren-wood?' Crosier Hilliard laughed, and pulled the girl called Cissie closer to him. I looked at the two dollymops: they seemed some-what sobered by the conversation, a little scared by the appearance of Harriet, a girl not too much different from themselves, and alarmed by the turn of the conversation. But they'd soon come round, I guessed: with two drunken gentlemen to wine and dine them, they would take what they could get, and then give what they had available in turn.

'Stay on, James,' Grenwood glowered, sitting down again, wrinkling his nose. He bared his teeth, half-regretting his outburst. 'Look here, the evening's young. Let's talk, see what we can do about that damned *Running Rein* business. I tapped up my old man but–'

I shook my head. I'd had my fill of Grenwood that evening. 'I'd better get Wilkins back to the Inn.'

I called for assistance from the waiters: they were well used to this kind of thing and two came forward immediately. When I finally managed with their help to get Charlie lurching out into the street he was barely able to stand. One of the waiters called to a waiting cabman outside the Adelphi Theatre: he cracked his whip and rattled forward, scattering the small knot of hopeful whores at the stage-door entrance. I pushed my drunken colleague into the hansom cab and he immediately collapsed in the corner and began to snore. I climbed in beside him. There was a smell of damp leather in the

47

close darkness. 'Serjeant's Inn. Then on to the Inner Temple.'

As we clattered down into the darkness of Maiden Lane it began to rain, a fine light drizzle that thinned the clinging yellow mist, and I shuddered, drew my *roquelaire* more closely about me. It was an old cloak, and the style was going out of fashion. I'd have to get a new Chesterfield, I thought gloomily, as Wilkins belched, farted, and muttered incoherently in his stupor.

We reached the corner of Maiden Lane and turned towards the Strand. It was then that, in one of the doorways, head down, arms crossed over her breasts, huddling against the rain, I caught sight of a young woman. She was familiar; I wondered briefly whether it was Harriet, and I hesitated, was tempted to call on the driver to stop. But I made no move; then we were rumbling on and I sank back in his seat. It was Grenwood's business, I told myself. It was not for me to interfere.

Looking back now, I realize that was a fateful error: if I had interfered, things might have been so very different, for her, and in the long run for me too. If I had stopped the cabman, got out, spoken to her, who knows but I might have taken a different path in my life? I doubt it, but who can tell?

We clattered and lurched on through the

damp streets. I deposited Wilkins with the gate keeper at Serjeants Inn and went on in the hansom to my own chambers at Inner Temple Lane. I felt vaguely depressed. The fire had died. I shook out my cloak, took off my boots and settled into an armchair to partake of another brandy and water alone in my rooms before making my way to my lodgings on the floor above. I contemplated looking over the papers my clerk Villiers had prepared for me, but then discarded the dispiriting thought. There'd be time enough in the morning I lied to myself. After another brandy and water I went to my chamber.

I slept badly and when I woke it was still dark, perhaps four in the morning, and the feeling of depression was still with me. I drifted back into a semi-comatose state and finally rose, later than usual, groggy with snatched sleep; I was due in court at nine o'clock. Bewigged and gowned, I barely made it in time, clutching the unread brief papers that Villiers had prepared.

To my amazement, when I entered the Old Bailey I saw that Charles Wilkins was already there, bright-eyed as a squirrel and beaming about him. He nodded a cheerful greeting to me and then, papers in hand, rose to his feet. He seemed completely unaffected by his night's activities. He clapped his hand upon my shoulder. 'An enjoyable evening, what I remember of it,' he said, and winked. 'I gather it was you who conducted me back to the Inn: you have my thanks.' He grinned wickedly. 'We must do it again some time.' He looked about him. 'Meanwhile, your clerk's been looking for you.'

Sure enough, that scoundrel Villiers was standing near the door. He caught sight of me, hurried forward, apologized for missing me at my chambers. 'Mr James, I need to speak to you. I've arranged an appointment for later this morning, at Mr Cockburn's chambers.'

I raised my eyebrows. An appointment with one of the leading lights at the Bar? Alexander Cockburn, QC? 'What's Cockburn want with me?'

The collar of Villiers' shirt was grubby. He fingered it in his usual obsequious fashion. 'It's the *Running Rein* business. As is commonly known, Colonel Peel has defaulted. Mr Ernest Wood has taken out a writ. It is reported that the case will come on in the Exchequer Court. The Solicitor General has been retained for Colonel Peel. Mr Cockburn has accepted the brief for Mr Wood.'

I can still remember the surge of anticipatory excitement that travelled through my veins. But I managed to retain my casual tone. 'So?'

Villiers handed me a document, tied in

pink string. 'Mr Cockburn will naturally require a junior to support him. Mr Wood has requested that you be briefed.'

I stared at the writing on the face of the brief. The solicitors were identified as Bulstrode and Bulstrode from Exeter. But I also saw other names. Cockburn and James. A fine combination. And it would mean a fine fat fee.

It was my first step on the ladder to success. I knew it, instinctively. What I did not appreciate at the time was that it also signified the first step on a long, slippery slope downwards, to disgrace and ignominy.

You know, my boy, when you're at the top of the tree, it's a long way down. And the sad thing is, there's no bugger waiting at the bottom to break your fall.

But just then, standing in the courtroom with the brief for *Wood v Peel* in my hands, knowing it would be a hearing that all of London would want to attend, all I could think of was that my financial problems would now soon be over.

I could ride to glory, on the back of *Running Rein*.

3

That foxy little bastard Cockburn kept us waiting, of course, in his anteroom, just by way of making an unspoken demonstration of his importance. But the delay gave me the opportunity to become acquainted with the briefing solicitor Mr Bulstrode.

I could see at a glance that the burly Mr Bulstrode thought he knew a Great Man when he saw one. He came towards me, with a deferential bow.

'You come highly recommended, sir,' he averred in an obsequious tone. By the corn merchant, of course. This, on the basis of a card handed to a triumphant – now infuriated – horse owner. I'd been lucky, if unprincipled.

In the next few minutes I realized that Bulstrode was also the kind of person who considered himself to be no fool.

'I tell you, sir,' he confided in me as we waited, 'there are those who assume that, because I have a West Country accent and affect gilt buttons on my waistcoat, my wits are not as sharp and my judgment as measured as other London solicitors. They might think me a dandy...'

It was exactly how he impressed me, with his high-collared, dark-blue coat and stiff stock, the satin ornamented with a small diamond and pin connected with a thin gold chain.

'But to make assumptions about my perspicacity from such evidence is, in my view, shortsightedness on their part,' he averred.

I listened with interest, and kept my eyes on the diamond and pin. He was not yet forty years of age, he advised me proudly, and had already established a successful practice in London, from the Exeter firm his father had founded: Bulstrode and Bulstrode were now a force to be reckoned with in both the West Country and the metropolis. He was a relatively wealthy man and did not need to seek work, but he enjoyed the bustle and excitement of the London courts and the Home Circuit. And though he did not say so, he clearly enjoyed rubbing shoulders with Great Men.

Alexander Cockburn, as we both knew, was already a Great Man. A Queen's Counsel with a considerable reputation. And I had been highly recommended, so Bulstrode already regarded me with respect. He kept me entertained with views about his own connections in the West Country but leapt eagerly to his feet when Cockburn's clerk asked us to enter the chambers, and even stepped aside to allow me the privilege of preceding him.

Alexander Cockburn, confident in his social and professional superiority, made no attempt to rise from behind his desk when we entered. Small in stature, neat in appearance, vain, red-haired and somewhat vulpine in features, Cockburn had built himself a powerful reputation over the years. Not just in the courts, I should add: I had heard he'd scrambled out of numerous windows in his youth, just before irate, horsewhip-in-hand husbands had burst into marital bed-chambers. But the wild young bachelor was now considered to have matured into an eminent, sage and successful pleader before the courts, known for the vehemence and in-sistence of his cross-examination technique. At the Bar, of course, I still heard whispers of liaisons and visits to married ladies in the afternoons, but they were muted, and the talk now was of the significant successes that Cockburn had won in cases of moment.

So there I was that day in Cockburn's chambers, briefed in my first big case. I was convinced about the implications. *Wood v Peel* was destined to launch me on the road to fame and wealth.

I did not realize, of course, that it would also hurl me into eventual infamy, poverty and disgrace. At the time, I saw it only as opportunity.

'This is not going to be an easy matter to handle,' Cockburn announced in his thin, squeaky tones, tapping the brief on the desk in front of him. He took a delicate pinch of snuff, brushing some of the grains from the front of his coat as a stray shaft of sunlight gleamed in his thinning, reddish hair. 'On the one hand, we have an Epsom corn mer-chant – our client, Mr Wood. On the other hand, formidable opposition: a Member of Parliament and brother to the Prime Minister...'

'Ranged with Lord George Bentinck, Baron le Tissier, and the worthies of the Jockey Club itself,' I made so bold as to add. 'The considerable weight of the Establishment.'

Cockburn eyed me warily, weighing me up with a suspicious lifting of an eyebrow but Bulstrode was clearly excited at the prospect of battle. He intervened eagerly. 'There is a point in our favour, however. I understand there had already been a degree of internal dissension prior to the running of the Derby itself. Baron le Tissier and Lord George have been at odds. There were arguments about *Running Rein* before the race was run. This dispute between Colonel Peel and Mr Wood has been the culmination of a long established dispute involving other parties and it seems to me that our client Mr Wood might be able to take advantage of this situation...' His voice tailed away as he caught the hostile gleam in Cockburn's eye. He licked his lips nervously. 'I would of course defer to the consideration of the strategy you would wish to employ...'

'Strategy,' Cockburn humphed, and tapped a doubtful finger on the pink-stringed brief in front of him. 'It will be all important if we are to sway the jury.' He hesitated, eyed me once more in a speculative fashion. He knew I was a mere junior, not yet fully blooded. 'What thoughts do you have on the matter, James?'

I hesitated, aware of the self-important figure of Bulstrode beside me. It was there the purse-strings lay, not with Cockburn. And the solicitor wanted a battle. I affected an air of sagacity. 'I believe the strategy should be a bold one. The dissension Mr Bulstrode has identified is a weakness in their defence: mention of their disagreement needs to be brought out into the open; the dispute between Lord George and Baron le Tissier needs to be highlighted, because it tends to undermine Colonel Peel's case. We need also to obtain more information on the betting syndicate that is behind the whole thing. There are shadowy figures behind the scenes, putting pressure on Peel to raise this issue in court.'

Bulstrode shivered with excitement. Cockburn smiled drily: he clearly felt my description of the situation would be more in keeping for the courtroom argument than a sober discussion here in chambers. But I knew it was important that Bulstrode should be hooked.

'Shadowy figures, yes,' the solicitor murmured sagely, making an eager note in his pocketbook. 'I would agree, we would be well advised to attack those who are working behind Colonel Peel.'

Cockburn frowned. He knew it would be a dangerous sea to venture upon. His slim fingers touched his freckled cheek: he had a passion for sailing and had indulged himself over the weekend in his yacht, the *Zouave*. His skin burned easily, and there was an angry redness about his forehead despite the precautions he had taken with a wide brimmed hat. Somewhat testily, he said, 'Just so ... but how are we to bring these issues out? Mr Wood can of course testify to the original dispute between himself and Lord George Bentinck over the age of the horse. After all, that is what this case is all about, in essence.'

Bulstrode nodded vigorously. 'Yes, but it seems Lord George earlier lodged an objection before the Jockey Club, claiming that *Running Rein* was not eligible for the Derby. At the ensuing hearing the Chief Steward, Baron le Tissier, refused to countenance the objection.'

'We'll need to bring that out,' I suggested. 'And that means we must put Lord George and the baron on the witness stand.'

Cockburn's narrow little eyes shifted to me, as he noted the determination in my tones. 'That would be a strategy of high risk,' he suggested.

'But necessary,' I insisted boldly. Bulstrode's eyes gleamed.

Cockburn was doubtful. 'We need to be

careful. Lord George Bentinck and Baron le Tissier are supporters of Colonel Peel; if we call them, we'd be in danger of giving them a platform on which they could launch an attack on Mr Wood's case.'

'The Solicitor General will surely call Lord George to give support to Colonel Peel,' I suggested. 'We're going to have to deal with him on the witness stand in any event.'

Cockburn opened the snuff box on the desk in front of him, tipped some snuff on the back of his hand, indulged himself and sneezed, then took out his pocket handkerchief. He listened as I continued, 'The Solicitor General won't want to call Baron le Tissier, if there really was a dispute between the two of them about *Running Rein,* before the running of the Derby.'

Cockburn nodded slowly. 'You're thinking we could quickly establish both Bentinck and Baron le Tissier as hostile witnesses–'

'And treat them accordingly,' I added.

Cockburn smiled thinly. He could see I would want to get my forensic teeth into two hostile witnesses and perhaps it wouldn't be a bad idea to give me the opportunity. Slowly, he nodded. 'Were you to be addressing the jury, how would you describe the nub of the case, James?'

'A conspiracy by senior members of the Jockey Club, against an honest corn merchant, to deny him his rightful winnings after a fairly run race.'

Bulstrode almost bounced in his chair and beamed. He truly was in the presence of Great Men. 'I'll make sure the necessary papers are served as soon as possible.'

I smiled. 'I think we should also attack Lord George's own history, as far as the Turf is concerned.'

Cockburn's glance was cool and calculating. 'You think we can raise some ... ah ... interesting issues here?'

'I've heard a number of rumours over recent years. There are people I can talk to,' I said confidently, while Bulstrode wriggled in delight.

Cockburn pursed his lips. Like me, he had a reputation as a sporting man. He was himself well enough aware of the information that could be picked up in the clubs as well as at the racecourse and the prize ring, although of late Cockburn himself had tended to somewhat distance himself from such obvious pleasures. Women and sailing, yes, but the gaming tables and the night houses were now a distant distraction for him 'You're suggesting we should be trying to muddy the waters.'

'It will serve our purpose.'

'Hmm.' Cockburn frowned. 'Lord George Bentinck's reputation ... but we also have a problem of reputation to confront us.'

'Why so?' Bulstrode pricked up his ears. 'Mr Wood is a man of propriety, and recognized integrity who is only seeking to make Colonel Peel honour a debt arising from the winning of the Derby.'

'Mr Wood has owned *Running Rein* for a short period of time only,' Cockburn countered coldly.

'I don't see that this is a matter of significance—'

'The significance lies in the identity of the gentleman from whom Mr Wood obtained the animal,' Cockburn interrupted.

Bulstrode consulted his notes. 'A Mr Lewis Goodman,' he said after a few moments. 'I have no information—'

Cockburn cocked a quizzical eyebrow and turned to me. There was a gleam of malice in his eyes. He had clearly heard more than a few rumours about me. 'I imagine you will know him, James.'

There were few who frequented the West End cigar divans who had not heard of Lewis Goodman. I hesitated. 'I've heard he has certain ... interests in premises of entertainment.'

'You might call them that,' Cockburn said drily. 'One or two clubs off St James's. He's a frequenter of the race track and a provider of doubtful ... entertainments. This is the man from whom our corn merchant bought his horse. The other side will certainly want the jury to take a view of Mr Lewis Good-man.'

'We'll have to call him,' I stated. 'Mr Wood will give evidence as to the purchase, of course, but the history of the horse can be provided only by Goodman.'

'And back we return to high risk strategy.' Cockburn sighed. 'Our witness Mr Goodman will, I'm certain, prove to be a smooth, efficient and well-versed provider of evidence. He will speak with confidence and I've no doubt he'll stand up well to the Solicitor General's attack in cross-examination. But will the jury believe him?'

'If the man tells the truth–' Bulstrode began to bluster. I stared at him. His innocence was appalling.

Cockburn cut him short. 'The Solicitor General will raise issues about Goodman's background which could be damaging to Wood's case. It'll be up to us to attempt to limit that damage. Consequently, we will need to have the supporting evidence of others – grooms, stable boys, trainers ... not the most reliable, or highly regarded people in society, but knowledgeable.' He fixed the solicitor with a steely glance. 'You will apply to Mr Wood for names, Mr Bulstrode?'

'Certainly, Mr Cockburn,' Bulstrode replied, hurriedly making notes.

Cockburn smiled. A vain man of short stature and even shorter temper, he liked to

61

see how his personality could cow others. 'Well, gentlemen, I think that will do for now. We will require another conference before trial, of course, and if any major issues arise in the meanwhile, I'm sure Mr Bulstrode will keep us both informed.' Cockburn paused, fixed his eyes on me. 'Perhaps you would work closely with Mr Bulstrode on this matter, James.'

I was under no illusions. This case would be a sensation. The Press would be there in force. But it had shaky foundations as far as we were concerned. That was the sole reason why the shifty Cockburn was putting me in the driving seat. Cockburn would want the praise, if all went well, and he would get it as senior counsel. But if the case collapsed Cockburn would certainly not want to bear the responsibility. In his head, he was already preparing his ground. I had the feeling he might give me my head, while he took the fattest fees. But I was not averse to the challenge: it could make my reputation.

Bulstrode and I left the Great Man taking snuff in his chambers.

On the narrow, winding staircase Bulstrode paused, smiled broadly, nodded enthusiastically to me. 'Mr Cockburn, and of course yourself, sir, should give the Solicitor General a run for his money.'

'Ah, one should not underestimate the

opposition,' I replied, injecting a note of doubt into my tone.

'I approve of your strategy for attacking the Jockey Club itself. It's high time these people—'

'It's likely to be expensive, Mr Bulstrode,' I said shortly. The thought that followed made me hesitate, but I took the step nevertheless.

It was to be a fatal one, I may tell you. But Bulstrode was an innocent, and I had outstanding debts, and when one is in the hands of moneylenders... At any rate, I took the decision.

At the foot of the staircase I stopped, preventing the solicitor stepping out into the shadowed courtyard that led down towards the Temple gardens. I held his glance, with a conspiratorial frown. 'I think there's a great deal of work to be done if Mr Wood is to be successful. Cockburn has already suggested that you must get up a list of names of witnesses who can support Wood and Goodman. But this is a matter in which I could possibly provide some assistance.'

Bulstrode gulped. 'How so, Mr James?'

I linked my arm through the solicitor's and gently steered him into the courtyard. Surprised, for it was unusual for barristers to demonstrate such a friendly bearing towards the men who briefed them, Bulstrode allowed himself to be towed along through the sun-dappled gardens, beaming with pleasure at this intimacy.

'Though I'm a member of the Bar,' I announced cheerfully, 'I enjoy a life outside the Temple.' I winked confidentially at Bulstrode, one man of the world to another. 'I enjoy the theatre, I attend Epsom, the prize ring notes my presence from time to time – and a growing Old Bailey practice brings me into contact with all manner of unusual and interesting persons ... from all walks of life, if you take my meaning.'

Bulstrode glanced around him, leaned forward to whisper as though we were in danger of being overheard. 'You think you might be able to find out ... useful information?'

'At all relevant levels of society,' I stated solemnly. 'But it takes a little time ... and not a little tin.'

Bulstrode hesitated. 'Your brief fee–'

'Is for my work, of course, in court and outside it. But time presses, and a brief fee usually arrives late in the day ... sometimes many months later from some solicitors of my acquaintance, though I feel sure that you, Bulstrode–'

'Oh, I assure you, Mr James,' the solicitor interrupted hastily, scrabbling at the gilt buttons on his coat, 'I am always prompt in my payments of brief fees!'

'I don't doubt it, Bulstrode.' We stood at

the entrance to the Temple Gardens over-looking the noisy river, where Mr Bazalgette's Embankment now extends. We looked out over the river where the wherries and steamers plied their trade; pigeons cooed in the trees of the Temple gardens and a hansom cab clattered its way beyond the trees that protected the gravelled walks. There was the perfumed hint of roses in the air. I breathed deeply, aware that my bait was being taken. 'However, there are certain people I could contact, engage to undertake further investigations...'

There was a light grunting sound in Mr Bulstrode's chest as he gazed about him, considering my words: I guessed he was excited at the hint of using the services of raffish members of the London underworld. But this was an important case; it could help the firm of Bulstrode and Bulstrode significantly. He licked his lips and swallowed hard. 'If you think an approach to certain persons might be advantageous and supportive of Mr Wood's case...'

'I feel sure it would,' I said gently, admiring with detached approval the shady walks of the Temple garden.

'It's possible I could arrange for a certain advance of funds, Mr James. I could talk to the clerk in your chambers.'

I nodded soberly, restraining the relief in my voice. 'I think that the expenditure would be worthwhile. But,' I added, my voice dropping a tone as I leaned towards the Exeter solicitor with a confidential air, 'I don't think a conversation with my clerk would be advisable. What we are discussing here is a little outside the usual arrangements. The people I would be dealing with ... well, perhaps I should say no more. However, payments will be necessary – in advance – and I would suggest the best way forward would be the creation of a ... ah ... small floating fund from which drawings could be made. Fully receipted, of course.'

Bulstrode's lips were dry but the suggestion excited him: it gave him a daredevil feeling that was new to him – an opportunity to step beyond the constraining boundaries of the provincial city within which he normally worked, and to edge into the wider world with which I was obviously very familiar. He nodded, swallowing hard. 'I'm sure an accommodation can be arrived at, Mr James.'

I tapped Bulstrode on the shoulder, almost affectionately. 'The sooner the better, then, so we can move into play. I will take my leave from you now ... but I will be hearing from you?'

'At the earliest opportunity, Mr James.'

The solicitor bobbed his head, tugged at his gilt-buttoned waistcoat and proceeded up the lane towards the entrance into Fleet

Street where he would be able to hail a cab. I watched his plump, self-important figure waddling away for a few moments, satisfied with myself. I sighed with relief. I could foresee I was now about to get rid of some burdensome financial obligations. I turned, humming a tune and made my way back to my chambers in the Inner Temple.

It was time to send a messenger to Ben Gully.

Chapter Two

1

I met Ben Gully at the Blue Posts Inn. A man of the world yourself, you might have heard of the establishment ... no?

The Blue Posts was down at the lower end of the Haymarket. During the day it served as an ordinary public house but after the closing of the theatres and the dancing halls in the evening it changed its character notably and became a regular adjournment place for those still seeking entertainment. At midnight the passage from the outside door and the large space in front of the bar was packed with pleasure-seekers, and men and women thronged the stairs leading to the upper rooms. There was always a roar and a din in the thick, confused atmosphere, reeking with spirits and tobacco, but the Scots couple who kept the inn maintained a tight control within the limits they set. During the day, it was quiet, and thinly frequented.

It was the reason why I arranged our meeting there.

My boy, I need to tell you about Ben Gully,

who did much work for me in those days. A man of consequence. He wasn't a tall man, perhaps five feet six in height and his overall build made him seem even shorter. He had a thick neck and broad shoulders, a chest like an *armoire,* a cicatriced forehead in a face that had been rearranged from time to time, and the kind of legs that wouldn't stop a pig in a passage. He had fists like hams, and his knuckles were knobbled and scarred. There lurked in his eyes a cynical appreciation of the artifices of man, and it was clear from his demeanour that he was one well experienced in the darker activities of the metropolis.

Ben Gully was a man of knowledge. The throbbing heart of the London underworld lay at Ben Gully's fingertips. He knew all the larcenous families who flourished in Whitechapel, and those who carried out the acts of highway robbery, burglary and shop-breaking in Whitechapel, Southwark and Lambeth. He could explain how the parish of St James was notable for drunkenness, prostitution and vagrancy while Clerkenwell harboured the horse-stealers under the control of a ring led by a man from Smithfield. He could point out the centres for coining and uttering counterfeit coin, run by two Jewish brothers, in Covent Garden; he knew the embezzlers of Islington, the arsonists in Marylebone and could identify the thirty two illegal pawnshops in Mile End and Lambeth. He knew who frequented the four-penny brothels in Lambeth, and was well aware of what went on in 60 and 64 Regents Quadrant. Curious sexual activities I can tell you ... but that is another story.

Ben reckoned the smelliest part of London was Bermondsey: the south bank opposite the Tower of London was where the dog turds gathered by street urchins were used to tan skins and hides into leather, but the most dangerous area of the lot was Clerkenwell, because of the murders and manslaughters committed there. He could quote verbatim the reports of the Constabulary Commissioners who had access to the main sources of information, but his own network of informers and spies, vagrants, thieves and cutpurses gave him a wide range of additional information to supplement official returns.

He was proud of his knowledge and achievements. I had been informed at one time that Gully had spent his early years among the wooden galleries and tidal ditches of Jacob's Island, lived in cheap lodging houses down at the Docks and it was said that at one time he had robbed and assaulted with the best of them, emerging from the rookeries and vanishing again into their depths when the alarm was raised. But he got caught in the end, of course, by

Inspector Whicher himself, on a charge of passing counterfeit bills. Charlie Dickens wrote about Whicher, you know – called him Witchem. And that sly, womanising reprobate Wilkie Collins, now – he used Whicher as the model for the rozzer in that book of his ... what was it called? *The Moonshine,* that's right. Or something like that. Inspector Cuff, Collins called him... The charge against Ben Gully was trumped up by Whicher, naturally. Ben assured me that he had never in his life handled forged bills – but he couldn't complain because he'd had a long run.

Still, the spell in prison and the treadmill and the cockchafer convinced him there were better ways to earn a living for a man with his knowledge and understanding of the stews of London. Over the years he'd turned that understanding and knowledge of the London underworld to better account. He was now an enforcer, a purveyor of information, a servant to all those who wanted information and could pay for it. A boon for a lawyer seeking information. I was one of them.

And that's why I arranged to meet him. I had recognized specialist talents when I saw them, even then, as a young man. Though I have to admit it was Serjeant Wilkins who first introduced me to him.

'It's a delicate matter, Ben,' I announced

with an air of caution, after I had outlined the case in which I had been briefed. I leaned back in my chair in the quiet corner away from the bar in the main room of the Blue Posts and waited for Gully's response.

Ben had the ability to swivel one eye alarmingly to make an important point. He made use of that unique facility at that moment. 'You want me to find out about the man who sold Mr Wood the horse. You're talking about Lewis Goodman. That's a matter that's not just delicate, it's dangerous.'

'Come now, you exaggerate,' I replied in an airy tone. 'All I'm asking is that you let me have whatever information you can dredge up on Goodman. I've heard of him, of course, as a result of his ownership of night houses, but rumours are vague. If you could place a few discreet questions here and there so I can have the background information that'll be useful in the court hearing, I'd be much obliged.'

Gully frowned thoughtfully. 'You want to attack him in court?'

'No, no, certainly not! The likelihood is that the Solicitor General may attempt to impugn his reputation. I don't want our side to be caught out by any information the Solicitor General may have up his sleeve.'

Ben Gully scratched at a recent scab on his shaven skull. A fracas down at Rotherhithe, I'd been led to believe. He shook his head in doubt. 'I doubt there'll be much for the Solicitor General to go on, apart from rumour. Lewis Goodman is a smart character, a slippery customer who keeps all his affairs at a distance. He don't get caught with fingers in tills. He's sharp, Mr James – too sharp for flats like the Solicitor General.'

'But not too sharp for Ben Gully, hey?' I encouraged him with a wink.

Gully brought his errant eye back under control and observed me sourly. 'You can forget the flattery, Mr James. I'm telling you Lewis Goodman is dangerous. He's got interests and connections in London at all levels and some of those connections can be violent. A lot of people owe him, and he's a man who collects his debts ... one way or another.'

'You sound as if you're afraid of him, Ben.'

Ben Gully hunched his powerful shoulders. He did not care for the raillery in my tone. He wrinkled his battered nose and looked down, as though inspecting his clothing. On this occasion he was dressed soberly, like an undistinguished clerk in the City. But I'd caught sight of him at Epsom occasionally, dressed as one of the swell mob. I'd also seen him recently emerged from the rookeries where he'd been in search of information: on such occasions he was almost unrecognizable from the neatly attired man in front of me now. He dressed the part for the job in hand. But he didn't like the comment I'd made and he scowled. 'I'm not afraid of anyone, Mr James, but that doesn't mean I don't know when to go careful, like.'

'Then go careful by all means,' I replied, sipping my brandy and water. 'But find out what you can, so I can be prepared against eventualities. And then there's the other end of the scale.'

'Such as?'

'What do you know about Lord George Bentinck? I don't mean about his activities in Parliament – I mean his activities on the Turf.'

'Depends what you want to know, Mr James,' Ben Gully said, eyeing me carefully.

I wanted there to be no room for mistake. I leaned forward confidentially. 'Look here, Ben. I'm pretty sure Bentinck is behind the attack on my client. He's the man who's stiffened Colonel Peel's determination to bring the case. And he may be able to prove some sharp dealing went on. But he's been involved with the Turf for years. And that can only mean that his own hands won't be entirely clean!' I snorted contemptuously. 'He announces to the world that he intends to expose the corrupt practices and behaviour of those who frequent the races, but from time to time there have been rumours... For instance, I heard at one stage that he himself ran a number of horses under assumed names – Jones, Edwards, Bencliffe...'

'Nothing illegal about that, Mr James. And I heard tell it was because he didn't want his ancient father to know how deeply involved with racing he was. It's out in the open now, anyway, that old story.' Gully scratched at his broken nose thoughtfully. 'There's no mileage to be gained in starting that hare.'

'But there are other ... hares?'

Gully shrugged. 'When a man regularly frequents the race track, or the Berkeley Club for roulette and chicken hazard, there's always the likelihood of hares.' His errant eye swivelled in my direction.

I smiled ruefully and winked, so that Gully knew the shot had gone home. He would be aware of my own recent losses at chicken hazard at Almack's. I watched Gully carefully for a few moments. 'As far as Lord George is concerned, I did hear a rumour, something ... somewhere ... about a horse called *Crucifix,* a year or so ago.'

Gully shrugged. 'There was some kind of story going the rounds, as I recall.'

'You could find out if Bentinck was up to something fishy. Something I could use to discredit him in court if he gets up and starts spouting about morality and honour...'

'Aye, I could ask around. The jockeys, the trainers, the stable boys ... they'll know a few things, I don't doubt.' He eyed me warily.

'But it won't come cheap. It'll cost, Mr James.'

'Don't it always?' I smiled and finished my brandy and water. 'And it usually costs more when there are tight time scales involved, ain't that so?'

'When do you want the information?' Gully asked, nodding.

'The hearing is set for mid-July.'

Gully frowned. 'That is tight, Mr James.'

'Too tight?'

'Not at the right price.'

'It'll be paid, Ben, never worry,' I replied, nodding, and rising to my feet.

Not that I'd use all of Bulstrode's silver, of course. An appropriate commission would be deducted for myself. But, as I shouldered my way out of the bar of the Blue Posts and passed the grimy window, I looked back to the hunched shape of the man seated inside. Ben Gully had not moved from his position: he had remained seated in the quiet corner, staring moodily at his beer. He seemed constrained. And yet I knew he would normally take pleasure in bringing down one of the aristocracy. Lord George was a preening, arrogant man who'd made enemies enough. I guessed Ben Gully would enjoy slipping some of the mask aside to help expose Bentinck for what he was.

But it was clear he thought Lewis Goodman was another kettle of fish entirely. It would account for his gloomy expression as he stared at his beer. Ben glanced up, saw me staring at him through the window. His eyes fixed on mine and then, involuntarily, he shivered suddenly, as though someone had walked over his grave.

A presentiment.

Presentiments are wonderful things, my boy. I've had a few when I had certain cards in my hand. Trouble is, they rarely came off as you'd expect. So I shrugged this one off. All I could think of was the glittering career ahead of me if I could pin a prominent member of the Jockey Club Committee to the wall. But there you are: when a man's riding young, and full of confidence, he don't realize all the ditches there may be in front of him. And he's likely to tumble in more than one of those damned ditches, believe me.

As I did.

2

I was talking to your mother about you last night, about some of the voyages you took down Valparaiso way, and she tells me you don't like the climate here in England. Different from South America! I am forced to admit, here in 1880, it's been wet and miserable of late, with the yellow fog, and the infernal stink from the Thames – they only did half the job, you know, after I'd protested in the House of Commons, in my days as Marylebone's MP, about the state of the sewage in the river. Mind you, it was really bad then, in the 50s ... in those days we had to wrap our lower faces in vinegar-soaked kerchiefs... That was when I had built up a considerable reputation at the Old Bailey and was sought by all... A long time ago.

But I digress.

The weather was different, the time I'm talking about. In fact, it was hot and dry that summer of 1844. The sunshine seemed perpetual. June saw no hint of rain. In between hearings at the Thames Police Court I used to enjoy the air in the Temple Gardens, away from the noise of the river traffic and the hurly burly of Fleet Street. But by the time the case came on in early July, I had no leisure for the Temple Gardens: the weather had still not broken and the avenues leading to Westminster Hall were crowded as people from all walks of life converged on the Exchequer Court, which was where *Wood v Peel* had been scheduled. To get to court I had to muscle my way past journalists and pie sellers, fruit stalls and print makers and all the other riff raff who shared Westminster Hall with the lawyers in those days. Inside the vast hall there was quite a hustling: Jockey Custance made an early appearance, paying at the door for entrance to a good seat, and an unobstructed view of the entertainment. Others of the sporting fraternity were shouldering their way about, various members of the swell mob had made an appearance, and then, a little later when the carriages arrived at the steps there were deposited numerous gentlemen of note, members of the Ten Thousand, with their ladies legitimate and illicit fluttering fans, pink with the excitement of the occasion.

In the courtroom itself there was a certain amount of not so good-natured stamping, hissing and catcalling when Lord George Bentinck himself made his appearance. He was never popular with the mob. It was all an entertainment, you see. Was, and still is. And in those days you even had to pay to get in unless you were one of the principal actors in the drama, like me.

The old courts have gone now, but in those days the Exchequer was wider than the other designated rooms in Westminster Hall, and boasted tiered seats for counsel, witnesses and the public so all could obtain a good view of what was going on. I beat my way through the sweating, noisy crowd and took my seat beside Alexander Cockburn on the open, front row. I noted that the Solicitor General was already seated at the far end, poring over his brief, flanked by two junior counsel I vaguely recognized. Lord George Bentinck had taken a seat beside him. Baron le Tissier and Colonel Peel were seated stiffly in the row behind.

I'd arrived early because the benches allocated to the barristers employed were sometimes seized by idlers who were difficult to dislodge before the judge made his appearance on the bench. As it was, I'd been forced physically to eject one importunate, half-inebriated fellow who seemed to think he was in his rights, lounging on the bench with his half-soled boots on the table in front of him, before I could take my place. Bulstrode and one of his clerks were in the row just behind us.

I can still almost feel the way it was that day. There had been a late sitting the previous night: the air was still thick, odorous and musty and the dilapidated walls of the courtroom were damp. Mind you, I've seen the walls running with water on other occasions because the ventilation was so abominable, but by arriving early we were granted the leisure to inspect the dingy pictorial nudities which had been sketched on the peeling walls by bored witnesses, suitors or unemployed barristers the previous evening. Some of them were quite inventive, even to my experienced eye ... it's surprising what one could learn about life from the Exchequer Court walls. Though I have to say that the walls of the Old Bailey were even more instructive.

The courtroom filled up rapidly and the babble of noise was reaching a crescendo as the mob fought for the remaining seats. Like all the courts, the Exchequer was as I told you, a place of entertainment for the idle. And they knew *Wood v Peel* could well prove entertaining enough to the mob.

Baron Alderson took his seat on the Bench at precisely nine o'clock. He was a seasoned product of the Northern Circuit, a large, heavy man who gave the impression he was only half as pleased with himself as he had reason to be. He was a man of uncertain temper who was reputed to have a sense of humour. I never experienced it. Certainly, that morning he was clearly ill-tempered to a particular degree: his florid features were more flushed than usual and there was a malicious glitter in his eye. Bed bugs perhaps, or a female termagant with an even sharper bite. Rumour had it he was ruled by his wife, at home. He made up for that domestic humiliation in his courtroom by his treatment of counsel. His expression that morning made me feel the riding would be hard. Alderson was a strait-laced individual who was known to have little sympathy for or understanding of the sporting fraternity and held decided, somewhat puritanical views about their reported behaviour.

Once the jostling on the benches had subsided the learned judge glowered around at his kingdom and invited Alexander Cockburn to open in *Wood v Peel*.

As always, my foxy little leader was clear, concise and relevant, indulged in no wild rhetoric, but he was so brief that I wondered whether he had another case pending elsewhere and was eager to get away. Even so the courtroom listened with interest as they heard Cockburn claim that Ernest Wood, the corn merchant from Epsom, had bought the colt *Running Rein* and entered it in the Derby.

'The animal had a good pedigree,' he said, 'and I will shortly prove that the dispute between Mr Wood and Lord George Bentinck had really arisen prior to the running of the Derby. The reason behind the dispute? Not the age of the animal that eventually won, the dispute had arisen because Lord George had a runner in the race, was concerned about the form of his animal, feared the danger presented by Mr Wood's entry, and so earlier conspired to prevent the entry of *Running Rein* by unfounded claims. But he failed in his attempt. Later, after the race was run and his own horses lost, he persuaded the Jockey Club to support Colonel Peel in a refusal to honour bets made against the winning animal.'

Baron Alderson was already unhappy. He shifted uncomfortably on the Bench, glowered at Cockburn and sniffed. 'I wonder whether learned counsel would make something clear to me,' he growled.

'Certainly, my lord.'

'Precisely who is supposed to be the defendant in this case?'

'Colonel Peel, my lord.'

'From your opening remarks you would seem to be suggesting that it is Lord George Bentinck who should be the defendant, but I see his name nowhere in the pleadings.'

Cockburn's thin nostrils were pinched. 'There is a thought that Lord George Bentinck *should* be the real defendant in the case—'

The Solicitor General jumped up to intervene. Small, plump, soft-fingered, fussy of dress, precise of diction and careful of language, Fitzroy Kelly was one of those men who had got on at the bar in an uncommon fashion, by marrying the ugly daughter of a judge. Though come to think of it most daughters of judges are ugly... Kelly was also one of those benchers of the Inner Temple who did for me, years later, with trumped up charges. I disliked him in 1844: my dislike grew over the years.

That day in the Exchequer Court he exuded his usual air of finicky self-confidence. 'As your lordship rightly points out, Lord

George Bentinck is not a defendant here: the issue is a clear cut one, which Colonel Peel will defend to the death. The colt known as *Running Rein is* nothing but a–'

'Mr Kelly, I need no assistance from you,' Baron Alderson interrupted sourly, raising one hand. 'You will have your opportunity for argument later.'

Unabashed, Fitzroy Kelly regained his seat. But he always was a thick-skinned man. Applepip Kelly he was called, after making the preposterous defence in one poisoning case that the deceased had passed away as a result of eating apples.

As Cockburn continued his opening speech, I glanced across to the tiered witness seats. Ernest Wood, the plaintiff, was there, pale, his mouth uncertain, clearly unnerved by the situation. A great deal had been said of recent weeks: innuendos had flown about; it was understood he had been cut by certain members of the Jockey Club and some of the gentry had implied that he was lowering himself in the eyes of polite society, bringing this case against the Prime Minister's brother. But there was a doggedness about his eyes, I noted: he had steeled himself to see it through. His honour had been impugned: Colonel Peel had welshed on a bet.

Beside Wood sat a small, wiry man with a bald head and fashionable muttonchop whiskers. He had quick, intelligent eyes and a tanned, wrinkled skin: a man of the out-doors. He was leaning sideways, listening to a lean, younger man with short cropped hair. I checked his witness list: the younger man would be John Marsh, a stable boy we would be calling to testify as to the age of the colt; the older, clean-shaven individual was the man Ben Gully had traced and persuaded to come to court.

John Day.

There should have been another witness from the stables, but I could not pick him out. As I looked around I saw that Ben Gully himself was in court, quietly tucked away on one of the end seats where he could escape the court easily if proceedings became boring, or his presence was required elsewhere. I nodded briefly: Gully rolled his errant eye at me in silent acknowledgement.

Seated behind John Day was Lewis Goodman.

Goodman cut an impressive figure. He was tall, clean-shaven and slimly built, with athletic shoulders and a dark, somewhat swarthy skin. His smooth black hair was thick, neatly swept back on his head. He was of an almost Mediterranean appearance, the flash kind that would appeal to the ladies. His coat was expensively cut, a collar of velvet, the overall appearance fashionably moderate, apart from the heavy gold chain that adorned his vest. He would like gold, this man. Heavy eyebrows shielded Goodman's eyes which seemed almost black. He caught my glance and held it, raised one eyebrow, riveting my attention. There was a certain appraisal in his eyes. Before I looked away, I noted that a slight smile touched his firm, confident mouth; it was as though he had summed up my character, filed away in his mind a picture of who and what I was. It made me feel uncomfortable as I turned away, leaned forward, to pay attention to Cockburn's opening.

I kept glancing back in a surreptitious manner, seeking out Goodman for a while, irritated by the impression he had made on me. I tried to match his attitude by making my own summation of the man. I concluded he was a little too elegant, too well dressed, too confident in his air of cool confidence. He was almost flash, as though he was trying too hard; his rolled collar waistcoat was not flamboyant but its cut was too precise and his satin stock was a little too rich for my taste, as was the diamond pin that gleamed on his breast. Lewis Goodman was a gentleman trying to *prove* he was a gentleman, and there would be reasons for that. I had heard some of those reasons lay in the dark corners of the Haymarket and the Strand, and at Epsom; they were backed by a clientele that would use him but perhaps never approve of him.

Ben Gully had said he was a dangerous man.

It was just then I began to feel uneasy, as I looked away and glanced around the packed benches. I still couldn't locate the missing witness. I inclined my head towards Bulstrode, seated behind me. He leaned forward, eagerly. I tapped my brief with an irritated finger. 'I've got a name ... Bartle. Where is he?'

Bulstrode grimaced, glanced sideways to John Day and wriggled unhappily. 'I regret ... it seems he has not put in an appearance this morning.'

'Where the devil is he?'

'No one seems to know. He works at *Running Rein's* stables, but he just hasn't turned up this morning to give evidence.'

I was far from pleased, I can tell you. Even in those relatively inexperienced days I never did like missing witnesses. They were like unseen shore cannon to a man-o'-war: they could send an over-confident ship to the bottom of the sea. I went back to my brief and the notes that Ben Gully had provided concerning John Day. Perhaps we wouldn't need the missing stable hand, Joe Bartle. He was only there to support the evidence to be given by Lewis Goodman. He was there for corroboration, but even so his non-appearance made me nervous.

I waited as Cockburn wound up his opening statement. He then called Ernest Wood. We soon got to the nub of the matter, as the mob drummed impatient feet on the tiered benches.

Ernest Wood was sweating, but determined in his evidence. 'Prior to the race large sums of money had been laid upon horses other than my own – notably, *Orlando* and *Ionian*. When I proclaimed the intention of entering *Running Rein* I was informed that a protest had been lodged.'

'By whom?' Cockburn asked, glancing around the courtroom theatrically.

'Lord George Bentinck.'

'Why do you think such a protest was lodged?'

'Because Lord George–'

'My lord,' the Solicitor General rose to his feet, twitching his robe about his plump thighs in a pompous gesture. 'Mr Wood is in no position to describe the state of mind of Lord George.'

When Baron Alderson agreed grumpily Cockburn smiled. 'I waive the question. The matter can be dealt with later. Please continue, Mr Wood. What happened then?'

'The protest was taken to the Committee of the Jockey Club.'

'What was the result of the objection?'

'It was refused.'

'And then?'

'The rest is a matter of undisputed fact,'

Wood said stoutly. '*Running Rein* was permitted to run and won the Derby. Colonel Peel's horses *Orlando* and *Ionian* lost. And then, to my surprise, Colonel Peel refused to honour his bets. I was thus forced to bring this action.'

'The details of the betting, and the amounts involved, are to be seen in the affidavits, my lord,' Cockburn drawled. He began to go through the individual amounts until Fitzroy Kelly rose and announced airily that the amounts of the debts were not in dispute. I could guess why: he didn't want the extent of Bentinck's betting, and interest in disputing the identity of *Running Rein* to be emphasized in open court. The mob didn't like it and feet drummed again. Baron Alderson scowled them to silence.

As Cockburn ended his examination, the Solicitor General rose to cross examine the corn merchant, and as might be expected, went straight to what the other side saw as the point in issue.

'How long did you own the horse before entering it for the Derby?'

'Three months.'

'From whom did you purchase the animal?'

'A Mr Lewis Goodman.'

'And what was the ground on which Colonel Peel has refused to honour the bets placed?'

Wood hesitated, flushing. 'He claimed that *Running Rein* was not eligible since it was in reality a four year old.'

'Thank you.'

Fitzroy Kelly sat down. He had made no reference to the enquiry before the Committee of the Jockey Club. It was something we could use to twist the knife.

Cockburn nodded to me to deal with re-examination. I rose and smiled at Wood, putting him more at ease, injecting some confidence into him, even though the blood was hammering in my own veins. My first big opportunity, with a baying mob and a courtroom full of reporters...

'Is *Running Rein* a four year old, Mr Wood?'

'Certainly not.'

'And are you alone in your opinion?'

'I have the animal's pedigree from Mr Goodman.'

'And this claim of Colonel Peel ... that the horse is really a four year old, had not this claim been dealt with elsewhere previously? Had it not already been answered on a previous occasion?'

'Of course,' Wood said quickly, recognizing my drift. 'It was the substance of the protest made prior to the race, to the Jockey Club, by Lord George Bentinck.'

'Which was...'

'Refused, sir.' Indignantly, Ernest Wood

appealed to the judge. 'The Stewards of the Jockey Club supported me, but Colonel Peel still refused to pay out after the race was won, because of the insistence of Lord George Bentinck!'

A storm of hissing and catcalling broke out as the unruly mob at the back of the room stamped their feet and expressed their support of the corn merchant against the might of the racing aristocracy. Bentinck was scarlet-faced with anger as he leaned forward, thick fingers clamped on his gold-topped walking stick. Baron Alderson hammered at the bench, and the lady seated beside him fluttered her fan while her companion Lord Stradbroke leaned forward to assure her all was well and this scene would not be comparable in its conclusion to the storming of the Bastille. When the noise finally subsided, I sat down and Wood was released from the witness box.

Cockburn smiled slightly at me, nodded, satisfied with the uproar, and then rose to his feet. It was time to call Lewis Goodman.

Goodman was well over six feet in height. There was a great deal of chattering in the courtroom and it was evident that his appearance was well recognized by the sporting fraternity who were present. The ladies in particular leaned forward to get a better view of the witness. There was a certain amount of fan-fluttering and sighing, amid a great deal of cat-calling from the mob.

Cockburn took Goodman through his evidence quickly. Goodman stated that the colt had been bred in Ireland where it had been trained by one Sam McGuire. Mr McGuire was presently in Ireland and was unable to be present at the hearing. Goodman had bought the animal as a one year old and had trained it. The man he had employed as trainer was one Joseph Bartle...

I ground my teeth, feeling a premonition again: Joe Bartle, the missing witness.

Goodman stated he had bought the animal at Malton in Yorkshire. He had run it at York and Chester before selling it for personal reasons to Ernest Wood. He was able to present Mr Wood with a full pedigree for the animal. He himself had placed certain bets on *Running Rein* for the Derby, but he agreed he had also placed bets on other horses. He was aware of the enquiry into the horse's age by the Jockey Club and fully supported their conclusion: he had provided them with reports and they had confirmed that the animal was indeed a two-year-old colt. He had no connections either with Mr Wood or Colonel Peel beyond those he had stated. He had no financial interest in the case itself: his own bets had been settled as matters of honour. He smiled when the crowd hissed at the implication: the Prime Minister's brother was not a man of honour.

'Give it to 'em, Goody!' someone yelled at the back of the courtroom as his evidence was concluded. There was a further brief outburst of cheerful pandemonium before the ushers restored order. Two members of the swell mob were expelled, as I recall.

The Solicitor General rose, tugging at his gown, and shuffling the sheaf of papers in his hand. He paused for a little while, allowing the air of expectation to grow about him: I liked that touch. Fitzroy Kelly looked up finally, puffed out his pigeon chest and gave the witness a thin smile.

'Your name, sir?'

'Lewis Goodman.'

Kelly frowned, made a play of consulting the sheets in his hands. 'Lewis Goodman ... But here I have ... surely it is Levy Goodman?'

Goodman's eyes hardened. 'No, sir.'

'You've changed your name, then.'

'I have not.'

Fitzroy Kelly affected a puzzled frown, and shook his head doubtfully. 'Perhaps I have been misinformed ... Mr Goodman, you are of the Christian persuasion?'

'I am.'

'Not of the Jewish faith?'

'No.'

'You don't owe allegiance to the synagogue rather than the–'

Alexander Cockburn rose almost lazily,

uncoiling himself from his seat. 'My lord, I must protest this line of questioning. In seeking to ascertain the identity of a horse it can be of no relevance whether or not Mr Goodman is a practising member of the Church of England – or any other, for that matter.'

The Solicitor General waved a dismissive hand at the objection. 'It is a matter of veracity, rather than religion, that I seek to place before the court, but no matter... Mr Goodman, do you have any interest in a club called Rouget's, in Castle Street?'

'I do. But it is an eating house, not a club.'

'Whereas the premises in Panton Street are best described as a ... night house?'

Goodman paused, a thin smile on his lips. The diamond pin sparkled on his vest. He remained at ease when he replied, 'A place of entertainment.'

There was a drumming of feet from the mob and approving laughter.

'A place of entertainment ... of a certain kind. Are you aware the night house in question is normally referred to as Goody Levy's?' Kelly displayed a feral smile. 'A distinctly Jewish name, would you not agree? A name derived from your own, as proprietor?'

'My lord–' Cockburn began to rise once more to his feet.

Fitzroy Kelly beat him to it. 'I am merely

attempting to sketch for the benefit of the court the reputation of the gentleman who calls himself Lewis Goodman. But I can move on to perhaps more relevant matters which will equally well serve the purpose. Mr Goodman, have you ever been banned from a racecourse?'

'Never.'

'Have you ever appeared before an enquiry of the Jockey Club?'

'Twice.' Goodman raised an eyebrow and gave a confident smile. 'Successfully.'

'You place heavy wagers at the races?'

'I do – as do most noble lords present today in this courtroom. Heavy wagers, yes. But certainly not as much as Lord George Bentinck.'

There was laughter at the back of the court and a further drumming of feet. Fitzroy Kelly was annoyed, and pressed on sharply. 'Do you know of a horse called *Maccabeus?*'

'I do not.'

'Or *Gladiator?*'

I'd been well briefed by Ben Gully. There was danger here. Cockburn was silent, so I lunged to my feet. 'This hearing is about a horse called *Running Rein!*'

Fitzroy Kelly rounded on me. He gave me what he considered to be a withering glance. I remained unwithered as he continued, 'No, sir, it is about an animal called

Maccabeus masquerading under another name – that of *Running Rein*. And it is also about a horse called *Gladiator,* entered under the name *Lysander–*'

'My lord, my confusion must equal your own!' I protested to the Bench.

But Fitzroy Kelly was launched. 'I intend to prove that *Running Rein* is what the sporting fraternity describe as a ringer – an animal substituted for another. I intend to prove that the horse entered as *Running Rein* is really a four year old called *Maccabeus;* that there was another horse entered as *Lysander* when it was really *Gladiator;* that both animals were once owned by Lewis Goodman, and that the man in the witness box, who lies about his own name and identity is guilty of perpetrating a criminal conspiracy–'

'Is this a cross-examination or a closing speech?' I yelled above the growing din and catcalling that had arisen throughout the courtroom. A fight seemed to have broken out on the back tiers and ushers ran forward to separate the struggling men. Infuriated, Baron Alderson was banging his gavel thunderously and when order was finally restored, I knew I'd got it right. He glowered at the Solicitor General.

'Mr James is correct. This is supposed to be a cross-examination on evidence already given. By all means seek to discredit the witness, but stick to the matters in issue. As for you, Mr James...' I wasn't going to have it all my way. Alderson's jowls were quivering dangerously and his eyes held angry little points of light. 'I will keep counsel in order in my courtroom. I don't need your help to do it.'

I acquiesced mildly, sitting down, but well satisfied. Cockburn was watching me with an odd light in his eye.

The Solicitor General had lost control; now he gritted his teeth and attacked Goodman in the witness box. He dredged up the matter of the Haymarket clubs, pressed him about alleged welshing, about incidents of violence at Epsom the previous year. He questioned him about the bribing of trainers and jockeys and the practice of deliberately losing races in order to raise odds at subsequent events. And he questioned him about his general reputation. But he was unable to shake the witness: Goodman remained cool, a slight twitch in his cheek only occasionally betraying the tension he felt, and to all Kelly's insinuations he merely repeated his denials. It was clear there were no proofs to be forthcoming, and his confidence remained unaffected. Ben Gully had told me Goodman would be a cool customer: Kelly was unable to breach his defences.

And as for the horses named by the Solicitor General, Goodman claimed he had not the faintest idea what was being talked about.

It was almost three in the afternoon before Goodman stood down. It was then I told Cockburn one of our witnesses was missing. It would have been a good time to introduce Bartle, to swear to the colt's identity and its training in Ireland, in support of Goodman and Wood. But he was not in court. I smelled conspiracy.

We were saved by Baron Alderson. 'We'll adjourn for lunch,' Baron Alderson intoned, and the court rose as he left the bench.

Cockburn leaned towards me, irritably. 'Try to find out what's happened to this man Bartle. And these other damned horses Fitzroy Kelly's referred to ... I've had no briefing about them.' He gathered up his papers. 'In my chambers in twenty minutes, if you please.'

We were there within the half-hour: me, Bulstrode, Ernest Wood and our next witness John Day. Cockburn tapped an impatient finger on the table in front of him. 'We are going well enough so far but there are issues which cause me anxiety. If we are to adequately represent Mr Wood we need to know what the other side are likely to come up with – and this attack upon our witness Goodman, and the talk of these other animals...'

The corn merchant was clearly out of his depth. He shook his head. '*Maccabeus* ... I know that Bentinck made this claim weeks ago but Baron le Tissier ruled it out in the Jockey Club enquiry. As for the others...'

Cockburn sniffed. He turned his head and observed John Day closely. 'And you, sir, do you know anything about these animals?'

Ben Gully had told me there was little John Day did not know about the skulduggeries of the racing fraternity. Now, the little man hesitated, scratched his lean, lined cheek. 'There have been rumours...' He glanced around him. 'But they're rumours only. It is said that Mr Goodman did indeed own two colts – *Running Rein* and *Lysander*. The one he sold to Mr Wood, here. The other, it is said, was run in someone else's name, but was really owned by Goodman.' He shrugged. 'There's no way of proving it.'

There was a short silence. 'So...' Cockburn said heavily, 'what about this charge that these horses are not what they seem?'

John Day's features were expressionless. 'I don't know about that, Mr Cockburn. If the Solicitor General says *Running Rein* is really *Maccaebus,* and *Lysander* is really *Gladiator,* let him prove it. *Lysander* fell early on, anyway, so it don't signify much.'

Cockburn sighed, unconvinced. 'So we're no further forward.'

'Before Fitzroy Kelly goes any further, I

think it's time we attacked the other side through Lord George.' I suggested.

'By way of your evidence, I believe,' Cockburn said, sliding a serpentine glance at John Day.

John Day's eyes narrowed and he licked his lips. He seemed uneasy. 'There's no love lost between Lord George and myself.' He hesitated. 'He ... let me down. I'll say no more than that. But I know a great deal about Lord George. Some of it I've written down for Mr Bulstrode, here. The rest–'

'The *Crucifix* case,' I prompted.

Day nodded. For Cockburn's benefit I narrated how Bentinck had bet heavily on a horse called *Crucifix* running for the Oaks, but had put it about that the animal was lamed, until the starting price fell. In the subsequent race he had made a great deal of money. 'Through fraud and lies.' I added.

'You can give evidence of this?' Cockburn asked Day.

John Day hesitated, then ducked his head unwillingly. There was silence in the room for a little while. I glanced at Bulstrode. The solicitor was sweating profusely. Beside him, Ernest Wood looked thunderstruck: things were getting complicated and he was clearly regretting what he had got himself into by bringing this case against Colonel Peel.

Alexander Cockburn twitched his nostrils and rose slowly to his feet. 'I think, Mr

100

James, I'll let *you* deal with Lord George Bentinck.'

He had seen the way a rush of blood had earlier sent me dancing to my feet. He knew I was young and aggressive. Cockburn had no desire personally to attack the Jockey Club. As for me ... I was inexperienced, perhaps reckless. And I had a reputation to establish.

And that really is how the *Running Rein* case all began to fall apart.

3

The evening session of the court in those days began at five. As was the fashion, Alderson had partaken of a generous lunch in Judges' Lodgings, including copious quantities of wine, and would have relaxed over the after lunch port. At least, he seemed in a somewhat more mellow mood when we resumed. We had sent runners out to the stables but there was still no sign of Bartle so Cockburn called to the witness box the stable hand John Marsh, who gave evidence supportive of Lewis Goodman's testimony.

'*Running Rein* had been bred in...'

'Ireland, sir, by Mr Sam McGuire, he it was who brought him across.'

'And trained him?'

The boy nodded nervously. 'At Malton,

sir, the stables in Yorkshire, and he was then entered to run a few races.'

'Before he was sold to Mr Wood.'

'That's correct, yer honour.'

'What can you tell us about the age of the horse?' Cockburn asked sharply.

'I was allus led to believe, and been told by Mr Wood's trainer Joe Bartle that *Running Rein* was a two year old.'

'Have you ever heard of *Maccabeus?*'

'No, sir.'

Cockburn sat down, satisfied and allowed the Solicitor General to rise. Fitzroy Kelly cross-examined the stable boy briefly and contemptuously, implying he was a hired man in the pay of a group of criminals led by Lewis Goodman. Then he sniffed out a weakness in our presentation.

'And who is this man you mention ... Joe Bartle?'

'The trainer, sir.'

'The person who averred that the horse was truly a two year old. But he has not been called to give evidence. So this comment of yours is hearsay. So where, pray, is Mr Bartle? Can he not speak for himself?'

There was a short silence. The boy giving evidence seemed frozen. Cockburn rose to his feet. He struggled to conceal his reluctance. 'The witness is missing, my lord. We hope to call him later.'

'To come up with the same weak farrago

of lies, no doubt,' the Solicitor General opined. 'It is what is to be expected. Horses being entered under assumed names, missing witnesses, a stable boy called to attest to something he's merely been told...'

'Stinking fish!' someone called out from the back of the courtroom, there was a burst of laughter and the Solicitor General waved an arm as though in agreement, and sat down.

Alexander Cockburn had no further questions of Marsh, and dismissed him. He faced the bench. 'My lord, it is clear that the Solicitor General is of the opinion that Mr Wood, as plaintiff in this case, seeks only the support of those who may be described as unreliable witnesses or of the criminal fraternity. To show that this is not the case, we now wish to call to the witness box someone whom the Solicitor General can surely not suggest is of that ilk ... I call Lord George Bentinck.'

There was a moment's pause, a silence in the courtroom, and then the silence was broken by an outburst from the tiered seats, a stamping of feet and a storm of protest from the Solicitor General and Lord George Bentinck himself.

Empurpled, Fitzroy Kelly jumped to his feet. 'You can't do this! This is outrageous...! Lord George is *our* witness. He will be called to testify in support of Colonel Peel!'

There was shouting and laughter and a rolling about on the benches at the back of the courtroom, while Baron Alderson himself raised his stentorian voice to call for order and Lord Stradbroke's female acquaintance leaned against his shoulder with her handkerchief to her face. The gavel pounding continued, the crowd roared, fights broke out and Fitzroy Kelly and Lord George Bentinck even ended up shouting at each other. I really quite enjoyed it all. The reporters were scribbling like mad. And we got our way. Even so, it was ten minutes before a grim faced Lord George Bentinck stood in the witness box, facing counsel.

As the noise subsided, Cockburn smiled foxily. 'I need hardly ask permission of the court to treat Lord George as a hostile witness,' he began, 'since he has already openly declared his support for Colonel Peel.'

'Hostile as they come!' Bentinck snapped angrily, hammering his stick on the floor of the witness box.

Cockburn inclined his narrow head gracefully. 'Then I will leave the examination of the witness to my learned friend, Mr James.'

My time had come.

I had trained for it. You know, like a lot of other young men seeking a career at the Bar, I had gone first to a school in the Strand which prepared those who wished to appear on the stage. It was the recognized way forward if you sought a life at the Bar. Why? Well, you obtained skills that would stand you in good stead in the courtroom. You learned declamation; you were shown how to project your personality; use exaggeration of movement, the use of the hands, as well as the voice. You seem surprised ... lawyers and actors training together? But that's the reality of it all. In the court room you had to put on as much a performance as you would on the stage. Including lachrymosity. I'm proud to say I was as good a weeper as anyone at the Bar. And in addition, they taught you fencing. There was a lot of it on the stage in those days. Though I have to admit I was never lissom, even as a young man. But I learned the basics.

And fencing, it helped in dealing with a witness: you must treat witness examination almost like a duel, for it is much like using an epee or a sabre. Prick and cut and slash. But cross-examination, like examination of a hostile witness, now that is something else again. You can't be trained to do it. You must have it in you. You know, would you believe that in my later career I was the most feared cross examiner in the Old Bailey? When I rose to my feet, strong men would pale; admirals would lower their colours; generals would bugle a hasty retreat. Tears would flow, copiously, at my inferences, doggedness, and cutting remarks. More than a few ladies fainted, from my questions rather than their stays. I once brought on a heart attack in a witness. It's all about cutting and pricking, and then digging in your claws, you see: stripping flesh, if you like, tearing off strips of skin, slowly, deliberately, painfully. I've had grown men crying in front of me, even vomiting before they faced me in the box. Charlie Dickens might have held me up to ridicule later in *A Tale of Two Cities*, but I tell you, if I'd ever got *him* in the box over his rumoured relationship with his sister-in-law Georgina Hogarth, or that affair he had with his actress Nelly Ternan ... well, the sparks would have flown.

Ah, well. Lost opportunities. A forensic duel with Dickens ... it would have been a sensation, but it never happened.

But that day I stood up to face Lord George Bentinck in an expectant courtroom. Even in those early days I dressed carefully for the appearance before a judge. Everyone needs a certain air ... I always affected white gloves in the courtroom: it was a little dandyism that I enjoyed, and I now showed them the mannerisms that were to make my name: I spent a moment fiddling with my white gloves, twitched my gown back over my hips and placed one hand on the bench in front of me. I glanced around the room, with a confident air, keeping them all waiting, even the scowling judge. It's style that does it, you see ... style.

'Fraud, falsehood, selfishness and greed. Is that how you would describe what this hearing is about, Lord George?'

'You've summed it up in a nutshell, as far as your side is concerned,' Bentinck sneered.

I ignored the comment. 'You're very active at the Turf, are you not?'

'I own a stud. I race them.'

'How much did you win on your horse *Mango,* in the '37 St Leger?'

Bentinck hesitated, taken aback. He blinked, then shrugged carelessly. 'It's well enough known. Fourteen thousand pounds.'

After the gasp died down in the court-room, in the ensuing silence I asked, 'How much did you win at this year's Derby?'

'Not as much as I had expected.'

'Because *Running Rein* won and your horses came nowhere.'

'Because a fraud was perpetrated on Colonel Peel. The horse was a ringer.'

'And you had already protested this?' I asked gently.

'Of course.'

'To the Stewards of Epsom. Was there an enquiry?'

As I'd hoped, Bentinck grew warm. 'There was. But Baron le Tissier was misinformed from the outset. He took the word of Mr Wood as a gentleman, even though I told him that it was that damned Jew Levy Goodman who was behind the scenes on this one. I know what goes on in racing, I know all about the bribery and the corruption, the falsehoods and the nobbling, and there were plenty of rumours–'

'So are you suggesting that Baron le Tissier, as chairman of the enquiry, was guilty of dishonest motives in reaching his decision?'

Bentinck glowered at me. 'Of course not! I never said that!'

'You were dissatisfied with the result of the enquiry,' I suggested.

'Of course. I knew that damned horse wasn't the Malton colt–'

'And it was you who pushed Colonel Peel into welshing on his bets after the race was run.'

'I *advised* him, as a friend, that he had been subjected to a monstrous fraud, perpetrated by that evil Jew trickster Goodman–'

'This had nothing to do with pique, or revenge because you had lost money on the race?'

'Certainly not!'

'So what was your motive?'

'Friendship!' Bentinck roared, empurpling, losing control of himself. 'A desire to see justice!'

'The avoidance of fraud?'

'Of course!'

'The avoidance of fraud and falsehood and selfish corrupt greed?'

'Certainly!'

I set the trap. 'So you see yourself as the Conscience of the Turf? You feel that you must press this case, to clean up the sport, to make an example of someone you regard as a rogue?'

Bentinck saw the jaws open in front of him. He hesitated, prevaricated. 'Colonel Peel brought this action on his own account.'

I raised my voice, waved a white-gloved hand, appealing to the muttering crowd on the benches, fanning their mood. 'But only under pressure from you, and others. Who are the others, may I ask? What sinister syndicate is there behind this disgraceful action against my client? How much have you all lost, in your secretive cabal? Could you not take your losses like men? Did you have to visit this foul calumny on my client simply out of pique at losing vast sums of money? You claim our witness Goodman is a rogue. But is not a man who welshes also a rogue?'

The stamping of feet started again. Bentinck's face flamed with anger and his fingers gripped the edge of the witness box. His voice came out almost as a roar. 'You impugn my honour, sir! When gentlemen place stakes on a race it is done in an honourable way! I resent your implications that we have grouped to attack an honest man. It is Goodman who is behind all this and I swear that I'll get him booted off every race track in the country before I've finished with him!'

A crescendo of hissing and whistling arose behind him and the incensed baronet turned and shook his fist at the mob on the upper tiers. This only served to increase the noise and Baron Alderson hammered ineffectually at the table for almost a minute before the noise subsided. The judge's eye was beady with malice when he turned it on me.

'Mr James. I agreed you could treat the witness as hostile. But this badgering must stop. I trust you will stick to the issues that should be before us: the identity of the animal known as *Running Rein!*' He glowered at me. 'No more red herrings.'

The mention of red herrings had drawn catcalls from the mob. The noise fanned my own excitement. I knew the crowd was behind me, and there'd be headlines in *The Times* tomorrow. I was not now prepared to give way.

'The fact is that a foul slander has been raised and spread about my client. His colt won the Derby fairly. Colonel Peel, out of pocket and out of temper, was persuaded by Lord George Bentinck and his syndicate, to welsh on the bets. Lord George points the finger at our witness Goodman, but I point the finger at Lord George. He holds himself up to be the saviour of the honour of the Turf, the cleanser of the Augean stable of vice and corruption and unfair dealing. But I now intend to prove that there is another man behind the mask. I intend to prove fraud, falsehood, selfishness, on the part of the man who is seeking to claim such behaviour on the part of my client, and my witness! More, I have it in my power to prove bribery–'

I tell you, my boy, there was a great outburst of cheering. The pandemonium in the courtroom was immense. The lady had fainted on Lord Stradbroke's arm. Baron Alderson was purple in the face as he pounded at the bench in front of him. The ushers ran frantically about the tiered benches, ejecting struggling mechanics and battling supporters. Somewhere a woman screamed.

'This courtroom will come to order!' Baron Alderson thundered.

Gradually, the noise subsided. The judge was standing; he glared down at me. Flushed with premature triumph I held up my head, glared at him, jutted out my chin in defiance. I was still young then...

'I hold you responsible for this outbreak, Mr James. You have now made statements which, outside a court of law, would be slanderous. That is for your conscience. It may well be that you could absolve yourself, by producing proofs concerning the matters you have raised. *But not in this courtroom.* The matters you are raising are nothing to do with this enquiry. I deem this name-calling has gone far enough. I do not intend wasting my time presiding over a bear garden.'

He took a deep breath; I could hear a ragged sound deep in his throat. Chronic dyspepsia was catching up on him. He belched angrily, and even at a distance I caught the odour of stale wine. He fixed me with a baleful eye. 'It is my view that we need hear no more argument. No more witnesses, but one. The issue, it seems to me, is a simple one, and I so direct the jury to attend to it.'

Facile a dire, as they say.

I could see the smug look on Cockburn's face. He knew I'd put a heavy bias into the case. But neither of us was prepared for what that old badger Alderson was about to do.

The judge leaned forward, cold and deliberate in his malice. 'It is clear from the evidence so far that Colonel Peel has refused to pay debts honourably entered into. Mr Wood has demanded payment. The issue can be resolved by obtaining the answer to one question and one question only. *How old is the animal in issue?* If it is a colt of two years, judgement should be entered for Mr Wood. If it is a four year old – of whatever name – Colonel Peel is proved right, and the matter should be allowed to drop. So I now intend to adjourn this hearing. On Monday morning I will have the answer to the question. You will produce the animal in court for my inspection of its teeth, along with a court-appointed veterinary surgeon. *The answer, of course, lies in the mouth!*'

I sat there stunned. Cockburn's own mouth dropped open. Beaming at his own malicious triumph Baron Alderson rose and swept from the room. Behind him he left a scene of complete disorder.

Chapter Three

1

You won't have known my grandfather, naturally. He was long since dead, before I even met your mother in New York, after the collapse of my first marriage.

My maternal grandfather. Harvey Christian Combe. An eminent man in the City, a member of Common Council, a well known personality in his day. Like his political friend Charles James Fox, he had been a great gambler. He'd made his living as a brewer and accumulated a large fortune. I think it was the prospect of succeeding to the old man's wealth that had led my father to marry my mother: I can't think of any other reason that might have persuaded him.

But marry her he did, and it stood to reason that when I was born I became a favourite of the old man. His daughter looked like him; I looked like my mother. We could all three have been pugilists. It was natural he would lean towards me: his look-alike.

So before we reconvened at the Exchequer Court on Monday it was only sensible that I spent the weekend down at Combe Park, hoping to tap the old man – again – for some financial assistance. But he'd heard rumours about my reckless gambling and was getting niggardly about the support he was called for. He gave me a lecture instead – as though I didn't get enough of those from my father.

I wouldn't have minded so much if my grandfather hadn't been so well-known as a whist player, and had bet with the most extravagant in society, in his younger days.

However, my Sunday morning visit was unsuccessful and I came away empty-handed. So you'll understand that I was more or less *forced* to go along to Hampstead Heath that Sunday afternoon, to see if I could make up for my dire financial state by placing a few perspicacious bets.

The occasion was a battle between two of the better-known fist men of the day ... all but forgotten now, of course. One was a rather portly gentleman by the name of Porky Clark. Unsurprisingly, he'd once been a butcher. His opponent was Sam Martin, an ex-porter from Hythe who was suspected of eating raw meat before a fight to get used to the taste of blood – usually his own. His speciality was taking a beating for twenty rounds before nailing his opponent when the man got tired of the sport of hammering seven bells out of him.

In those days, what, forty years ago, pugilism depended very largely on aristocratic support, you understand. Prize fights were arranged by noble patrons who raised funds for the stakes and supported favourite boxers during training. Lord George Bentinck, naturally enough, was a member of the Pugilists Club that had been set up in 1814. The club established codes of conduct, hired gangs to keep order at the ropes and tried to keep purses modest, though the sums were bolstered by side stakes. It was where I was hoping to pick up some cash: supplementary stakes were arranged by the Fancy at the Castle Tavern and it was towards that establishment that I first directed my steps after leaving my grandfather: I placed a wager with the little available money I had among the usual company of aristocrats who were there rubbing shoulders with tradesmen, peers and pickpockets. I didn't see Lord George there: nor did I have any wish to see him. But I was pretty sure he'd be at the Heath.

There was quite a crowd there, of course: Sunday afternoons on the Heath were a fixture during the summer months for the pugilistic fraternity. The police knew all about it of course and were supposed to intervene in the illegal pursuit, but the crowds were too big for their interference: they stayed on a little knoll some distance off, waiting for the inevitable riot that would accompany the almost guaranteed disputatious verdict.

Proceedings had already commenced within the ring when I arrived and I was gladly surprised to see that one of the two men sparring was none other than my acquaintance Lester Grenwood ... who still owed me money against that accursed bill. Amateurs such as he often put on a show before the main event of the afternoon and Grenwood fancied himself with his fists but I knew him well enough to be aware that once his nose got bloodied, he'd retire. In the hope of grabbing a little quick return I placed a quick bet on his opponent, but got it wrong again. Within the first few minutes, after a bit of wary circling, Grenwood landed a quick one-two, struck a blow in his opponent's kidneys and ended up with a fierce knee in the groin which brought water to everyone's eyes. No Queensberry nonsense in these amateur bouts those days, you know.

The crowd howled loudly – though not as loud as Lester's opponent writhing on the ground and clutching at his precious jewels. It was clear the fight was over. I was still making a hasty agreement with my creditor by way of a piece of paper, when Lester Grenwood came through the throng with a towel around his neck and a broad smile on his face. He had his arm around the shoulders of his Hussar friend Crosier Hilliard.

As he was wiping the sweat from his handsome features with the scruffy-looking towel he caught sight of me. He raised a triumphant hand.

'James! How about that, then! Did you see that right of mine? And that trick with the knee?'

Crosier Hilliard whooped. 'Hope you had your money on the right man, James!'

'If not the right horse,' Grenwood shouted gleefully. 'See you got nailed in court too, the other day, in the *Running Rein* business,' he crowed. 'The papers are full of it! Produce the nag, hey? Does Alderson really expect that to happen? Draggin' a horse into the courtroom? It's got all London by the heels!'

Slightly annoyed, as well as to some extent gratified, I countered, 'And how's that little dollymop of yours? She got *you* by the heels yet?'

He was too delighted with his pugilistic success to be offended. 'Sweet Harriet, you mean? She'll have long since gone back to her countryside pursuits. Talking of which, James, Hilliard and I have got a little party going on tonight down at Swanscombe and if you want to join in, stop being such a dull dog and–'

'I've got the hearing Monday morning,' I cut in, shaking my head dolefully. 'Got preparations to undertake. But talking of

Running Rein, what with the sum you owe me and those bets you laid off for me–'

'Ha, don't worry old friend. Keep fleet of foot and they won't catch up with you for a week or so. Besides, the tin you'll get from this *Running Rein* brief of yours should keep them wolves from the door, hey?' He hugged Hilliard, and pulled at the man's whiskers. 'Away then, Crosier, let's to the fleshpots!'

I put out a hand to detain him but, flushed in the face, he was being dragged away by Hilliard in the midst of a congratulatory group of successful punters, eager to express their appreciation and admiration for him in a local tavern. Disgruntled, I made my way around the fringe of the restless crowd, waiting for the main event of the afternoon. I could see Porky Clark limbering up chewing on a half-cooked steak and glugging a bottle of beer, all white, hairy, scarred flesh and chunky jowls. His opponent Sam Martin was across the other side of the rope barrier, stripping off: he was taller, almost ten years younger than Porky, carried less fat, and had the scarred, bristle-featured look of a man who intended bloody business. Porky was going to be no match for him that day.

I watched the two men as they completed their preparations and then undertook another judicious bet, on credit, of course. And received some more wigging from various acquaintances on the *Running Rein* business. After which I edged my way into the crowd, shouldered my way close to the ropes, to see how Porky shaped up to Sam Martin.

You know, I always regarded myself as an acknowledged expert on horseflesh, bare-knuckle fighters, and women. Mind you, I don't know that I ever made any money on a pugilistic encounter. Not even when I was acting as manager of John C. Heenan, when he was champion of the world. You didn't know about that stage in my career? I'll get around to telling you about it, in due time. But Heenan, I *should* have made some tin out of him, particularly when I came back from New York with him in tow, fixed him the challenge fight of the century with Tom Sayers in Ireland, only for Heenan to pull out at the last moment. To get *married,* by all that's holy! But then, to be fair, what a woman! It's Adah Mencken I'm talking about. The sensation of the New York and European stage... Now I lost money on her too: she had cost me the security of my first marriage ... but I'm digressing again. I'll tell you about that later.

To put it shortly, you need to know that it was age, if not beauty, that did for Sam Martin that day on Hampstead Heath. At least, that's what the sporting press said next day. The fact is Sam Martin didn't seem up to his usual cunning tactics: he took the blows but he seemed slow, sluggish, not as aggressive as he was reputed to be. There looked to be no weight in his slugging hand; his legs seemed rubbery from the start and there was a vacant glare in his eyes that made it seem as though he was somewhere else than the Heath. And there was no sign of the usual comeback when the fight was far advanced. Anyway, in the eighteenth round, as the blood was spattering the bawling mob around the ropes Porky Clark laid one on him, high on the temple, and poor Sam went down and according to some accounts I read later in the sporting press didn't wake for a week. He never did regain control of his speech after that, now I come to think of it. Not that he ever had anything particularly interesting to say.

It wasn't a good day for Sam Martin, but it was worse for me – first my grandfather hadn't come through with anything other than a homily, I'd lost some ready by betting against Lester Grenwood, and now Porky Clark had done for me with his right fist.

It was time for me to make myself scarce. The disaffected crowd was breaking up into a few isolated battles as they disputed the legitimacy of the verdict ... even though Sam Martin was still stretched unconscious on the muddied sward, but I avoided them easily enough. I pushed and barged my way through the sweating supporters, avoiding the eyes of the bookmakers I dealt with, and saw the peelers beginning to come down from their hill to separate some of the more violent squabbles. There were a few hansom cabs waiting on the road that fringed the Heath and I headed for them. Before I reached them however, I noted there was some kind of celebration going on near the bushes adjoining the highway, just behind the line of cabs. A couple of hats were knocked off, thrown in the air, and there was a degree of shouting. The unusual thing was that no great crowd had gathered, just a small group of the swell mob.

I thought I caught a glimpse of none other than Lewis Goodman among them before I turned aside, began to fight my way past a noisy group heading for the nearest tavern. It was then that I observed one man who stood watching the celebrating group, his back to me: there was something rural about him, a stocky, broad-shouldered fellow with a mass of red hair and muddy boots. His hands were on his hips, but his fists were clenched, and his head was lowered like a threatening bull. I glanced at him curiously. He was clearly in an angry, dangerous mood; he stared after the small group of whooping revellers, then slowly walked after them. His gait was stiff-legged: he reminded me just then of a belligerent fight dog, a bull mastiff entering the ring.

But it was none of my business. At least, I thought so at the time.

I reached the cabs, negotiated a price, and by supper time I was back in town. Still almost penniless.

I met my leading counsel, Alexander Cockburn, during breakfast at the Inn on the Monday morning. Like me he had spent a thoughtful weekend. Since his early struggles on the West Country circuit Cockburn had become much sought after by London solicitors and the briefs that were brought to his chambers were numerous. He could afford to pick and choose but it was clear to me from his demeanour over our kidneys and steak that during the weekend he had thought deeply about *Wood v Peel* and he was beginning to consider that he had chosen badly with the *Running Rein* case. It was always likely to be a *cause célèbre*, and I've no doubt that had attracted him for Cockburn enjoyed the limelight and was a sporting man by inclination. But he clearly felt we might be on dangerous ground: somehow the thing was all unbalanced.

'I spoke to Baron Alderson at dinner, at the Inn last night,' he growled unhappily, as he ladled some more kidneys onto his plate. 'He has a clear disposition towards the other side. He considers it unwise of us to rely so heavily upon evidence from a man like Lewis Goodman: his name is a byword in racing circles and there's every chance that the gullible Mr Wood was taken in by him.'

'Mr Wood's not the one on trial.'

He eyed me sourly, his narrow little eyes red-rimmed with displeasure. 'Perhaps not, but I suppose you've heard the latest news from Bulstrode?'

I shook my head. 'I haven't seen him and–'

Cockburn's mouth twisted unpleasantly. 'He tells me that not only Bartle has gone missing. It seems the damned animal has also disappeared!'

I was thunderstruck. 'What! But Baron Alderson–'

'The judge wants to see the horse, and now we can't produce the animal.' He paused, took a mouthful of kidney, chewed it in distaste and eyed me coldly. 'I trust you have properly loaded our barrels,' Cockburn observed, as though it were all my fault.

I could see what was about to happen: he would be handing the problems to me. A witness had gone missing. Now the horse was not to be found. And the judge had already been nobbled by the other side.

It was with a heavy heart that I followed him as we made our way on foot from the Inner Temple to the Exchequer Court.

I've already emphasized that in those days courtrooms were regarded as places of entertainment. And *Wood v Peel* was turning into high theatre. There was the usual crowd milling about outside, and the shaggy-faced, blue-coated Cerberus on the doors greeted us warmly, happy that the sensationalism of the case and the rumbustious press reports had enabled him to raise entry prices to the benefit of his pocket. Then, as we entered, close to nine o'clock, Cockburn, already in a cantankerous mood, went as red as a rooster in season: Lord George Bentinck had seated himself between the Solicitor General and junior counsel.

Cockburn literally danced in anger. 'I don't think this is appropriate, Kelly. Lord George is *my* witness: I called him. I can't have him sitting beside you!'

Kelly sniffed, smiled and ignored him.

There was a scuffling at the entrance to the courtroom. I looked around: Bulstrode was coming in, his face flushed, dragging with him an unhappy, reluctant, bow-legged little man. Bulstrode approached me, muttered that Ben Gully had advised it: the new witness was a stableman by the name of Cornelius Smith. A replacement for the missing Joe Bartle, who seemed to have gone to ground like a hunted fox.

The usher entered a moment later and called for all to be upstanding. As the crowd hustled about and those on the benches rose to their feet the usher was followed by the

125

heavy, cantankerous figure of the judge. Baron Alderson was barely seated before the irate Cockburn, stiff-legged, made his application. 'My lord, I wish to move that Lord George Bentinck be required to withdraw.'

'Withdraw?' Baron Alderson grumbled, gathering his robes about him, peering around the room like a disturbed, suspicious owl, and adjusting his heavy wig. 'On what ground would you wish him to withdraw? It was you who called him to give evidence. You can hardly object to his presence now.'

'Then I would beg your lordship to request that Lord George sit elsewhere. It is most inappropriate that he should be seated with counsel for Colonel Peel.'

The judge glared at him, then swept the room with glowering eyes. He saw Bentinck, jutted his lower lip, and turned back to the protesting advocate. 'Where would you *have* him sit, Mr Cockburn?' Baron Alderson growled in a dangerously cool tone.

'Anywhere but *there*, my lord!' Cockburn snapped to a chorus of hooting and laughter.

'I cannot see it makes any difference where Lord George sits,' Baron Alderson replied above the din, 'providing we get down to business. I believe we are waiting upon you to produce the primary evidence so that we may reach judgment in this hearing. I refer of course to the animal itself, the subject of this dispute.'

Cockburn sat down abruptly. He'd had enough. 'You take it, James,' he snarled. I was to be captain on the sinking ship.

As I rose, I flicked my gown in a show of confidence I hardly felt. Airily, I waved a white-gloved hand. 'My lord, we have already proved the identity of the horse—'

'To your satisfaction, perhaps. But now we'll have a look at the animal,' Baron Alderson growled, not to be deflected. He nodded towards a sober-looking gentleman in a brown coat, seated to one side of me. 'The court has commissioned a veterinary surgeon to carry out an inspection.'

I swallowed hard. 'My lord, I greatly regret that these circumstances have made so great an impression on your lordship's mind, but if you will only—'

Baron Alderson held up an admonitory hand, cutting me off. He looked about him, scouring the court and I obtained the sudden impression that he was beginning to enjoy himself hugely. 'Do I detect an anxiety on your part, perhaps an intention to conceal this horse? I ordered it to be produced this morning.'

'But, my lord—'

'Produce your horse!'

There was thunder in his tone. The room was shocked to silence. I swished my gown nervously. It had to be faced. I hesitated, licked my dry lips and put on a pleading expression. 'I regret, my lord, that I cannot!'

There was a long deep silence, and then almost like a wave breaking on the shore a great uproar broke out. Baron Alderson's features were twisted with rage as he rose to his feet and hammered with his gavel on the bench: he was almost beside himself when the gavel broke and the head of the instrument went spinning across the courtroom, almost beheading the usher. The man ducked, and the flying missile laid out the man standing up and bellowing on the seat behind him.

Above the growing tumult, I yelled, 'My lord, I can explain if I may call to the witness box Mr Cornelius Smith...'

Baron Alderson glared at me as though he could hardly believe his ears. Then he calmed, nodded to the usher and sat back grimly in his seat. The uproar subsided only when the bowlegged stable owner was sworn in. He stood sullenly in the witness box, head down, mouth reluctant, the squint in his left eye more prominent than ever under the strain of a court appearance. I had had time only for a brief conversation with Bulstrode while Cornelius Smith was sworn in. Cockburn was picking at his nails. In a moment, I knew, he'd skulk out of the courtroom, murmuring something about another hearing elsewhere. I stumbled to my feet. 'You are Mr Cornelius Smith, the owner of the stables at—'

'One moment,' Baron Alderson growled threateningly, 'I think I will conduct this examination myself.'

I began to protest. The judge raised a peremptory hand.

'This is very likely to be a matter of contempt of court, Mr James. Sit down.' The baron turned to the stable owner. 'You are here to explain why the horse is not here as directed?'

'It wasn't my doing, my lord!'

Baron Alderson's tone was gritty. 'What happened?'

'I wasn't to know, your lordship,' Smith said sullenly. 'They just came to me and they took the horse.'

'Who did?'

'I didn't know them, my lord.'

The judge sat back, astonished. 'You allowed *strangers* to take the horse from your stables, when you knew the animal was the subject of a court hearing?' Baron Alderson asked in rising fury.

'I didn't have no control of *Running Rein*,' Smith replied sullenly. 'He's not my colt, I was just stabling him.'

'But you handed the horse over to strangers!'

'They said they'd come on instructions from the owner, Mr Wood.'

I heard Ernest Wood struggling to his feet behind me. His voice was high-pitched, nervous, faltering. 'I gave no such instructions! I sent no one to take the horse from the stables!'

Among the cat-calling of the crowd Baron Alderson glared balefully at him until Wood sat down. Then the judge turned back to the stable owner. 'Tell me exactly what happened.'

Cornelius Smith shuffled in the witness box. His voice was nervous, edged with uncertainty. 'It was about half past six yesterday evening, your honour. I was at the stables when these two men came down. They had a message from Mr Wood, they said. *Running Rein* was to be taken by them to a stable nearer the court. Ready for the hearing this morning. I had no reason to argue: they seemed genuine enough to me. So I let them take him.'

'Where did they take the horse?'

'I dunno, your honour. Honest.'

'And you don't even know who they were?' Baron Alderson ground out.

'Never saw neither of them afore, your honour.'

For some inexplicable reason the court suddenly went quiet. Baron Alderson leaned his head against the back of his chair. He sat still for a little while, glaring at the unfortunate stable owner and then he turned his heavy head. He glowered at Cockburn's retreating back as my leader made his careful way from the room. That left just me. Alderson's piggy eyes held a certain satisfaction as they dwelt upon me.

'You have a motion to make?' Baron Alderson grunted in a low, dangerous tone.

'My lord, if I may ask a few further questions of the witness–'

'You may not,' Baron Alderson snapped. 'It would serve no purpose!'

I stood there speechless, twitching nervously at my gown. Baron Alderson continued to glare at me for a while, then slowly turned his bewigged head to look directly at the jury. The silence in the courtroom was complete: all waited on the judge's words. There was a contemptuous curl to Baron Alderson's heavy lips. 'So there we have it, gentlemen. Mr James wants to ask questions of the witness. Yet there is but one question before this court: the age of the horse. It can be settled quite simply: by producing the animal called *Running Rein* for the inspection of the court. It is owned by Mr Wood. It was sold to him by Mr Levy Goodman. The animal has been in the custody of Mr Cornelius Smith at his stables, at Mr Wood's request. But now it has disappeared. The horse cannot be produced. It has been taken by strangers. Its whereabouts are unknown.' He raised his eyebrows, shaking his head in disbelief, then turned back to me. His tone was evil. 'You cannot go on without the horse, Mr James.'

There was no choice left open to me. I swallowed hard, glanced at the pale-faced owner of *Running Rein* and shrugged. Wood seemed thunderstruck as in a lame voice I muttered, 'I regret, my lord, that my client is forced to withdraw his complaint.'

Pandemonium ensued. The withdrawal was not to the liking of the sweaty mob on the back benches of the courtroom. There was a storm of hissing and catcalling that rose to a crescendo when Lord George Bentinck and Colonel Peel were seen to be shaking hands, smiling, congratulating each other. I looked around. Ben Gully was no longer in court. Lewis Goodman was still there, standing near the doorway, seemingly unconcerned. I noted that he was talking quietly to none other than the prize fighter Porky Clark, whose face was a mass of bruises, but who bore a satisfied smirk on his swollen lips.

I wondered if Goodman had a financial interest in Porky and I began to wonder whether the battle with Sam Martin on Sunday at the Heath had not been all it seemed to be. The beaten man had seemed sluggish throughout the fight. It wasn't un-known for something to be slipped into a man's drink...

But my thoughts were wandering. That battle was yesterday. Today was another story. Here in court, Goodman did not seem particularly upset by the situation: there was a slight, cynical smile on his handsome features. The noise spilled around us as with a brief nod in my direction Goodman pushed his way out through the doors of the Exchequer courtroom, some of the swell mob surging out in his wake, but leaving Porky Clark behind, leaning against the wall.

Baron Alderson sat solidly, quietly on the bench, for once making no attempt to quell the disturbance, but his passivity was menacing and gradually that menace came through to the crowd. Silence slowly fell. And I became aware of a drumming against the filthy windows. The drought was over. Rain began to hammer against the dirty panes, streaking the filth down to the street, cleaning the gutters, sending more filth down into the already polluted Thames.

Baron Alderson glanced around the court and turned his head to stare directly at me. He took a deep, sighing breath. 'This has been a case beyond my previous experience. I have heard of trickery, ringers, betting syndicates; I have heard performances from counsel which are a disgrace in that they have sought to attack persons who were seeking only for truth and justice; I have heard slanderous comments made...'

His piggy eyes seemed to drill into mine. 'These may well be adjudged in another place. But ... in my view a most atrocious fraud has been practised – there can be no other explanation for the plaintiff's failure to produce the horse in question. I do not seek to blame Mr Wood personally in this matter: he has clearly been misled by others of a more dubious reputation, although he would have been well advised to heed the doubts raised earlier by Lord George Bentinck within the purview of the Jockey Club. But it is a matter for great regret that I have seen gentlemen associating with persons much below themselves in station.' His steely, angry glance swept over me, and then turned on Ernest Wood. 'If gentlemen would associate with gentlemen we should have no such practices. But if gentlemen will condescend to race with blackguards, they must expect to be cheated...'

I stayed slumped on my bench after the judge rose and the crowd thinned. There had been enough in Baron Alderson's demeanour to tell me that not only were my hopes of fame – the right kind of fame – dashed. There would also be a report on this whole matter to the Benchers of my Inn. My climb to the stars was now in high jeopardy.

Cockburn would keep himself well out of the furore. That left ... me.

As it happened, the collapse of the trial was not entirely to my disadvantage.

While it was not the kind of attention I had hoped for, the coverage in the newspapers after the trial was at least extensive: *The Times* thundered on in two columns – I think it was John Delane's work, he never liked me you know, and years later when he was editor of the newspaper it was he who sidled up to Prince Albert, poured poison into the pious, priggish royal ear to stop me getting the knighthood I deserved...

But where was I?

Ah, yes, *The Times* attacked me, the *Spectator* joined in the clamour, as did the *Morning Post*. Among the weekly journals, *Punch* even produced an unflattering cartoon of a horse having its teeth inspected by a bemused barrister. Me, in effect. And I received a verbal caning in their usual doggerel.

By dealing out invective vain
From his instructions false and idle,
The advocate of Running Rein
Proved that his tongue required a bridle.

The *Law Times* was even more censorious: it

took the general view, sympathy for the corn merchant, described as the innocent dupe of unscrupulous tricksters, but as far as the trial was concerned brought its guns to bear on my 'wild and unfounded accusations' against Lord George Bentinck.

But not a word about my leader, or his absence from the courtroom when Alderson thundered out his judgment.

I was left to face the music. And my creditors were queuing up at my lodgings.

But on the other hand a new trickle of briefs came to my clerk Villiers, as solicitors were asked by their clients to use the man who had so violently attacked the aristocrats. But I knew I was still on a knife edge.

On the Wednesday of the week following, Charlie Wilkins came down from high table at the Inn to sit beside me. 'A word, James? In the library?'

I followed his portly, affable figure way across the busy hall, up the steps and past the portraits of eminent Benchers of the past, to the discreet, little used library. Little used by me, anyway. Like most barristers I had never been much for reading, particularly of law books. You get to learn the law by practice, not book-reading ... and besides you could always get some other poor soul to devil for you, get the case up so you could use your own personal oratorical gifts, make an effective presentation in court. That was one of the tasks I delegated to Villiers.

So there we were, Wilkins and I, together among the shelves of musty leather-bound, rarely consulted books. Wilkins eyed the dusty bindings with displeasure and confirmed my own experience. 'Always say it's better not to get bogged down with law. Appeal to the emotions; wring the old heartstrings. Get to the twelve good men and true. It's why I always drink a pot of stout at midday.'

'What?'

'A pot of stout. Nothing like it to fuddle the brain. That then brings me down to the intellectual standard of the average British jury. Not to mention the judge.' He winked, expansively. 'But you know all about that, hey? You're already being reckoned to be a capital man with a jury.' He eyed me, carefully. 'But not over *Running Rein,* hey?'

'The issue never reached them,' I muttered. 'If only–'

'Yes ... *Running Rein* ... and the attitude of the Benchers.' Wilkins twitched at his whiskers thoughtfully. 'I understand there's a degree of ... dissatisfaction about your performance. The attack on Lord George Bentinck was deemed in certain quarters to have been extravagant. They've been considering hauling you up before them.'

'Cockburn–'

'Has gone sailing. They won't touch the jumped up little bastard. Too big these days. Heading for honours. But a junior like yourself, well, they like the taste of fresh meat in their jaws occasionally. Just to lay down some markers for other juniors.'

I was bitter and angry. 'My attack on Bentinck was justified. There are stories about him; there's evidence that demonstrates what a humbug, what a hypocrite he is—'

'That's as may be, James, but he's a powerful man, with powerful friends. However, no matter. I put a word in with the Benchers. After the Cider Cellars the other night, well, a man knows who his friends are, hey? But be certain, my boy. The Benchers are gunning for you. Be careful, James. Tread a more cautious line.' He grinned suddenly, linked his arm in mine. 'There, that's done. Duty completed. So, what do you say to a grog? The *Café Chantant* suit you, my boy?'

It suited me.

So, in spite of the attacks on me by the yellow press and the muttering behind closed doors of the Benchers, the reality was that my practice suddenly began to look more promising. The number of briefs that came to me increased. Solicitors had seen enough of me at the Exchequer Court to become interested: clients like a bulldog who snarls and snaps in court, you know.

They feel they're getting value for their money, even if they lose. But even so, I wasn't happy. I felt ill-used. Cockburn had pushed me into the firing line and ducked his head behind the parapet. Bentinck and the Jockey Club were smugly pleased. The Benchers were watching. I was smarting.

I met Ben Gully at The Blue Posts to discuss the whole thing. He confirmed what I was feeling.

'You need to tread careful, Mr James. Lord George didn't like the way you handled him: he's arrogant, and touchy, and he makes a bad enemy. And he's got the Jockey Club behind him.'

'I'm taking a beating in the newspapers, Ben,' I replied sullenly, 'and I don't like it.' I contemplated my brandy and water. 'So, what exactly do you think happened to *Running Rein?*'

Ben Gully's errant eye wandered thoughtfully. He shook his scarred head. 'I don't know, Mr James. He's been hidden somewhere, I don't doubt, safe enough in some up-country stable. Valuable piece of horse-flesh, you see. But the whole thing was sleight of hand. It was like the thimble-riggers and the sharps and bonnets you see at the race course – tricksters all. First you see it, then you don't.' He sniffed. 'We had a witness, name of Bartle. He didn't turn up. We had a horse. It got spirited away. You never stood a chance, Mr James, not when the cards were really down on the table.'

My gut growled irritably. 'Do you think Bentinck was involved? In spiriting away the horse, I mean? If so, what did he have to gain by hiding the horse?'

Ben Gully sniffed again and traced a stubby finger on some grog that had spilled on the table in front of us. 'He'd shouted long enough about a ringer in the Derby. But he could have been wrong. You can never tell in the courtroom, can you? If the judge had held *Running Rein* was what his owner claimed he was... Bentinck wouldn't have liked losing face.'

I eyed Ben Gully carefully. He'd still not given me his own opinion. 'Do you think *Running Rein* was a two-year-old colt?'

Gully shrugged. 'Mr Wood was pretty sure of it.'

I didn't like the evasion. 'The way things are, Ben, nothing's been proved: Goodman can stick to his story, Mr Wood has lost a deal of tin – and I feel I've been led by the nose.'

Gully was silent for a little while. He took a pull at his porter, then said, 'Look upon it as experience, Mr James.' Then, seeing the expression on my face, he added, 'If you intend following up the matter, Mr James, best leave Bentinck alone.'

'That leaves Lewis Goodman.'

Ben Gully stared at me portentously. 'I'll be straight with you, Mr James. The track gossip is there were indeed ringers in the Derby. Possibly two. Both put up by Lewis Goodman. And several men of consequence have had their fingers burned.' His glance slipped away. 'I hear Lord Havermere's son has been caught, among others.'

Lester Grenwood. I nodded. 'Grenwood mentioned it to me.' At the Cider Cellars I'd learned from gossip that both he and that popinjay Hussar Hilliard had been in a syndicate. We sat silently for a while, mulling things over.

The truth is, I should have left well alone at that point. It was Ben Gully's certain view: I could tell from the way he looked at me. But I disliked the mud the newspapers were throwing; I didn't like scornful fingers pointed at me, or sniggers in the clubs. I'd been frustrated unjustly by Baron Alderson because of the judge's dislike of the Turf and friendships in the Reform Club; I still writhed mentally under the lash of the newspaper comment and the attitude of the Inner Temple Benchers; and I was angry at the way in which Alexander Cockburn had manoeuvred himself out of the limelight at the appropriate moment.

'You're taking this too personally, Mr James,' Gully murmured after a while. 'That's bad, sir.'

'I'd damned well like to discover the truth of it all.'

Ben Gully emptied his mug. He shook his head doubtfully. 'So what do you want me to do?'

'Make further enquiries.'

Gully wrinkled his battered nose doubtfully. 'Could be a waste of time and money. Everything's gone quiet. No Joe Bartle. No *Running Rein*. No information on the street, other than the usual ill-informed gossip.'

I frowned. 'What about this man Bartle? Why did he just disappear?'

Ben Gully shrugged. 'Paid, I reckon. Maybe gone off to darkest Yorkshire. Or lying low in London. He was to give evidence supporting Goodman's story so I wouldn't put it past Bentinck to suborn him. Lord George can afford it to save his own reputation.'

'And the horse?'

Ben Gully drew a deep, reflective sigh. 'Now that's another matter. It could well be that Lord George is behind that. On the other hand it could be Goodman – he didn't want to take the chance of having the horse he'd sold to Wood shown up as a ringer in court. He'd have been taken aback by the judge's attitude... But going back to Bartle.' Gully tapped a fingernail against his teeth. 'I did hear there was a bit of a problem at the stables, on the Wednesday he left, but the stableman Cornelius Smith is keeping close.

My guess is he's been warned off saying too much – by Bentinck or Goodman, who's to say?' Gully eyed me covertly. 'You didn't happen to turn up at the Porky Clark–Sam Martin battle, that Sunday afternoon?'

'I was there.'

Gully frowned. 'I missed it. Business down at the docks. But one of my … advisers, he told me he thought he saw Joe Bartle in the crowd. So the stableman was still around at the weekend, on the day before your case collapsed.'

'Goodman was also there, on the Heath.'

'Well, he would be, with the rest of the swell mob. As for Joe Bartle, seems that he got himself into some kind of scuffle. Before he vanished again.'

'There was a lot of battles going on at the Heath that afternoon,' I recalled.

'That's nothing new,' Gully agreed.

I took a deep breath. 'This man Bartle. I think that's where the key lies. We need to talk to Joe Bartle. He was at the stable; he would have supported Goodman's evidence. But he didn't turn up, and now he's gone to ground. Get out into the streets, Ben. See what you can find. I'm sure if we can get to talk to Bartle, we'll find out what really happened to turn our case into a fiasco.'

'I'll do it, Mr James, but,' Gully added warningly, 'I have to tell you it's going to cost.'

'Don't worry about the money,' I replied confidently. I had an appointment with Mr Bulstrode the following afternoon.

3

'I've seen your clerk, Mr Villiers,' Bulstrode announced wheezily, settling back in the easy chair and accepting gracefully the glass of sherry proffered him. He stroked his flamboyant cravat in self satisfaction. 'Your clerk will no doubt have informed you that your fee has been paid in full, Mr James ... we always pride ourselves at Bulstrode and Bulstrode that we settle our debts promptly.' He licked a pudgy finger, smoothed his left eyebrow smugly. 'It's helpful, of course, to have an honourable man like Mr Wood who is also prepared to settle up quickly. As for the case itself, the outcome was a great pity, a great pity for Mr Wood. He is quite cast down.'

'He's been made a fool of,' I replied curtly. 'As we all have.'

Bulstrode eyed me, a certain anxiety creeping into his eyes. His tone took on a nervous edge. 'I admit things did not go well for us...'

'The dice were heavily loaded against us,' I asserted with vigour. 'It's clear to me that Baron Alderson was nobbled by members of the Jockey Club. The stableman Joe Bartle was probably paid to stay away from the courtroom. And the damned horse was stolen away from under our noses.'

'It's all been most unfortunate,' Bulstrode muttered unhappily. 'And it's too late to be remedied now, of course, but the whole affair leaves me very angry of disposition.'

I knew I'd have to play my West Country solicitor carefully. I affected a cynical air. 'Do you enjoy being made a fool of, Bulstrode?'

The West Country solicitor wriggled uncomfortably and sipped his sherry. 'Made a fool of ... I'm not sure I'd go that far, Mr James.'

I injected anger into my tones. 'I would. It's been nothing less than a conspiracy from the beginning. We've been caught in the middle of a great confidence trick, Bulstrode, perpetrated by one or the other, or even both sides! We have that tricky villain Goodman on the one hand, and we have on the other Lord George Bentinck and his aristocratic friends. Colonel Peel, it seems to me, is as much a gull as Ernest Wood in this matter. Both have been pulled by powerful forces. Evil forces. The underworld on the one hand, and the reprehensible use of power and privilege on the other. Don't you agree, Bulstrode?'

'Well, I'm not sure...' Bulstrode hesitated. I

poured him another glass of sherry to stiffen his sinews. 'I suppose there is something in what you say,' he admitted unhappily, staring at his highly polished boots.

'Absolutely right! And I think it's up to us, as men of probity and honour and determination, to do something about it!'

It rang the right bell. Bulstrode preened a little at my choice of words. He sipped his sherry. 'Probity and honour and determination. Well, of course, we did our best in the courtroom...'

'But that was not enough! The undoubted fact is we were overcome by powers of darkness. But you and I, we are men of law, are we not? It's up to people like us to surmount such difficulties, fight on in the pursuit of truth and justice!'

Bulstrode's eyes gleamed. He enjoyed the ring of my words. He was clearly flattered by my suggesting we were seekers of truth and justice. 'I'll drink to that, Mr James,' he replied boldly, raising his half-empty glass.

I eyed him carefully. 'So you agree we should not let this sleeping dog lie, then?'

Bulstrode finished his sherry in a gulp and set down the glass. 'Indeed ... absolutely not!' He frowned. 'But how...?'

'I don't think we should let these evil-doers get away with it,' I growled truculently. 'We should look into the possibility of another trial.'

Bulstrode sighed and shook his heavy head. 'I don't think Mr Wood is quite up to that. He's quite devastated, poor man. He's taken to his country house in Gloucestershire, and is avoiding society at the moment. Another trial...'

'We'd have to get the evidence first, of course,' I intervened quickly. 'To demonstrate where the guilt lies. We can only expose the conspiracy when we have the evidence.'

'But without instructions from Mr Wood, or some other interested party—'

'But aren't *we* interested parties?' I insisted. 'You and I, Bulstrode? Men of law?' I thundered. 'Men who have been made fools of? Men of pluck and probity, determination and destiny? Haven't we a part to play, as seekers of truth and justice?'

It was the kind of rhetoric that became my trademark at the Old Bailey in later years. Bulstrode jumped in his seat, a little alarmed but also excited by my blustering tone. 'Well, yes, of course, but I don't see—'

'To find the truth, all we need is money,' I said confidentially, pouring the solicitor another glass of sherry from the diminished decanter. 'I have contacts, as I told you earlier. I feel sure we can get to the bottom of all this, and then we can call for a new trial, redeem Mr Wood, save his reputation, and confuse both Goodman and the Jockey Club!'

Bulstrode's eyes grew round. He accepted the refilled glass. 'I have to agree that the prospect is–'

'Exciting! Yes, I knew you'd see it my way!' My tone was confident. I waited as he drained his glass with an enthusiastic flourish then leant over and once more filled the glass to the brim. It was an investment. 'I can get Ben Gully on it right away. It'll need a small advance of course, say five hundred pounds, but I'm sure he'll be able to get us the information we need.'

'Five ... five hundred pounds.' Bulstrode paled a little and his hand shook as he lifted his sherry glass for the fifth time. 'But if we don't have a principal who will pay us...'

'Come, come, Bulstrode, you're a man of means! I'll put some of my own money into it, of course, but I'm sure you can find five hundred for a private investigation of the circumstances surrounding *Wood v Peel!* We're seekers after truth and justice, after all. And think of the glory afterwards, when we prove what's to prove. Consider the publicity! It will be the talk of the City! Bulstrode and James ... what a combination, hey? Irresistible!'

The images burned in his mind. I could see the pride in his eyes as Bulstrode beamed his pleasure and he waved his glass happily. But, as he drank, a little doubt crept back, and the doubts returned. He wrinkled his nose, picked at his lip with an uncertain finger, and eyed me a little uneasily. He sighed. 'It's not an easy matter, Mr James. The prospect is extremely attractive of course ... and you're absolutely right.' He hiccupped loudly, and put an apologetic hand to his mouth. 'We should ... we should regard this perhaps as a matter of public duty. But though I cannot dispute I am other than a man of some means, I've already expended a considerable amount of money on this case ... sums which I could not in all conscience call upon Mr Wood to furnish ... and I'm not at all sure that a further advance...'

His voice died away miserably. I allowed the silence to grow around us, embarrassingly. It requires patience to land a struggling fish. At last, I shrugged and in a careless tone, I said, 'Well, it don't signify. If you think the matter of insufficient importance...'

Bulstrode wriggled unhappily at the hint of contempt in my voice. 'I didn't say...'

'No matter. The villains will get away with it, but that's the way of the world.' I paused, eyeing the ceiling. 'So, you're up here in London for a few days, then, Bulstrode?'

'That's right, Mr James,' the solicitor replied, eager to get away from the painful subject of a further advance. 'I've just deposited another brief for you with Mr

Villiers. It's not going to be a *cause célèbre* of course, but it involves the second son of Lord Cantelupe, and a certain actress who is bringing a charge against him for breach of promise. There are some compromising letters–'

'Oh, I'm sure we can do something for the second son of Lord Cantelupe,' I interrupted, waving a hand dismissively. 'However, I take it you'll be staying in London overnight, of course.'

Bulstrode nodded eagerly. 'For a few days in fact. I have lodgings at...'

'I was recently elected a member of the Devonshire Club. Sponsored by Lord Clanricarde, as a matter of fact. I shall be dining there later tonight and if you don't happen to have an engagement this evening perhaps you'd care to join me there, as my guest for dinner.'

Bulstrode beamed. 'Mr James, I–'

'Count d'Orsay often puts in an appearance at the club,' I remarked casually. 'And the Earl of Chesterfield is a member, as is Lord Lytton. It's quite a good table, too. Sometimes there's whist afterwards. Or roly poly. On the other hand, perhaps it would be more to your taste after dinner to step out into the Haymarket...'

'Mr James,' Bulstrode positively glowed, 'I'd be honoured to accept your invitation!'

The line had been paid out, the hook

swallowed. The fish was almost netted.

In those days, during the daylight hours the Strand and the Haymarket were quiet enough, with occasional newsboys plying their wares, men strolling to or from their offices, carts and carriages rattling along to the West End. But as you might be aware, my boy, when dusk fell the character of the area changed. The night houses opened their doors in the Strand, the Haymarket, Oxford Street and Tottenham Court Road. Brightly dressed whores emerged from Catherine Street to parade in their finery under the gas lamps near the theatres, and the gin palaces, hotels, French restaurants, and oyster shops lit up the area, did a roaring trade while the coffee houses who had kept blinds drawn all day now gleamed their windows onto the street. The scene was all very familiar to me: Windmill Street crowded with flash men and fast women, cabs and carriages jostling along the cobbles to deposit young men out for an evening's entertainment, old hags selling fruit and flowers, dollymops arm in arm, giggling as they eyed up the young bucks with their curling whiskers. As the theatres emptied towards midnight the dancing saloons became crowded and the supper lounges were filled with bullies and whores, pickpockets and thieves, fools and rogues. At midnight they all came spilling out of the

Argyll Rooms calling for broughams, or hansom cabs, or staggering on to one of the numerous night houses: the army, navy, the universities, the Inns of Court, the City and the Stock Exchange all were well represented.

I was well aware that for a gentleman like Bulstrode, up from the country, it could be a dazzling, exciting scene: sherry cobblers and cigars in a Haymarket coffee house, a roaring chorus in the *Café Chantant*, comic songs in the Cave of Harmony, and the Judge and Jury Society in the Garrick's Head, under the lead of 'Chief Baron' Renton Nicholson.

'You'll enjoy this,' I assured Bulstrode as I paid the shilling to enter and manoeuvred the inebriated solicitor into a seat at the back of the crowded room. The fee included a glass of grog and a cigar and I was certain it would be money well spent. I pointed out to Bulstrode the notorious Renton Nicholson. A burly, coarse-looking individual with a red face and leering style, he sat at a raised desk railed off and facing a table set for 'counsel' and a makeshift jury box. He was dressed in tattered court robes with a wig worn askew and an eyeglass screwed into his left eye. 'Counsel' had been made up to resemble noted advocates and they gave exaggerated imitations of peculiar mannerisms and oratorical flights. One of them, I noted sourly, was wearing white gloves. They were already well launched into tonight's parody of a recent criminal conversation case with which most of the audience were familiar and Nicholson and his supporting 'counsel' were drawing from the participants as much by way of salacious comment, obscenity and *double entendres* as was possible.

When we had finished our grog, I called for gin and water, and Bulstrode sat gaping as the 'Chief Baron' demanded further evidence of the witnesses as to what they had observed of the adulterous relationship in question.

'So you applied your eye to the hole?'

'Not only my eye, m'lud!'

'And what did you see?'

'More'n I ever did see before, m'lud ... or *behind!*'

The drunken audience hooted with raucous laughter and Bulstrode reached for his gin. Sherry, wine at dinner, and now grog and gin had worked their spell. He raised the glass to his mouth shakily, spilling some of it over the gilt buttons of his waistcoat, and gaped at me owlishly. 'Shplendid evening, shplendid!' Then the glass dropped, and shattered on the floor. Bulstrode glared at it as though it had committed some unpardonable offence and then blinked, slowly closed his eyes and leaned back in his chair.

It had been a long and exciting day and the alcohol was finally getting to him. His blubbery lips pursed, a small bubble emerged and popped silently and a little sigh of satisfaction escaped him. He would remember little of the Judge and Jury Society.

'Strange company you keep, James!'

I glanced up: Lieutenant Edward Crosier Hilliard, with yet another dollymop. He was drunk, his mouth loose, his eyes vacant. 'May I sit down? Legs a bit tottery, don't you know.' He gave the bold-eyed girl he was with a shove. 'You can push off now; I found a friend.'

She began to protest but saw the danger in his eye, and after a moment flounced away. I glared distastefully at the hussar officer. The company was little to my liking, but Hilliard was drunk and it was easier to humour him.

'Who's your friend?' Hilliard mumbled, staring at Bulstrode.

'A professional acquaintance.'

'Up from the country, I see,' Crosier Hilliard said, looking him over and sneering at the cut of his coat, and the gilt-buttoned waistcoat. 'Can always tell, you know. They have a smell about them. What's his line? Cattle? Pigs?'

'He's a solicitor,' I replied in a cool tone.

'Same thing, begod!' Hilliard guffawed. He repeated the comment, finding it hilarious, and then jerked his head about, beckoned to the waiter, thumped on the table, calling for gin. He turned back to me, grinning wolfishly. 'See that dollymop I was with? Had her last week. But couldn't be bothered tonight. Stale meat, you know, James. You seen Grenwood lately?'

Hilliard's whiskers were stained with nicotine and his dress coat was marked at the lapels with spilled wine. I stared at him with contempt. While freely plying the Exeter solicitor I had kept my own drinking under control this evening, aware I would have to get Bulstrode back to his lodgings, and still with a task to perform. I shook his head. 'Haven't seen Grenwood since I came across the two of you at Hampstead Heath.'

'Hah! The Porky Clark battle! Yes, of course. The fact is, Grenwood's keeping close, you know. His old man ... Lord Havermere ... got him on a tight rein at the moment. Truth of the matter is,' Hilliard leaned forward confidentially, 'he's in a bit of trouble ... and he's not alone!' The hussar guffawed loudly, finding the comment incomprehensibly witty. 'Staying close to home, trying to persuade the old skinflint to get him off the hook.'

'What hook?'

'Different with me, you see,' Hilliard announced slyly. 'Got expectations, don't you know. Banker's daughter from Sheffield.

The delectable Miss Edge. So I'll get out of it, you wait and see.'

'Get out of what?'

'That damned *Running Rein* affair,' Hilliard belched.

I was intrigued suddenly. I glanced at Bulstrode, making sure the man was really asleep, head lowered on his chest. Confirmation came from the light snoring sound emanating from his open mouth. I turned back to Hilliard. 'I picked up some rumours at the tables in Almack's the other evening. Just what exactly is your involvement in that business?'

Hilliard winked and placed one finger along his nose. 'Ahah! Not to be bruited abroad, if you know what I mean. But you're a friend of Grenwood ... he came to me with a proposal. Form a syndicate. Bets on two horses ... good odds. Inside tip. And it all worked out, just as we'd been promised.' He frowned, and clucked his tongue. 'Except for that bastard Lord George Bentinck. Upturned the damned applecart, didn't he? And Grenwood and I, we'd had a hell of a job, raising the necessary tin, but made it in the end ... borrowed from a few people in the East End.' He shook his head ruefully. 'Stay away from them, James, those damned moneylenders. They'll have your boots and your teeth before they finish.'

They already had their hands on my

damned boots, that was the problem. 'But why is there a difficulty for you and Grenwood? Weren't the bets all called off after Colonel Peel defaulted?'

Hilliard shook his head fiercely. 'No, it all worked perfeck ... perfectly. *Running Rein* came in as we expected. And the other horse was shoved out of the race early, as we'd been told. These little jockeys ... they can be cunning buggers, believe me.'

'Yet you and Grenwood are in trouble. With the moneylenders?'

Hilliard stared at me, befuddled, a certain irritation appearing in his eyes. He tugged at his moustache. 'Nothing I can't deal with, James! But Grenwood ... he's in deeper than me, and it seems he can't raise the tin.'

'But with the defaulting...'

'It wasn't just that! The damn welshing by Colonel Peel came after we'd settled our bets. We got part of our winnings quickly enough, but only a fraction of the full amount before the storm broke and that damned man Bentinck started shouting the odds. So the money that was paid out, it was called back ... too many people waiting to see what happened in court. Fact is, you see, the bets were spread pretty widely ... lot of people involved. And after Bentinck put the word out, we found ourselves in trouble. With the wrong people, if you know what I mean. Both Grenwood and I, we soon used up what we'd received. And now, well, we're told that unless we settle up there'll be a visit from the heavy mob. So we're left ... Grenwood and I, that is ... with bad debts, and owing a hell of a lot to the moneylenders.' He grimaced. 'And Grenwood's been trying to recover the situation ... but the tables've let him down too. His paper's all over town, but they won't see much of it back, I warrant. He's having the most infernal bad luck. He even backed the wrong man in the Porky Clark-Sam Martin bout! Damnit, even I got *that* one right!'

Unlike me.

Hilliard nodded to himself and began to say something, then stopped. He glanced around him furtively, and shook his head as though reminding himself to be wary. 'We didn't come back to Town together from the Heath, you know, though. I left early: appointment in Town.' He leered. 'I gather Goody Levy gave Grenwood a ride ... and took him on to The Quadrant.' Hilliard snickered. 'I'm told that Grenwood lost a packet that night too.'

'This syndicate you've been talking about,' I said slowly, 'who put you up to it? Where did the information about the race come from?'

Hilliard looked at me as though he thought me slow-witted. 'Where else? Goody Levy, of course.'

A roar of laughter almost drowned him out as another obscene witticism from Renton Nicholson was received with raucous delight by the drunken gathering. My attention wandered for a moment.

'And when Mr Allcock was seen by you naked with Lady Plum ... just how would you describe him?'

'He was rising to the occasion, m'lud and living up to his name!'

The bellowing laughter disturbed Bulstrode; the solicitor swallowed, blinked and opened his eyes slowly, looking around him with an owlish expression, at a loss as to his whereabouts. I would have liked to question Hilliard more but now Bulstrode was awake I had other objectives to achieve. I nodded to Hilliard and took Bulstrode by the arm, dragging him upright from his seat.

'Time to go,' I said.

Hilliard was still sitting there, staring mournfully at his gin in the sudden depression of a drunk, when I steered Bulstrode from the noise, fumes and stench of the Garrick's Head to a cabman waiting under the hissing gas lamps.

In the end, the evening proved to be a successful one. I took Bulstrode back to his lodgings and entered the lounge of the small private hotel with him, for a late night drink to round off the evening. The solicitor was now more awake, but still inebriated: he kept expressing his gratitude for my providing an evening of such 'royal entertainment', as he put it; so grateful, in fact, that he cheerfully signed, with a drunken flourish, the paper I pushed in front of him. But it meant that I was late to bed myself, and with an aching head.

As a result I was not best pleased to be woken by a pounding at the door of my chambers at seven the next morning.

It was Ben Gully.

Still in my nightshirt, I let him in. 'Confound you, is this necessary?' I groaned.

'I thought you'd like to know as soon as possible,' Ben Gully replied coolly, standing slouched in the doorway.

'Know what, damn you...?' I muttered in a sullen tone, holding my head, and pouring myself a glass of water to counter the raging thirst I was suffering from.

'Can you come with me?'

'Now? Impossible,' I replied sharply. I took a long draught of water. 'I'm due at Old Court at eleven, and then I've got an indecent exposure in the Marylebone Police Office this afternoon. But in any case, come where, dammit?'

Ben Gully pushed his left hand into the voluminous pocket of his greatcoat. He drew forth a watch and displayed it to me. 'I've been doing the rounds. Putting the word out. There's a receiver I know, fences all kinds of goods ... name of Strauss. He owes me favours. I got this watch by way of him, in an indirect fashion. Came through his hands, to an acquaintance of mine.'

'So?'

Ben Gully snapped open the back of the hunter and showed me the inscription engraved inside the case. I peered at it, eyes still bleared with drink and foggy with disturbed sleep. 'What's it say?' I asked irritably.

Ben Gully turned the watch so I could see the markings more clearly. 'There's a name inscribed there,' he said quietly.

He paused. 'Joseph Bartle.'

Chapter Four

1

When my head cleared somewhat, we had a discussion, Gully and I, but arrived at no firm conclusions. We agreed that the watch was something a man would be reluctant to be parted from. It had landed up in the hands of a moneylender called Rossetti some time after he had acquired it from Strauss, some time after its owner would seem to have disappeared.

Ben Gully was suggesting we should meet the fence who had passed it to the money-lender.

'If I can root him out, that is. He's a bit slippery, if you know what I mean.'

But I had my court appearances to deal with so I left him to pursue that opportunity while I went on with what other business lay to hand. I needed to get to court, to set about earning a few crusts to relieve the distress of my creditors. There were attendances at Old Court, Marylebone Police Court, and I also had a guinea brief to attend to at the Thames Police Court. As far as I was concerned, Strauss would have to wait.

So after Gully left, I scurried about on my professional business. It was late afternoon before I set out for the Thames Police Court.

It led to a distressing experience that took my mind off the *Running Rein* business for a while.

I suppose I ought to admit to you, even though you're my stepson, that I've always been partial to widows.

It was Garibaldi himself who gave me a piece of very sound advice. You didn't know I was with Garibaldi that summer of '60, when he made his advance on Rome to establish the Italian Republic? Oh, yes, I was with him. Exciting times. Great days. A great man. A great patriot. But also a man who had known many women. And if I may say so, a personal friend.

I remember I was there with Guiseppe that day, at the camp in Salerno, a brace of pistols stuck in the leather belt around my waist, and a red scarf around my neck ... there was a photographer from the *Illustrated London News* present to preserve the moment for posterity. We were striking camp, making ready to proceed in great triumph up to Naples to secure the liberation of Italy.

We had a number of political discussions, Garibaldi and I (because in fact I was there acting under commission as a secret agent for Lord Palmerston, who was Prime Minister at that time). But Garibaldi also gave me the benefit of his views about women, along with sound advice. We were seated together in his railway carriage steaming north – his triumphal 'march' on Rome was done by steam train, you know – and I was telling him about my serious financial difficulties since becoming MP for Marylebone. I can remember his considered, confidential tone as he gave me his advice.

'My dear James,' he said, fixing his glowing dark eyes upon me and fingering his bushy beard, 'at your time of life, with all the troubles surrounding you, you should be looking for a widow, a lady of means, a lodging lady perhaps. You should marry her, against the possibility of a rainy day.'

Back in England it was a comment I repeated to Charlie Dickens, and of course, like the plagiaristic weasel he was he used it as a thought of his own when he libelled me in *A Tale of Two Cities*.

But it was certainly sound advice from Guiseppe Garibaldi and I took it, later in '61, when my professional bubble finally burst. That's right, my first wife, Marianne, she was a widow – just like your own mother, of course.

But where was I? Ah, yes, the point I want to make is that women are different, one from another – some women, widows or not, can be cunning as snakes; others can be weak as dishwater.

Take my first wife, Marianne. She was a great philosopher. She'd philosophized her first husband – none other than Crosier Hilliard – into a state of *delirium tremens,* which killed him. She thought widowhood was an impertinence of Fate, and further considered that by marrying me she could make me change my profligate ways. And as for Garibaldi's advice, well, it was already raining when I led Marianne to the altar after my disbarment at the Inner Temple. It wasn't a church wedding: the ceremony was held in the office of the British Ambassador in Paris. That's where the knot was tied.

Unfortunately, the rainy days didn't stop during the next eighteen months of marital disharmony, either. It was a relief when the court in the Bronx decided she had bitten off more than she could chew, and freed me.

That's how I came to be free to marry your mother.

But really it was all Marianne's fault. She just didn't know how to handle me.

But I digress again. An aged barrister, hey? What was the point I was alluding to? Ah, yes. Women are different. One will proceed with exaggerated caution, another will react precipitately from despair. I mean, they take things like love affairs, or pregnancy, so *seriously.* It came home to me vividly that day in the summer of '44, when I went by boat up-river, to the hearing at the Thames

Magistrates Court, still mulling over Gully's discovery of Bartle's watch, still smarting from the comments that were circulating about the farce of the *Running Rein* case...

As usual, the Thames that afternoon was soiled and darkened with livid false tints and packed with all kinds of river craft: barges, wherries, coasters and watermen's boats. Patches of fog, dense and dirty-yellow, were collecting along the river banks and the watery sun gleamed only fitfully through the gloom. I waited for *The Cricket* steamboat at the Temple Gardens. That was the paddle steamer that blew up later in 1847, there were some fatalities, and there was quite a public outcry about it. However, off I went that day, joined the scrambling crowd at the pier, and stood on the Temple steps as the boat edged cautiously in from the crowded river to the landing.

There was a lot of bad feeling around on the river at that time. One of the steamboats had recently run down a waterman in a skiff and killed him. The master was found guilty of manslaughter and got a four-month gaol sentence ... but there was always some kind of trouble between the watermen and the steamboat owners: both sides used to demolish the piers used by the opposition in their competitive struggle for trade.

Anyway, I waited at the steps above the landing in good time for the steamboat: they had a nasty habit, you know, of pulling away at full speed from the embarkation pier before everyone was on board, but I was near the head of the queue. Off we went with a great churning of the river water, the engine chugging away manfully against a background of the slapping sound of the paddles in the grey, greasy water. Groups of black-clad office workers crowded the deck, like attendants at a mourning. The sight did not improve my black mood.

As for the hearing at the Thames Police Court, I needn't tell you about the proceedings that occurred there that day: they were insignificant. I don't even remember much about them except that the magistrate was a fat pork butcher who sweated profusely on the bench, it being his first hearing. But whatever the case was, it came to an abrupt end when someone came rushing into the courtroom in quite a hurry, seized some of his companions, and rushed out. The pork butcher bellowed in indignation, found his gavel and slammed it on the desk for order but it was too late: the rumour quickly spread throughout the dark little room. There had been an accident on the river. And as the courtroom rapidly cleared the magistrate decided to adjourn the hearing when the usher whispered in his ear.

A moment later the pork butcher was scurrying outside as fast as his fat little legs could take him. I recall picking up my papers wearily, aware that my paltry guinea would have to be worked for some other time, and followed the crowd outside.

I made my way down to the crowded, heaving embarkation dock and realized that a crowd had gathered there to witness what really was an incident of note. Through the rising yellow mist I could just make out where a decorated barge of some considerable size had collided with the piers of Westminster Bridge. There was a deal of distant shouting, much coming and going of wherries and steamboats, and a procession of wooden skiffs busy disembarking bewigged gentlemen from the barge: it was clear that they were persons of consequence from the crowd that had gathered on the bridge itself, and the waving of hats and cheering as notable individuals were rescued.

At the Devonshire Club that evening I learned that the accident had occurred to the *City Barge* carrying the Lord Mayor, the Sheriffs, the Aldermen and the Secondaries (among whom was my father). The barge had collided with one of the piers. All had been thrown from their seats in the collision with the mace, decanters and glasses from the hospitality tables thrown down and rolling about on the floor. At a distance, I watched the excited scene for a while but was soon bored by it: rather, I became

168

somewhat irritated, because with all the roiling about on the river, and the ferrying of the Lord Mayor's party to the shore, and the halloing from the massed boats with cheering spectators, there would be little chance of my obtaining even a skiff to take me back to the Temple within the next hour or so.

Moreover, I found myself standing next to another barrister of my acquaintance ... Ballantine, who later wrote so disparagingly of me in his memoirs. I always did dislike the man, who had obtained his position in the profession as a result of his father's influence as a Police Court magistrate. He was a long-nosed, slimy enough fellow, and on this occasion seemed inclined to button-hole me and engage me in conversation. Perhaps about my humiliation before Baron Alderson or my brush with the Benchers. This did not appeal to me. Accordingly I decided to forgo the pleasure of his company on the next available boat and turned to walk along the bank, to make my way back to the street where I might find myself a hansom cab.

I left the dock and proceeded to make my way along the riverside. This entailed scrambling over scattered river detritus, mud flats and decaying timbers at first, until I reached the narrow, dusty pathway that traversed the riverside. The track was fronted by rank, head-high weeds behind which decaying hovels lurched dangerously on the steep banks that led up to the main thorough-fares.

My boots were filthy. I was about to turn into one of the cobbled, narrow, rubbish-littered streets that led up to the highway, where I might find a cab, when my attention was distracted by a small group that had clustered about one of the ancient jetties that lay above the mudflats. I hesitated, curious.

At first I had thought that they were watching the shouting crowds on the bridge where the mayoral barge had suffered its collision, but soon realized there was more *purpose* to this group. A wherry had been drawn up at the edge of the mudflat; several brawny workmen were dragging at what seemed to be a kind of net, which resisted, surging heavily in the filthy water. They were paying no attention to the events at the bridge, and they were supervised by a man in a blue frock coat and tall, black-varnished hat. The supervisor's hands were locked behind his back; he was staring at the thing the men were drawing with difficulty from the river, and he bore an air of square-shouldered, imposing authority. Curiosity got the better of me and I walked towards the jetty, until I was standing just behind the man in the blue frock coat.

170

My steps echoed on the ancient, rickety timbers of the jetty. At the sound of my approach the man in the varnished hat turned slowly. He was a lean-featured fellow apart from his mastiff jowls; he wore reddish-hued side whiskers, and his small, deep set eyes were a startling blue. He was a little above average height, narrow in the hips, but the hands locked behind his back were large and meaty. His sharp glance met mine and I stopped: he observed me for several seconds, as though appraising me, and then nodded slightly, raised a hand to touch his hat. The carefully polished gilt buttons on his coat glittered in the watery afternoon sunshine. I did not know him, but I felt I caught a glimpse of recognition in his sharp glance as he looked at me. A moment later the suspicion was confirmed.

'Mr James, is it not?'

I was surprised. 'You have the advantage of me, sir.'

He smiled. His teeth were yellow-stained, wolfish. 'Inspector Redfern. I have seen you on occasions at the Thames Police Court, and once at the Old Bailey, sir.'

A policeman, evidenced by his uniform coat and hat; I had been blind not to have realized it. I stepped closer to the officer, peered past him to the men grunting and heaving at the jetty's edge. 'So what's happening here?'

Inspector Redfern glanced back to the workmen then turned back, observed me calmly. 'An unfortunate, Mr James. We come across many such. This time, it seems, a young woman.'

I stood there just behind him for several minutes and watched in horrified fascination as the men succeeded finally in dragging the thing caught up in the net out of the muddy water. The clothing was sodden, the grey cloak heavy and stained, hair plastered to the skull, features swollen as a result of the woman's immersion. There was an ugly sucking sound as the corpse was lifted over the gunwale of the skiff, then a deep trail was marked in the mud as the skiff was dragged across the mudflat towards the jetty. Inspector Redfern seemed unmoved by the activity, standing with his hands once more locked behind his back, almost indifferent to the scene, but it was the first time I had seen a corpse recovered from the river and I remained just behind the police inspector's shoulder, horrified, nauseous, yet fascinated.

Over his shoulder, Inspector Redfern commented after a thoughtful pause, 'There was thirteen children went overboard from a steamboat last year: three of them died this way. Not much chance of survival if they inhales the filthy water. Bound to be accidents, of course.' He nodded casually in the direction of Westminster Bridge, still packed with spectators observing the hapless Lord Mayor's barge. 'We calculate there's two hundred steamers constantly navigatin' the Thames apart from the three hundred or so sailing vessels carrying coal from Newcastle and the barges bringing grain and building stone up from Kent. And with the Diamond Company now taking wives and families down to Gravesend or Ramsgate for the summer, bound to be even more accidents, I reckon.'

He shook his head dolefully. 'I mean, they're crowding people aboard at a shilling for a fore cabin and eight pence for an after cabin.' He paused, glanced at me, leered, showed yellow teeth. 'Makes it a bachelors' week for the husbands in the City though, don't it, till they rejoin their families at weekends.'

My mouth was dry. I was unable to tear my glance away from the drowned woman being stretched out on the dock. 'You think that's how she died? Falling overboard from a steamboat?'

Inspector Redfern took a doubtful breath and shook his head. He removed his black varnished hat and polished the crown, absent-mindedly. 'No, my guess is this one was a jumper. They throw themselves off the bridges at high tide, you know. Sometimes it's weeks before they wash up on the shores, depending on the tides; other times they fetch up just days, or even hours after they go in. It's usually because they're poor, starving ... or are in an unwanted, *interesting* condition.' He paused, sniffed, leaning forward as the corpse was laid out on the jetty. 'Not that this one was struggling against poverty, if I could hazard a guess from her clothing...'

She wore a dress buttoned up to the throat; her petticoats were soiled from the water. The dress had been torn at the shoulder, exposing the flesh of her upper arm: her skin was white and unmarked. Her eyes were wide, staring sightlessly at the sky but strands of wet, bedraggled hair spread across her face, half-hiding her features which had begun to bloat. But there was something about her, and the soiled grey cloak about her waist that brought back a memory...

Inspector Redfern replaced his hat. 'Sometimes the fishes have feasted well from 'em,' he murmured, almost to himself. 'But this one, she don't seem to have been in the water long, the crabs haven't got at her...'

The body was laid on the jetty at his feet. Her head lolled to one side, her limbs were spread negligently, her skirts failing to hide her shapely legs. One of the labourers, a middle-aged man with a pockmarked face, leaned over her and with surprising solicitude rearranged her clothing more decently, smoothed back the strands of hair away from her face and stood looking down at her in compassion. He would have seen many such in the river, I did not doubt, but he had not yet become inured to such occurrences ... or perhaps it was the youth of the victim that was affecting him. I too stared at her, unable to drag my eyes away from the pale, bloated features. My eyes seemed to look beyond the ravages the river had wrought, and other images crowded into my mind. I was hardly aware of Inspector Redfern's orders as he instructed one of the men to arrange a cart for the corpse to be taken away to the mortuary. I remained rooted to the spot, shivering slightly in spite of the warmth of the clouded sun on my back. Slowly, my senses returned and I became aware that Redfern was frowning, staring at me strangely.

'This your first river corpse, Mr James?'

His tone was solicitous. I nodded dumbly. He kept his deep set eyes fixed upon me. I glanced away from him, across to the south bank, down to the crowded, cheering bridge where the mayoral party were still being rescued, then finally back to the body at our feet. A deep silence had settled among the small group in front of me as they contemplated the thing they had drawn from the grey water, a silence broken only by the rattle of cartwheels on the jetty, and hoof-beats on the weedy, misted cobbles. My mouth was dry, and my heart was pounding.

Inspector Redfern sighed. 'Aye, well, you get used to it. I was there when Samuel Scott, the American diver, took his first flying leap from the topgallant of a coal brig off Rotherhithe, you know. His end came when he tried to emulate that dancing on air performance with a rope around his neck. He got strangled at Waterloo Bridge in front of ten thousand spectators. Last year, that was. But this young lass ... ah, she'll have had no cheering spectators when she took her fall. For her, poor soul, it would have been a lonely, night-cloaked entry into eternity...'

I remained silent. I looked about me at the mist-shrouded lines of ships, the spiderweb of rigging up and down the dirty river, and I thought of the desperation that must have been in the young woman's mind when she leapt into the darkness to the black waters below.

'You are returning to the city, Mr James?' Inspector Redfern asked quietly after a brief interval.

I swallowed and nodded. My tongue was thick in my mouth. 'To the Temple.'

'Please permit me to offer you transport to the Inn,' Redfern offered, caressing the gilt buttons on his frock coat. 'I have a cab waiting. My men here will now attend to this business.'

I was reluctant, and hesitated.

'It will be no problem,' Redfern assured me, 'and I would be honoured to offer my assistance.'

Without being certain why, I wanted to refuse him, but could not find the words. I dragged my glance back to the woman on the jetty. Redfern stepped closer. 'Your first river corpse, Mr James,' he murmured. 'I understand your natural distress. But if I may be so bold ... I seem to detect something else...'

My senses were reeling. There was a great pounding of blood in my ears. My mind was filled with images ... how long ago had it been? A drunken evening with Serjeant Wilkins snoring in the cab beside me, a dark street, a lonely, distressed young woman at the street corner. I could have stopped, got out, found some way to help her, console her, but now it was too late.

'Am I correct, Mr James, in assuming...?' Redfern's voice was soft, gentle yet oddly menacing.

I chewed at dry lips. I knew what he was asking. I was unable to utter a denial. After a short interval, I nodded, gazing in horrid fascination at the sad bundle at our feet. 'Yes,' I muttered. 'Yes. I can't be certain, but...'

'You are able to identify her?'

'I think so,' I muttered. 'Only days ago ... but yes, I think I know who she is ... was ... might be...'

Inspector Redfern shuffled closer to me, touched my elbow respectfully. 'I will take you back to the Temple,' he said quietly.

He led the way from the jetty and I brushed past the workmen as they lifted the corpse into the mortuary cart. I followed Redfern up the cobbled slope between the overhanging balconies of the wooden slum dwellings until we reached the thoroughfare beyond. The rattle of cabs, carts, and the squabbling calls of a flock of geese being taken away from Leadenhall Market brought me back to my senses. Redfern's cab was waiting, a caped, disgruntled driver huddled in his seat, whip in hand.

Inspector Redfern opened the cab door, stepped to one side to allow me the privilege of entering first. As soon as I was settled he climbed in to sit opposite me and called out directions to the cabman. With a lurch and a clatter we were off, rattling over the cobbles and I settled back against the horsehair-padded seat, uncomfortably aware of the challenging scrutiny of the police officer's eyes.

'I have been reading the proceedings of the debate on the Brothels Suppression Bill, introduced by the Archbishop of Canterbury,' Redfern announced after a few minutes. 'Lord Foley has expressed the view that putting down such houses of ill repute will lead only to their transfer and re-establishment to other parts of the city.'

I was glad of the changed subject. I licked my dry lips. 'I understand the Bill has been withdrawn.'

Redfern nodded. 'I believe that is so. The result will be that, among others of her persuasion, Black Sarah will be able to continue her nocturnal activities in the Ratcliffe Highway.' He paused, meaningfully. 'I take it you are acquainted with Black Sarah?'

'I've heard of her,' I replied stiffly.

Redfern shifted in his seat and stared gloomily out at the dreary buildings we were passing. 'Perhaps it was in that area around the Ratcliffe Highway you might have met the unfortunate woman we've recovered from the river?'

Stung, I retorted quickly, 'What do you imply, Inspector?'

His tone was calm and measured. 'Forgive me, Mr James. I am applying logic, that is all. You are a young man who spends much time in the Temple. Your profession is a demanding one. Court proceedings run late into the evening. Your chambers are close to places of entertainment. I am aware that many of your colleagues frequent the night houses in the town; I am also aware that the young woman we have just recovered from the river, while reasonably well dressed, can hardly be described as one of the Upper Ten Thousand.'

A certain irony had entered into his tone.

Irritated, I snapped, 'You're suggesting that the dead woman was a whore.'

'You will have made her acquaintance in some other capacity, Mr James?'

We lurched our way into a crowded Fleet Street, pausing while the cabman cursed vociferously at the driver of some skeletal horses bound for the knacker's yard. They were dragging a cart piled with already dead nags. I answered the police officer with a surly stare. 'I have met the dead woman on only one occasion.'

Inspector Redfern raised his eyebrows in surprise. 'Yet you recognized her almost immediately, even though the river has somewhat changed her features?'

I hesitated. 'She ... she made an impression on me at the time.'

'And am I correct in assuming she was a whore?' Redfern pressed.

I wriggled uncomfortably on the odorous horsehair seat. 'I did not say that. I have no way of confirming the suggestion, except that...'

'Yes?'

I sucked at my teeth, thinking carefully. There were people to protect here. 'All I can say is that I met her just once. It was in the Cider Cellars. She was in a state of some distress, I felt a certain sympathy for her. Then, when I left the night house, as I made my way back to the Temple I caught a glimpse of her at the street corner. She was huddled in a doorway. She seemed distressed.'

'The Cider Cellars ... she was with a man?'

I shook my head. 'She entered alone. And she left again within a matter of minutes.'

'Yet she was in an unhappy state, so much that you clearly observed her.' The police inspector leaned forward, elbows on bony knees, frowning in concentration. 'Do you know what might have caused her distress?'

Now you have to understand that there was a matter of loyalty to friends here, even though I must admit I've never been strong on loyalty *per se*. But, apart from loyalty, more seriously, Lester Grenwood owed me money and I did not consider it sensible to place him in any kind of jeopardy, however much I might have disagreed with his behaviour that night when I had escorted Serjeant Wilkins back to his lodgings. In my opinion the whole thing was none of my business, and the death of the young woman, occasioned possibly by despair over her pregnancy, was a matter about which I could do nothing. It was done; it was over;

and for that matter the girl's death might have had nothing to do with Lester Grenwood.

In short, I had no desire to become further involved.

'I observed her,' I replied carefully, then added the lie, 'but the reason for her distress was unknown to me. I saw her briefly; I noted her distress; she left and after observing her in the street I saw her no more.'

'Until today,' Redfern murmured. His cold glance was riveted on mine. I gained the impression that he knew I was lying but he also knew that there was little he could do about it. 'Are you able to give the dead woman a name?'

I hesitated, then shrugged. 'I believe she was called Harriet. It is the only name I heard.'

Inspector Redfern stared at me for a few moments then leaned back in his seat and lapsed into silence. After a while, he tapped at the roof as the cab clattered along beside the alley leading to the Temple Church. As the driver hauled on the reins I put my hand on the door and looked at him. 'So what will happen now?'

Inspector Redfern's tone was cool, almost unconcerned. He shrugged. 'A dead woman of an uncertain reputation, recovered from the river where it would seem she probably entered of her own volition, and a name,

Harriet, the only identification we are likely to receive ... there is little more that can be done.'

'You will make no further enquiries?'

'There will be a report, then a coroner's enquiry as a matter of form,' Redfern replied diffidently. 'If any further information is received proceedings may be undertaken, but such an occurrence is unlikely. Desperate women enter the river daily; identification is difficult where whores are concerned, and my guess would be that this ... this Harriet would have been at the edge of that particular world at least. So, Mr James,' he said as he bared his yellowed teeth in a mirthless smile, 'it is unlikely that you will be called upon to take any further part in this matter.'

Sweating profusely, but relieved, I got out of the cab, and closed the door. I paused, looked up to the policeman. 'Thank you for your assistance, Inspector.'

'And yours, Mr James,' he replied drily, leaning his head through the window, and raising one finger to his hat.

I watched as the cab clattered away down the thoroughfare. I was aware of a heavy feeling in my chest. The prospect of the low ceilings and confining space of my lodgings at Inner Temple deterred me. I made my way into the Temple Gardens and sat on a wooden bench under the trees overlooking the busy, crowded, deathly river. I thought about Harriet as I watched the curling mist...

As I suggested to you earlier, women can sometimes take things so *seriously*. I mean, there were the rich, unattached women who had lent me money and were unreasonably indignant when they found out about each other; there was my first wife, making so much fuss over that business with an actress...

Of course, the girl at the Cider Cellars had been pregnant. But was that a sound reason for taking her own life in despair? It was so *final* a solution. It's why I always preferred widows: they often have a more mature outlook on such matters. They know there are practised persons in the back streets who can always get rid of what we might call unwanted encumbrances. They tend to be more rational, more discreet. But to leap from a bridge into the filthy waters of the Thames!

Redfern had assumed Harriet was a whore. Somewhere in my chambers I had a well-thumbed copy of Snell's *Guide to the Metropolis,* and I was sure Harriet was not listed there among the professionals. I sighed, strangely depressed. Perhaps I should inform Lester Grenwood of the discovery in the river, but recalling his attitude that night in the Cider Cellars I guessed he would be not in the slightest interested, or concerned.

I slapped my hands on my knees. I rose to my feet, and headed for my chambers. It was done. There was no action I could take. I had my own life to get on with. My professional reputation to establish.

And numerous debts to settle.

2

Harriet was still on my mind that evening, nevertheless; I could not remove from my thoughts the image of the sad, soggy bundle drawn from the river any more than I could discard the memory of the sound of her pleading voice that evening in the Cider Cellars.

Thoughts of Harriet, the image of her life-less body in the mud of the river bank, the last view I had had of her when she was alive, they returned to my mind throughout the early evening, even though I knew there was nothing I could do for her. But a few glasses of brandy and water in my chambers and a refreshing cigar helped to settle my nerves as I dressed in preparation for my evening meeting.

The appointment had been arranged for me by my grandfather. It was to be dinner at the Canton Club with one of its more eminent members.

I've always appreciated the existence of gentlemen's clubs: they are oases of quiet conviviality where a man can feel at home without entering the bonds of matrimony.

I was already a member of White's, and Almack's, where I did much of my gambling and I enjoyed the company of actors, writers and painters at the Garrick but it was towards Canton House Terrace, the home of the Tory grandees that I made my way that evening. The meeting was to be with an old gambling acquaintance of my grandfather's: the Earl of Wilton.

Politics was something I was always interested in ... not least because when you're a professional young man seeking preferment it's more than necessary that one should rub shoulders with those who rule the country and make decisions that affect all professional lives. Many of the members of the House of Commons came from aristocratic backgrounds and could afford to while away their time in the House, having nothing better to do. But of recent years a growing number of lawyers had succeeded in elections to the Commons and I had it in mind to follow them for that was the route to political preferment and the highest honours of the profession: Solicitor General, Attorney General, even Lord Chancellor of England. All political appointments.

And, equally important from my point of view, there was the fact that Members of Parliament could not be arrested and imprisoned for debt. Of course, I hadn't yet reached the stage where imprisonment for failing to meet my financial obligations was becoming a realistic possibility, but I knew my own inclinations and I was aware the day might come (as inevitably it did!) when having the letters MP after my name might help solve many financial difficulties.

An interest in politics is one thing: loyalty to the stated principles of one party or another is something different. One trims one's sails to the wind. The fact is, I have to admit that I took a somewhat cynical view of the best route to take, to serve my ambition. The route to political success lay by way of the Government benches, and that meant membership of the Tory Party. The obvious first step in that direction was to obtain membership of the Carlton Club.

My grandfather, who had many political connections from the days when he played whist with some of the greatest in the land, had prevailed upon one of those acquaintances to put forward my name for membership. I did not know the Earl of Wilton personally at that time, but Grandfather was well acquainted with him. Indeed, I had heard rumours that Grandfather had in the distant past enjoyed certain amatory escapades in Wilton's company ... when the earl was still the Right Honourable Thomas Egerton and a noted libertine of the day. Be that as it may, Grandfather made use of the acquaintance to arrange for Wilton to issue an invitation to me to dine with him at the club. Consequently, that evening I thrust aside thoughts of poor Harriet, and Ben Gully pursuing his enquiries about Joe Bartle's watch, while I went back to the West End and prepared for my dinner with Lord Wilton.

His lordship was in his late fifties then; had a considerable paunch, sagging cheeks, hooded eyes; his dissipated, fleshy mouth hidden by a luxuriant, drooping moustache. Ten years later we were to come face to face in the courtroom when he was accused of introducing a whore to the Queen at the Hanover Ball and it was my duty and pleasure, to attack him in the courtroom for his social malfeasance ... or as some brayed, treason. The whole thing got me into some difficulty at the time, as I recall...

However, that 1844 evening in the club Lord Wilton proved on our first acquaintance to be a good host: we dined well on soup and duck and fish and saw off a bottle of splendid hock and a passable claret. No matters of politics were touched upon in our discussion: during dinner our conversation ranged, as I recall, over the prospects for the hunting season and the availability of whores in the West End, as he sat there proudly smoothing his thick, greying moustache. At any rate, the evening passed pleasantly enough, and at the end of it all, when we had retired to the smoking room where an aged waiter provided us with brandy and cigars, Lord Wilton was still passing informed comment on the relative merits of a certain Nelly Cook at Cleveland Gardens and a Mrs Murray who resided at Long's Hotel in Bond Street. He was clearly more interested in whores than politics but finally was forced to allude to the reason for my presence: my desire to be proposed as a member of the club.

'I'll be happy to put forward the name of a grandson of Harvey Christian Combe,' he pronounced grandly. 'And I've no doubt that my nephew, who is also a member here, will second my proposal.'

I murmured my gratitude, began to mutter something about the aims of the Tory Party, concerning which I knew as little as he, but was relieved when Wilton's glance began to glaze. After a few minutes he laid his head back on the antimacassar of his leather chair and half-closed his eyes, clearly regarding the interview as over. He was soon snoring slightly, twitching his lips in a half smile, his moustache puffing as he snorted in some sort of sensual half-dream. I finished my

189

brandy, laid aside my cigar. It was time to leave him to his lascivious memories. I was about to lean forward, touch his lordship's arm and take my leave when I became aware that someone was standing close by, watching us. I turned my head.

It was Lord George Bentinck.

For a few moments his brow seemed thunderous as he stood there regarding me, an outsider in his Tory stronghold and a man who had dared sully his reputation in court. Then, slowly the expression on his heavy features changed. He jutted his lower lip thoughtfully, raised an arrogant eyebrow and then slowly walked forward. 'Mr James. I was not aware you were a member here.'

I rose stiffly. 'I am present as the guest of Lord Wilton.'

'Indeed?' Bentinck said, expressing surprise. He glanced at the earl, who grunted, stirred, and wheezed away from his amative memories at the sound of our voices. Lord Wilton blinked, stared at Bentinck and grunted. 'Ha...! Lord George ... so you know young James here? Harvey Combe's grandson.'

'I had not been aware of that connection,' Bentinck admitted after a somewhat strained moment, as he frowned slightly.

'I'm proposing him as a member.'

Bentinck looked at me appraisingly. There was a cold calculation in his glance that I did not care for. And I had no desire to spend time in his company. I inclined my head towards my host. 'It is time I took my leave, my lord. I have some work to complete before I make an appearance at Bow Street in the morning.'

'Yes, yes, my boy,' Wilton replied, appearing somewhat confused and waving his dying cigar. 'You cut along ... pleasure to dine you this evening ... regards to your grandfather.'

I attempted to move away, stepping past Lord George Bentinck, but with a slight movement of his heavy shoulders he half-barred me. He smiled in a reptilian manner, his tongue flicking his teeth in predatory fashion. 'Before you leave, Mr James, I wonder whether I might be permitted to detain you for a few moments. There is something I'd like to discuss.'

He did not wait for my reply, but nodded to Lord Wilton, turned and led the way to a far corner of the room. Reluctantly, I followed. He waved me to a leather armchair placed just in front of the tall windows. I sat down, aware of the cobblestoned rattle of the dark evening streets beyond the windows. Bentinck took no seat himself immediately, but stood with his hands locked behind his back, staring at me with a certain contemplation in his cold eyes. 'So,' he murmured at last, 'a grandson of old Harvey Combe, hey?

He was Lord Mayor in '96, wasn't he? And wasn't he the man who carried out the first interrogation of Bellingham for the murder of Spencer Perceval in 1812?'

'I am told so,' I muttered. 'It was the year I was born.'

Bentinck grimaced, and nodded. 'And I seem to recall he was a great friend of Fox, and Sheridan too ... didn't the Duke of York visit him once at Cobham Park to play whist? The Duke of Cambridge too? He moved in exalted circles, your grandfather, for all that he was ... a *brewer.*'

Irritated at the sneer, I began to rise from my seat but Bentinck forestalled me with a raised hand. He flicked at his coat tails and took a seat in the armchair facing me. He rearranged his heavy features into the imitation of a smile. 'Not an aristocrat, but a wealthy landed gentleman heaped with public honours. And your father, recently become a Secondary in the City, I believe? He will have married Combe's daughter.' He smiled more broadly as he stared at me, allowed his glance to linger over my features. 'Hah ... now, in fact, I seem to detect a certain resemblance...'

A brief silence fell as I struggled to hold my temper in the face of Bentinck's sneering tone. At last, I said, 'There is something you wanted to discuss with me?'

Bentinck raised his thick eyebrows and

nodded slowly. 'Yes ... since you're here. Our recent common experience ... I suppose you're aware that the damned Jew Levy Goodman made a considerable amount of money out of the Derby? In spite of all the hullabaloo. Odds of ten to one, it seems. What about you, Mr James? Did you have much money yourself, backed on *Running Rein?*'

I had no desire to discuss the tattered state of my financial affairs with the Chairman of the Jockey Club. I made no reply. After a short interval, Bentinck curled his lip cynically. 'Ah, well, your business to be sure. But an unfortunate affair, entirely. And I must admit, it did not end to my satisfaction. Nor can I say that I enjoyed my experience in the limelight of the Exchequer Court, in front of that hooting crowd. Well whipped up by your, ah, forensic skills.' He grimaced, squinted at me reflectively. 'But one should not look back. One should move on, look to the future, suppress unpleasant memories, don't you agree?'

I made no reply, but waited.

'On the other hand, I must confess that you, Mr James, you made an impression on me,' Bentinck continued in a silky tone. 'Naturally, I did not care for your forensic arrows in my direction, but I admit there was a certain *vigour* in your attack in the courtroom, which is praiseworthy in a young advocate at *nisi prius*. A considerable practice could well lie ahead of you. With your father's connections in the City, your grandfather's reputation...' He paused, glanced around the room, rested his gaze on Lord Wilton who had already returned to his slumbers. 'Not to mention well-placed friends in a club such as this.'

The hairs on the back of my neck began to prickle. I could not yet see where this conversation was proceeding, but a stain of suspicion was beginning to cloud my mind. Though not my judgement.

Bentinck folded his big, reddened hands over his chest, drumming his fingers lightly on the buttons of his waistcoat. 'There are many lawyers in the House of Commons these days. Your grandfather was a member of the Council for London for many years of course ... so in seeking to become a member of the Carlton do I detect that you yourself at some stage might be interested in finding a seat?'

I raised my chin defiantly. 'I have yet a career to make in the courts.'

'Assuredly.' There was a hint of cynicism in Bentinck's thin smile. 'But if Wilton's support gets you into this club, where you will rub shoulders with the Prime Minister, and his brother, and senior members of the Conservative Party I feel sure that in a short time a borough might well fall into your lap.'

'I have no such grandiose thoughts at the moment,' I lied.

'That may be so, James, but...' Bentinck reflected, as his narrow eyes bored into mine. 'Nevertheless, I'm sure you're well aware that the first step is membership of this club. The problem is that, well, one's acquaintances can sometimes let one down. Particularly if a person is unwise in the choice he makes of roads to wander down. A person can sometimes follow his nose into alleyways that can lead to ... unforeseen consequences.'

You know, my boy, I learned very early in the courtroom that if one is quick-witted enough it is always possible to discern the blade that is hidden under the cloak, however well concealed it might be. Moreover, though Bentinck was choosing his words with care, he was no lawyer, he lacked the finesse for this kind of business, and his arrogance would not allow him to hide his feelings and intentions too closely. I was on my guard: I could already detect the half-hidden poniard.

'This rogue Levy Goodman, for instance,' Bentinck continued in a decidedly casual tone that fooled me in no manner. 'He is well known to be an undesirable, un-principled liar.'

It takes one to recognize one, I thought. But aloud, I said, 'I have no acquaintance

195

with the man, outside that day in the court-room.'

'Is that so?' Bentinck queried. Oddly enough he seemed surprised and was on the point of saying something more, but then hesitated, leaned back in his chair. He looked about him, raised a hand, gesturing to the aged waiter leaning against the far wall and ordered a brandy for himself. He offered me none. But he fixed me with a cold eye as he waited for his refreshment and said, 'Well, I may tell you he has something of a history: thuggery, race-fixing, pugilistic frauds...'

'But nothing *proved,* I understand.'

Bentinck glowered at my taunting tone. 'And then there's the matter of *Running Rein.* A bad business for everyone. But ... as I said earlier, one must move on.' His glance slipped away from me as he added, 'I am of the firm view that the 1844 Derby is a book that should now be regarded as closed.'

'You are not interested in what was the truth behind the affair?' I taunted him.

He frowned, raised his chin. 'We reached the truth in court! As far as I'm concerned, the issues were finally dealt with in Exchequer. Moreover, Baron Alderson's strictures were, shall we say, received unhappily in certain quarters. There is a view among many of my friends, men of consequence that these matters should now be laid to rest.'

'*Buried,* you mean?'

I was surprised by his reaction. His eyebrows shot up alarmingly. 'What do you mean by that?' he demanded angrily. I shrugged carelessly, and his stubby fingers drummed on the arm of his chair. He was always a man of uncertain temper, unable to control his emotions. Now, irked by my tone, he fully withdrew the poniard from its sheath.

'Look here, James, let's say it plain. It's my view, and that of the Jockey Club, that after Alderson's strictures matters should be let rest. But it's come to my attention that you are still involved in making certain enquiries...'

'I can't imagine where you might have heard that,' I interrupted stiffly.

'If my information is correct,' he responded with a surge of anger, 'you're sticking your nose into matters that are no longer of any concern to you. I think you should be made aware that any further enquiries will not find favour in quarters that have influence. The plaintiff, Mr Wood, has agreed to let matters rest. Colonel Peel has come to a suitable accommodation with the corn merchant. That reprobate Levy Goodman can be left to look after himself. There'll be another day for a reckoning there. But as for you ... there is no further reason for you to involve yourself in this whole business. Let the sleeping dogs lie. No more stones to be turned over.'

'Not even to discover the truth?' I asked sarcastically.

Bentinck brushed the thought aside. 'Let the matter end here, James,' he demanded roughly. He paused as the waiter bowed in front of him, the brandy glass offered on the small tray. He took the glass, swirled and sniffed at it, waved the waiter away and sipped carefully at the liquid. Over the rim of the glass he observed me with hot, angry eyes.

'You have what might be a glittering career ahead of you, James. You could enjoy a fine career at the Bar. Entry into Society. The friendship of great men. Perhaps political preferment. So don't be a damned fool. Don't damage your prospects. By joining this club, you might well be able to gain the friendship of the Prime Minister's brother, among others. But your proposed membership of the Carlton, that could be endangered if you persist in dragging up further matters connected with that damned horse...'

His meaning was quite clear to me. I knew all about the advantage of an inside track at the races, and I knew it was being pointed out to me that I could have an unhindered run as a member of the Carlton Club ... if I behaved. But, perhaps foolishly, I felt resentful, and my dislike of this bully of a man stuck in my throat. I rose, bowed slightly. 'Thank you for your advice, Lord George. I must now take your leave.'

Bentinck was enraged, hardly able to believe I was resisting him. His tone changed, threateningly. 'Damn it, James, I want your assurance that you'll leave this business well alone!'

'That is something I cannot do,' I retorted.

For Bentinck it was like a slap in the face. And leaving him sitting there, empurpling, well, perhaps it was ill-advised conduct on my part. I could have used more discretion, perhaps have even been accommodating. Bent with the prevailing wind. But I was unable to countenance further that man's arrogance, and the underlying menace in his tone.

My intransigence in the matter, well, I knew that almost inevitably it would cost me membership of the club. And with loss of membership there would also be lost the opportunity to rub shoulders with government ministers, gain influence, reach for a seat in the Commons in the government interest ... but it was not to be.

The result was predictable. The Earl of Wilton was as good as his word. He duly proposed me a few days later, his nephew seconded me, but a single blackball was sufficient to deny me entry to the Carlton Club.

I had no doubt whatsoever it was Lord George Bentinck's blackball ... or that of one of his minions from the Jockey Club.

3

The evening that I heard of my blackballing at the Carlton Club, fuming, I met Ben Gully and we had a further discussion about Joe Bartle's watch. He had had difficulty rooting out the elusive receiver, Strauss, who was rumoured to have gone to Amsterdam on business. The conversation ended with my insisting that Ben continued to pursue his enquiries further among his acquaintances in the St Giles rookeries and along the Ratcliffe Highway. It meant letting him have some more of the money I had squeezed out of the Exeter solicitor Bulstrode, which was making me run short once again with debts piling up. But I was furious about Bentinck's threats and behaviour; I was put on my mettle, and determined not to be thrust aside by such menaces.

Impetuosity, of course. I would have done better to heed Bentinck's advice, however bitter the draught might have been to swallow.

However, a few good things seemed to have occurred as a result of the *Running Rein* case and the hullabaloo that surrounded it. While I had been abused and humiliated by Baron Alderson on the Bench my ranting in court had certainly persuaded certain solicitors who dealt with the seamier clients in town that I was a man after their own heart. As a consequence the trickle of briefs that began to arrive at my chambers was still growing ... even if they were not of the most lucrative kind and I felt that at last I was obtaining the notice I deserved. And needed.

Moreover, *The Times* was taking an interest. In those days 'The Thunderer' used to devote two or three of its pages exclusively to law reports in which the correspondents spared no detail. It led to the Bishop of London spouting from his pulpit that the newspaper had become the 'only authorised unmoral publication' of the day. Be that as it may, the details published included flippancies the barristers and judges used to while away the tedium of the courtroom and one such comment I made obtained some prominence. That particular week I'd been briefed to act in another horse case where I'd described the animal as 'running faster at the nose than on the track', a turn of phrase that pleased the yellow press. I was also briefed to appear for the Quaker travel firm Thomas Cook Limited in a libel suit. It had been claimed that they had used one of their vans to transport corpses to the crematorium for the London Necropolis Company. Mr Justice Maule was on the bench: he passed the opinion that he could see no libel in the claim. I spoke up quickly: 'True or not, my lord, I consider it be a very *grave* charge!'

The judge chuckled, then laughed out-right at my quick pun; the well of the court responded, and a roar of laughter spread throughout the room. It was reported in *The Times* next day, and made an appearance in *Punch,* after which my reputation was made, if not as a black-letter lawyer, at least as a man of ready wit.

I see you grimace, my boy; the fact is, audiences were more easily pleased forty years ago.

However, while I was pursuing my prac-tice in the courts, yet still brooding over the injustice of Baron Alderson's strictures, Cockburn's betrayal, and the threats of that rogue Lord George Bentinck, Ben Gully was busy burrowing into the rookeries, talk-ing to people, following up suggested leads, and spending my money. Well, Bulstrode's anyway.

But Ben was always an honest man, after his lights. He left a note at my chambers on the Friday evening. He had traced Strauss at last. An assignation had been arranged.

I hate rats.

It's an incontinent, unreasoning hatred. Even though I recognize that fact, the rustle of their scurrying steps, the sound of their panicked squeaking, the general evil appearance of their little red eyes and predatory teeth have always made me shudder and break out into a cold sweat. So it was with a degree of trepidation that I fought my way along the street that Friday evening, thrusting my way through the chaos of peripatetic placard men, pedestrians with wheelbarrows or perambulators, small traders with donkey carts, cows being milked by maids outside houses, streams of animals, private carriages and omnibuses all inconvenienced by the gas and water companies repairing mains and the slum clearances that had commenced with a view to connecting the new railway to Whitehall.

The thing was, Gully had asked me to meet him in Bunhill Row, near Moorgate, for a certain sporting occasion.

Blood sports have always been popular in the metropolis but had been banned some nine years earlier: bullock-running, bull-baiting and bear-baiting, or throwing sticks at tethered cocks for fun were activities no longer to be seen in public places. But in the poorer parts of London, if you knew your way around, you could still watch specially-bred dogs fighting each other for the delectation of the Fancy ... or you could watch dogs fighting rats, if you knew where to look.

Ben Gully knew where to look.

A good ratting dog could fetch a high price in those days, you know. And rat-catchers could make a good living. One publican I acted for in court was reputed to buy over 25,000 live rats a year, at threepence each, mainly from the country about Enfield. His consequent sporting occasions drew the attention of titled ladies and noble lords, he claimed, and I believed him without attempting, or even desiring to attend one of his entertainments myself.

But that's where Gully was taking me that evening. A short cab ride together and I found myself following him into a two-roomed house in a dilapidated part of Bunhill Row. Gully had informed me it was used by a notorious dog-trainer who kept a dog pit in the house. At the front entrance a battered-featured thug tapping a thick cudgel meaningfully against his gnarled hand took the entry fee that Ben provided and we were allowed entry through to the back of the verminous, odorous house. Ben gestured upward: the pit was located on the first floor. There was no staircase: the upper floor was reached by way of a rickety wooden ladder that gave access to a ceiling trapdoor.

We clambered upward, Gully leading the way. The hot fug and stench as we entered the crowded room made me gag but it seemed to disturb in no way the cluster of men and women who had gathered around the pit. The noise was incredible. The inhabitants of the room were waving their arms, enthusiastically shouting out wagers, stamping on the wooden boards, screaming and yelling encouragement mixed with curses at the animals. The stench was inevitable because all the windows on the upper floor had been boarded up and light was provided by smoky, flaring gas jets which gave the room a shadowy, dancing, eerie appearance. The pit itself was in the form of a small circus constructed of wooden palings, some six feet in diameter. Its timbered floor was stained with blood and excrement. In one corner was a cage teeming with frantic, squealing, excited rats. I caught a glimpse of their likely replacements in sacks bulging with terrified movement, gripped tightly in the huge fists of men with rough clothing, scarred faces, heavy shoulders and merciless eyes.

It was a scene from hell, but in spite of my aversion I could not drag my shivering gaze from the activity in the pit.

As far as I could calculate, some dozen

rats had been let loose and set running in the pit against an untrained dog. Quick, efficient kills could set a high price on a ratter but this animal was not doing well, and no bids for the dog were being launched as it scurried around the pit, snapping a back here, a neck there, but failing dismally to deal with the squealing mass of rats as they sought cover in different parts of the circus, crouching against the boards, baring savage teeth, rushing away as the dog tentatively approached them.

The patience of the crowd was quickly exhausted. There was a chorus of disapproving cat-calls until the reluctant owner of the dog reached down into the pit, grabbed the animal by the scruff of its neck and hauled it out, swearing fiercely as he did so. My guess was that it would not have a long life ahead of it. There was a shuffling of feet, a rising jabber of conversation and I looked about me: men in rough jackets and caps, women in shabby dresses, a small group of clearly wealthy patrons of the sport in their rolled collar coats, top hats and cloaks. None seemed to be observing the ring now, as dead rats were scooped up with a broad-bladed shovel; rather, money was changing hands, bets being scribbled on scraps of paper, and then the cage was being refilled with a sack of scrabbling, snapping, squealing vermin.

I was sweating profusely, my throat was thick with panic, and yet I confess to being fascinated, unable to move as the next entertainment commenced.

The bull terrier now thrown into the pit was clearly well known. His left ear hung loosely, half torn away from a previous battle; he walked with a peculiar gait, perhaps occasioned by the bloodied flank on his left side, perhaps by the loss of one eye, the socket now merely a mass of solid scar tissue. There was blood, half-dried on his muzzle. Anticipatory saliva dripped from his jaws. He was an ugly, unprepossessing sight, but the crowd loved him.

And their bellowing rose to a crescendo as some fifty rats were let loose from the wire cage.

The rats behaved as perhaps threatened humans would: they huddled together, gathered in a panicked crowd, rushed to the far corner of the pit away from the cage, and bundled into a mass, those at the outer edge frantically climbing one over another to reach the presumed safety of the centre of the writhing, squeaking pile. But the bull terrier was upon them in a trice.

He was an experienced killer and worked with a ferocious sense of purpose, a committed determination, champing methodically with his wide, blood-streaming jaws, snapping backs and necks with a rigid conviction, throwing each stricken rat over one shoulder in almost the same movement as he turned and snapped fiercely at the next. The vermin made no attempt to break from the pack, stream about the pit, attempt to confuse the attacker. They snapped back, squealed in terror, but held their place as the bull terrier methodically chewed his way through the black, heaving, squealing mass. As bodies and blood flew in the air, spattering some of the onlookers baying above the pit, and as the black and brown corpses began to litter the sanded boards of the circus the remaining rats began, finally, to scatter, and voices were raised, timings being called out, a crescendo of excitement thundering against the slates of the tawdry roof.

I turned to Gully, part-nauseated, part-excited, part-appalled. 'This tumult ... won't the police hear it? Is there never a raid?'

'The peelers won't be coming down into Moorgate when the rat-catching is on. They know better.'

As I stared at him I realized he was not watching the killing in the ring. Instead, his gaze was fixed on a man leaning on the paling at the other side of the pit. Nor did his gaze waver. It was as though he was willing the man to raise his own eyes from the rat-catching, meet his glance, recognize him and acknowledge Ben's presence.

Through the haze of greasy smoke in the spluttering gaslight I could see that he was one of the better-dressed among the baying fraternity, albeit a little flamboyant and perhaps out-moded, a man seeking to keep up with fashion by buying second-hand clothes discarded by wealthier members of society. A silk handkerchief drooped casually from his yellow waistcoat, the green coat had once been of a stylish cut, and his wristbands were slightly grubby. His hair was black and long, composed with a careful disorder, combed forward, divided nicely so as to allow one greasy lock to curl on his forehead. His eyes were as black as his hair, I realised, as he looked up at last, caught Gully's eyes on him, and stiffened, holding the glance.

I thought I detected a certain enquiry in the man's black eyes, a concern, but the glances of the two men seemed to be locked for several long seconds before some agreement must have been reached, quietly, without words, for Ben suddenly turned aside, touched my arm lightly, and murmured, 'Come, Mr James. Let's go back downstairs.'

I was glad to follow him, escape down the ladder, get away from the whistling, cheering, raucous crowd and the stench of stale beer, cigar smoke, blood, excrement and human sweat. We stood side by side in the dim light at the foot of the ladder. Several minutes elapsed but Gully said nothing. Above our heads the stamping and shouting could be clearly heard: it would no doubt have echoed the length of Bunhill Row but people who lived in this area tended to mind their own affairs.

At last the steps on the ladder creaked above our heads and the man with the greasy locks made his careful way down to the ground floor. As he did so, Gully drew me away so that we were standing in the dark shadow of the narrow corridor, where only stray gleams of light filtered through from the floorboards above. In those gleams motes of dust drifted down lazily, escaping the thundering feet above. I stood beside Ben as the man reached the bottom of the ladder, and looked about him, then came forward.

'Strauss,' Ben said carefully, in a low tone.

'Mister Gully.' The man called Strauss spoke in a high-pitched tone, a foreign accent, slightly broken. He held his head to one side, at a curious angle. I wondered if he had ever survived a garrotting, or even a hangman's noose. 'I didn't know that you was a follower of the sport.'

'I ain't,' Gully replied gruffly.

Strauss leaned forward, bending slightly at the waist and peered curiously in my direction. 'And who might your friend be, may I ask?'

'No need to ask,' Gully snapped, bringing an end to the enquiry.

'A gentleman, perhaps, come to see some new sights,' Strauss suggested, with no clear expectation of obtaining an answer. 'Still, Mr Gully, if you ain't come to see the rats, maybe you come to see me. Now why would that be?'

'I have some questions.'

Strauss considered his reply, mulled it over with a slight shake of the head. 'Questions, questions. Them as ask questions expect to receive answers, that's my experience. But you know, Mr Gully, I ain't in the business of giving out answers.'

There was a short silence. At last Gully spoke in a quiet but firm tone. 'I know what business you're in. I've known you a long time, Strauss. Done you some favours, too, even when you didn't deserve them.'

Strauss bobbed his head carefully, weighing up his reply. 'I don't deny–'

'There was that business of the strangling at the penny gaff, for instance.'

'Now, Mr Gully, there's no call to dredge up that old business.' A pleading note had entered the man's voice. I realized he was older than I had first appreciated. And unsteadier.

'And I never said a word to the swell mob about the shiv that went into Tom Shepard's back, that time at Lambeth.'

Strauss whinnied, and gave what seemed a little shuffling dance of protest. 'Now you know that was none of my planning, Ben,' he pleaded. 'The stuff he tried to fence me, it was perilous and he wasn't honest with me...'

'Since when was the biggest fence in Clerkenwell dealing with honest folk?' Ben sneered. 'But no matter. This ain't a matter of negotiation. Like I said, we've known each other a long time. Something's come to my attention. I been asking around for a week. Talking to certain of my acquaintances in the rookeries around St Giles way. Mainly without success. But, finally, a whisper came to me. And the whisper, it leads finally to you.'

'What you talking about, Ben?' the old fence queried in a sullenly querulous tone.

'A watch.'

There was a short silence and when Strauss finally spoke there was a note of incredulity in his voice. 'A watch? This about a watch?'

'Story is you fenced it.'

'So, but a watch? What's so special about it?'

'That's my business,' Ben Gully replied grimly. 'And relative to the watch, I've got a couple of questions that need answers. Where did you get it? Who fenced it with you?'

Strauss glanced uneasily in my direction, shrugged, spread his hands. 'A watch? I mean there's a deal of stuff comes through my hands...'

Ben thrust his hand into his jacket pocket and pulled out the hunter. He held it under the nose of the doubtful receiver. 'It's a gold watch. There's an inscription on the back. A name. Joseph Bartle. I know who you sold it to, but I want to know who it was fenced it with you, Strauss. And I want to know *urgent,* like.'

It was more than a little while before Strauss replied, peering carefully at the watch, weighing up options open to him, no doubt, and concluding that Ben Gully was not a man to be trifled with, and to argue with him was a game not worth the candle.

It was then, finally, that he told us about the Puddler.

4

Much has changed in the City these last forty years. I saw many changes on my return from New York, after my ten-year sojourn there. The old rookeries swept away, vast areas of country built over in response to the hunger for houses among the growing middle class, the marvel of the underground railway... And change continues. It was all so different in the 1840s.

Living in London in those days meant you could never avoid the poor and wretched: they were ever present in the streets and after all only a few paces from the houses of the wealthy in Regent Street lay the teeming rookeries of St Giles whence most of the criminal classes eked out a precarious living among their fetid courts and rubbish-strewn, sunless alleys. I mean, you were certainly *aware* of them, even if you avoided them like the plague. And the main streets in the metropolis in those days teemed with the lower classes, tending to geese and ducks being driven to market past stables and dairies, cowsheds and abattoirs: even in the Strand there was a cowhouse in a cellar under a dairy. They used to lower the cows down by ropes as the packed traffic rumbled by.

So I'd seen a deal of London, was familiar with its sights and smells and its swarming humanity, but when Ben Gully took me with him in our search for the Puddler I entered a new world. I was of course a denizen of several different worlds already: I was familiar with the splendours of my grandfather's house at Combe Park; I still visited the village in Herefordshire where I had spent my early years before my father transferred his law practice to Bucklersbury; I had personal experience of the theatre stages in the West Country, particularly Bath, where as a young man I did a short stint in front of the lights, and I had come to know the Inns of Court, Westminster Hall, the Strand, Regent Street. I even had more than a nodding acquaintance with the St Giles rookeries: there had been occasions when a few of us in our cups had ventured down its reeking alleys in search of adventure of the whoring kind. But I'd only *heard* of Jacob's Island by reputation, and had never felt the desire to venture there. But that was where Gully took me a few days after meeting Strauss at the rat-catching.

We went by boat, just the two of us, and Ben Gully himself did the rowing. He'd removed his jacket and the muscles bulged in his shoulders and arms as he heaved on the oars. There was a damp, meagre mist on the teeming river, curling slowly upwards and ship sirens boomed plaintively along the length of the turgid stream. The air was cool, but Ben was soon sweating at his exertions. I huddled in my coat, feeling slightly nauseous. It was not merely the river ... though the smells were bad enough. It was the thought of our destination. I had met in the courts various denizens of Jacob's Island: it had an evil reputation.

After a half hour rowing against the flow of the river, Ben sculled us into a gloomy, mist-shrouded, branching creek. The entrance to the narrow stream was screened by tiers of ancient, battered colliers, disused now and moored to rot along the shoreline; the littered banks were lined with decrepit, shuttered warehouses that had long since fallen into decay: their half-destroyed walls, gaping onto the side of the muddy stream, were gap-toothed, green, odorous and slimy. The creek would have been supplied at one time by clear streams from the Surrey hills, but the ravages of man had changed all that: the creek was now an open drain for the refuse that spilled from what houses remained inhabited on Jacob's Island.

For Ben Gully I was aware it was a return to his early years: I could hear him muttering as he rowed along, almost to himself. At one point he glowered at me from under frowning brows. 'I remember well how I escaped this as a young lad ... the place still smells of the graveyard.'

My thoughts were elsewhere engaged. I closed my eyes and thrust away the surrounding images of Jacob's Island as I hunched in my cloak and ruminated upon events that had brought me here, and not least the burning desire to get my revenge on that scoundrel Lord George Bentinck. I was becoming more and more convinced that it was he who had put pressure on Joe Bartle, perhaps bought him off, so he would give no evidence in support of Levy Goodman. I was certain it was Bentinck who had also arranged for *Running Rein* to be spirited away. My conviction had been growing ever more firm since Bentinck had showed the extent of his malice by blackballing the proposal for my membership of the Carlton Club after I had refused to turn aside from my investigations into the Derby fraud.

The skiff lurched and I heard a grinding noise. I opened my eyes. Ben was pulling the skiff in at the side of a broken, weed-encrusted jetty. He tied the painter to one of the supports; I eyed it uneasily, wondering whether the jetty was capable of holding the boat, let alone supporting our weight, but though it creaked and groaned in protest when Ben scrambled onto the sagging planking, it held well enough. He turned, held out a hand to me and I heaved myself up reluctantly beside him. When I grasped the slippery timber of the jetty for support it left a coating of green scum on my hand.

Gully took a deep breath, looked about him with a reluctant eye, perhaps dwelling on old memories, then jerked his head silently, and led the way. Our boots echoed on the crumbling timbers of the jetty and we struck out across crazy, rotting bridges, clearly familiar to him for he showed no hesitation. I am forced to confess that I glanced down nervously as I stumbled along: the bridges spanned reeking ditches where the water was covered with a thick scum and floating masses of green weed. Floating in the water near the bridge posts were malodorous carcasses, swollen with putrefaction, unwanted cats and dogs as far as I could make out, and on the muddy shore were piles of stinking fish bones and oyster shells, sticking up like pieces of discarded slate from the mud.

It was my first time on Jacob's Island, and the place made a vivid impression on me. So much so that after all the intervening years, I can still taste the acrid reek in my throat, experience again the disgusting smell in my nostrils. Stumbling behind Ben Gully with a handkerchief held to my face, I looked about me at the staggering wooden houses behind the disused warehouses: they had been erected half a century ago with their galleries and sleeping rooms at the rear, standing on rickety, rotting piles above the dark flood. The scene reminded me of old paintings I had seen of Flemish streets except that these houses flanked stinking, undredged ditches rather than canals. Some of the dwellings had been built above the narrow creek itself, with house adjoining house over the filthy ditches, or linked by lurching bridges, and there were signs that they were still inhabited: yellowed linen had been left hanging out to dry along balustrades or staves, or run out on a series of long oars above the slow-heaving, tidal waters, scummed with the outpourings of faecal refuse from the houses.

We continued on our way along the muddy track past some old, broken boats beached on a scummy, weed-strewn stretch of land near a dilapidated wharf. Gully stopped to speak to an old, white-faced, cold-skinned man squatting in the dirt, leaning against the front of one of the houses. I glanced to the back of the house: there were pig sties there, and scratching hens and ducks, lean and ill-fed. The scrofulous old man was staring at me with watery eyes and he said something to Gully, nodding towards me suspiciously. Gully shook his head impatiently: there was a certain threat in his stance as he spoke roughly to the ancient, who cringed. The old man saw Gully's bunched fist and scowled; he swivelled his head on his scrawny neck and pointed across the tidal ditch towards a crazily-leaning, gape-windowed, dilapidated wooden house that seemed on the verge of collapse. The few remaining shutters of the house were tightly closed: I remember wondering at the time, somewhat fearfully, if fever had struck there recently.

There was no sign of life as Gully led the way around to the side of the house to a narrow, close court. It was almost completely shielded from any sunlight that

Jacob's Island might occasionally enjoy; the air in the courtyard seemed stagnant, and as noisome as the ditches behind them.

'Who in God's name lives in these hovels?' I asked, almost gagging in my handkerchief.

'These days, corn-runners and coal porters, mainly.' Gully shrugged with indifference. 'It's as much as they can afford. They can earn maybe twelve shillings on a good day, but then might get nothing else for weeks. The longshoremen and toshers are in a similar situation...'

There was a battered sign above one of the windows. I wrinkled my nose as I realized the dismal line of hovels beyond the court had been given the name of Pleasant Row: I wondered what wit had decided upon that name. Certainly no one had had the energy to change it, or even scratch something more appropriate on the sign. That would have required a sense of humour, or energy: I suspected both were lacking among the inhabitants of Jacob's Island. I picked my disdainful way through littered filth as Gully led the way through a cellar-like back yard past a ragged, female child nursing a half-comatose baby on a doorstep: she watched us pass with vacant, uninterested eyes. Gully turned into Joiner's Court, a group of four wooden houses huddled around an excrement-laden yard. He looked around suspiciously and then strode to the second of the houses and thundered with his fist upon the door. There was a short silence, then a shuffling sound from within. The door creaked open a little, and a dirty, shaven head appeared. The boy had deep-set, heavy-lidded eyes and his bruised skin was the colour of brown earth. Ben Gully said something that I failed to catch and the boy shook his head sullenly. 'T'ain't convenient,' he muttered, and began to close the door.

Ben Gully kicked out his foot and the door slammed open, taking the boy by surprise. He yelped as he fell backwards, and lay there gasping for a moment, then was quickly back on his feet. He lowered his shaven head and shot past us, out of the house, scuttling down the yard like a frightened rat. Gully looked back and ducked his head, intimating that I should follow him. With even greater reluctance than earlier, I did so.

The house was shuttered and dark, but in the dim light we were just able to make out the litter of rubbish that had accumulated at the foot of the stairs. Gully paid no attention to the downstairs rooms and I could guess that the inhabitants would almost inevitably want to use the rooms upstairs, if only to get away from the proximity of the malodorous ditches outside, to seek a little air above. The handrail to the stairs was broken; as we ascended the creaking steps we moved carefully, Gully warning me of some missing boards. We finally came to a single room at the top of the stairs: without ceremony, Gully thrust the door open with his broad shoulder and stepped inside.

The windows of the room had been long boarded up, and only faint chinks of light filtered through the split wood. For a few moments I could see nothing. Then as my eyes grew accustomed to the dimness I gradually made out in the filtered gloom a rubbish-strewn, uncarpeted floor, and a broken-backed chair and table. On the rickety table there lay an empty gin bottle, a wooden trencher and some scraps of stale, unidentifiable food. A three-legged wooden bed stood in the corner, half supported by a block of timber dredged from the river. On the bed there was a pile of ragged clothes. Over all hung a miasmic smell of must and dry rot, mingling with the odours from the creek, and I heard Gully growl deep in his throat. Too many memories, I guessed. He closed the door as he gestured to me to stand near the window; he himself took up a position just to the right of the door. We said nothing; I was still gagging into my kerchief. We waited in the dimness as the muted sounds of the island drifted up to us intermittently through the broken shutters of the window.

That damned rogue Lord George Bentinck had brought me to this. I swore fiercely under my breath.

Leaning against the door jamb Gully seemed content to wait. I grew impatient, and fought against the taste of bile in my throat. But I held my silence. It was twenty minutes before we heard a shuffling step on the stairs. Gully held up a monitory hand. A few moments later the door swung open and someone stood in the doorway, a narrow shaft of light picking out his features.

He stood there, stock still, for several moments, staring at me, a canvas bag slung over his shoulder, a long stave in his hand. I could see the boy was young, but his stance was confident and worldly. He was lean and wiry in build, narrow in the upper body but through his ragged shirt there were glimpses of well-muscled arms and chest. Slowly, he let the canvas bag drop to the floor and he stepped forward suspiciously towards me. As he entered the room Ben Gully moved quickly behind him, and in a trice had wrested the stave from his hand and slammed the door shut. The noise reverberated in the empty house like the knell of doom.

'This,' Ben Gully announced to me with a certain satisfaction, 'is the Puddler.'

The boy, startled by the sudden loss of his stave, stared at Gully. 'What's the 'ell's happenin' now?'

Gully ignored the snarling tone. He glanced at me and sniffed. 'The reports of the Constabulary Commissioners will tell you, sir, that the inhabitants of Jacob's Island suffer extreme lassitude and are deficient in energy, as a consequence of the inhalation of the mephitic vapours of the swamp ... and that drives them to the gin shops. Impaired digestion, languid circulation, depression of mind ... that's what the Commissioners say.' Gully grunted and smiled. 'But you and I know better, don't we, Puddler? We know you can crack a rat's neck with your fingers, and carry a heavy load of loot on your back. You won't yet be fourteen, but you know every stinking courtyard in the rookeries over at St Giles. You know the boatyards and the shoreline and every inch of its slime, and you can outpace any constable over half a mile ... after which, you're vanished! Ain't that so? You're a man of consequence and initiative, ain't that right, Puddler?'

'Who are you?' the boy snarled.

'The name's Ben Gully.'

There was a brief silence as the boy stood there, tense as a cat ready to spring. 'I heerd of you, Gully. You used to be from around here.'

'Used to be,' Gully almost spat. 'And it's *Mister* Gully to you, my young friend.'

After a short silence, the boy looked again

at me. 'Who's the swell?'

Gully stepped forward and prodded the shoreman in his chest, pushing him backwards down onto the filthy bed. 'It's no matter to you, Puddler, who my companion might be ... but watch your tone of voice when you talk to me. And I ask the questions around here.'

'There's no cot for you around here these days, Mr Gully, and I don't know what you want of me,' Puddler replied, somewhat subdued, but still casting a wary eye in my direction.

'What do I want of you? Merely a little information,' Gully said cheerfully, seating himself carefully on the edge of the bed, pinning Puddler's legs with a brawny arm. 'I'd like to know what you been up to recently. What necks other than rats you been cracking of late? What cribs you been breakin' into?'

'Hey? You got to know better than that, Mr Gully,' the young boy said, a note of alarm in his voice. 'If you know me, you know my trade. I work the underground, and an honest trade it is in spite of what the Commissioners say. If it wasn't for the likes of me, think what would be lost for ever! All I'm doing is plying a trade, collecting–'

'Thieving, more like!' Gully intervened sarcastically.

'That's not so!' Puddler started up, seemingly outraged. 'I only pick up what I find, where it's lost, and no one can say otherwise.'

'But you're not above breaking the rules here and there,' Gully suggested, almost conversationally. 'Like lifting something from a drunk in a gutter.'

'That's not my style, Mr Gully,' Puddler rejoined sullenly.

Ben Gully grunted in contempt. 'Aw, come on, there's days when pickings are poor down in the sewers, when you've got nothing to take to old Strauss... Did I happen to mention I been talking to him recently?'

Puddler made no reply, but there was a stillness about his body suddenly.

Gully smiled genially. 'That's right, my son, I been talking to him. He's an old friend. Keeps me informed, like all the fences do. I could cause them trouble, you see, a word here, a word there, so they confide in me. And old Strauss, now, when I met up with him at the rat-catching he left me with the impression that he's worried about you, in a fatherly sort of way ... well, not to put too fine a point to it, he tells me he thinks you've maybe changed the nature of your trade.'

Puddler shifted uncomfortably. 'I don't know what you're talking about, Mr Gully.'

'Ah, I know how it is, Puddler! Things are hard going, the sewers have been dry this hot summer, there's no great wash to the river, and pickings are lean. So how's a young man of talent to live? Bit of thievery, maybe. Bit of crib-cracking. And I hear there's been a bit of neck-breaking and garrotting down the West End, too. You coming up out of the sewer to do your bit of that business, Puddler?'

'I don't know what you're talking about, Mr Gully! Mr Strauss's got no call to say things about me that ain't true. You know me–'

'Yes, I know you, for a miserable piece of scum who'd sell his grandmother, if you only knew who she was!' Gully snorted. 'But no matter. I don't really care what you've been up to, not today, and not as long as you tell me where you lifted this little piece of plunder.'

Gully dangled in front of the shoreman the watch he had earlier shown to me. Puddler hardly glanced at it. 'Never seed it before.'

Gully was silent for a moment. 'I think you'd better look at it more carefully, my friend,' he said quietly. There was a subdued menace in his tone. 'Strauss tells me you fenced it with him, and he was a bit nervous of it like, since it had a name ... Joseph Bartle ... etched on the back, and he thought maybe you'd have lifted it from that gentleman's pocket. So he passed it on, and it finally came into my possession through a contact...'

Puddler detected the threat in Gully's lowered voice and looked at the watch nervously. He shook his head again. 'I never–'

Gully's left hand shot out and grabbed the shoreman's throat. I stepped back, startled, as there was a wild thrashing in the bed but Puddler could not escape the grip, his legs were pinned under the weight of Gully's body, and though the boy tore at Gully's choking left hand he was unable to loosen the pressure of the man's powerful fingers.

'Lissen to me, Puddler,' Gully hissed. 'If you're found dead around here there's none to mourn, none to question, and none who'd dare point a finger at me, even if they cared. You'd be no loss to society, just a nameless grave in the swampy ditch out there. But my companion here, he's an important man, a busy man, and he's no time to waste on scum like you. He don't like the air around here, and as for me ... I'm tired of it too. Now I seen Strauss, and he's told me a little tale, and now I want you to tell me a little tale too. Sort of confirm things, like. Strauss says you came in and fenced this watch ... and a chain ... with him. Now I just want the answer to some simple questions. Where did you lift this watch? Was it in some back alley? Was the owner drunk in the gutter? Is he holing up somewhere and had to use this to pay for accommodation? And how the hell did you get your dirty little hands on it?' He thrust his menacing features closer to the struggling, choking boy. 'What you been up to, Puddler?'

The shoreman's head was thrashing around, his eyes beginning to roll up into his head as the fierce grip of Gully's fingers increased. I thought that if Gully did not release him soon the boy would expire; even as I thought so and put out a warning hand, Gully glanced at me, then slackened his grip. He thrust his head closer to Puddler's. 'Well?'

The boy nodded desperately, and then as Gully released him he fell backward, racked by a paroxysm of coughing and retching. He sat up, head lowered to his chest and fought for breath. It was several minutes before he was able to speak. Gully remained silent, waiting, watching the boy's convulsive movements dispassionately. At last, in a tone that was almost gentle, he said quietly, 'Talk to me, Puddler.'

Puddler shook his head desperately. 'All right. I seed it before. But it wasn't no thievery, Mr Gully, I swear.' He rubbed his sore throat and gagged. He swallowed painfully and stared in reproach at his tormentor. 'You know that ain't my caper, Mr Gully. I ain't changed my style. I found it, Mr Gully,

I found it.'

'Where?' Gully insisted in a quiet but threatening tone. And the boy told us.

I really ought to explain to you about Puddler.

He was one of those lads for whom the overpowering stench that pervaded the outlet to the main sewer emptying into the river at Shadwell was merely just part of a day's work. He was impervious to it: he had worked the shores since he was eight years of age and he was well used to ignoring both the stench and the foul, evil-smelling sewage that trickled from the outlet in a black, turgid stream dripping into the river. Every day he'd trudge through the mud, turning into the main outlet where the Commissioners had yet to install the brick walls and strong iron doors that they had erected elsewhere to prevent flooding. The doors were so arranged that at low tide the pressure of sewer water beyond the door would force them open, to spew forth the accumulated filth of the city streets and dwellings. When the tide rose the door was forced shut against the wall so that the shoremen could not enter. But the Puddler knew how to get around that problem.

From what the boy told us, a few days after I had faced humiliation in the Exchequer Court at the hands of Baron Alderson, inside the main sewer outlet Puddler had lit his dark lantern and adjusted his bag on his back. The air was not too bad that day, apparently: it was always somewhat better when the spring tides caused the water to rush through the sewers, bursting up through the gratings into the streets, and flooding the low-lying districts in the vicinity of the river. There were times when Shadwell and Wapping came to be intersected by muddy canals but those were not the good times for Puddler. It made his task – grubbing out a meagre living from pickings in the sewer – that much more difficult. And the spring tides were past. The dry spell had caused accumulations of filth in the sewers, but he had worked in worse air.

You ask what was he about? Well, he had learned his trade early from the toshers who travelled along the muddy shores beside the ship-building and ship-breaking yards. You know about them? The toshers picked up iron bolts, copper nails, lengths of rope, anything of value, stuffing their prizes into the vast pockets of their greasy, velveteen coats. The shoremen wore old shoes and dirty canvas trousers to shuffle through the mud, testing their foothold with long poles at the end of which were large iron hoes. Puddler had learned how useful, indeed necessary, such a pole was when he had been caught one day, struggling in a deep set of sewer mud. The more he'd struggled the deeper he'd been enmired. The pole had saved him: by hooking it into some crumbling brickwork he'd been able to draw himself to safety. His own version was a five foot stave with an iron hook on one end and a stout hoe on the other. He never worked the shore without it.

When Puddler had started, working with gangs of four other boys, he would have heard tales of sewer hunters beset by giant rats, of skeletons that rattled their bones underfoot, or fell clawing from the decaying brickwork of the walls of the sewer tunnel, and of the mythical, vicious wild hogs that lived and fed in the underground tunnels. Puddler learned to discount these tales: there was more danger from the nosys who peered down through the street gratings. They could claim a reward of five pounds offered by the Commissioners for information leading to the apprehension of sewer hunters like himself so the gratings were to be avoided, or passed with care.

He had learned his trade well before leaving the gang to look for 'tosh' on his own: he knew better than to scramble over the heaps of rubbish in the darkness of the criss-crossing tunnels by grabbing at the overhead brickwork: the slightest tug and he might be buried in an avalanche of old bricks and earth. He also knew it was dangerous to branch into the smaller sewers leading off from the main run: apart from the discomfort of stooping low and crawling in the noisome mud under a four foot heading there could be foul air and gas accumulated in the confined space. And that's where the rats nested: they could be ferocious and vicious if disturbed. And there was also the sluice gate which was shut down by high tide and opened by low tide – the water could burst out in a torrent, sweeping everything away in its path.

I gathered that Puddler had no idea what his real name might be: brought up on Jacob's Island he had always been called Puddler, he knew not why. He could not recall who had first set him to work in the sewers nor who had first given him a canvas apron and a dark, bull's-eye lantern, and it was a good three years since he had split away from the gangs of boys, to strike out on his own as a sewer scavenger. He was lean, wiry, thirteen years of age and he was able to look after himself, scraping a reasonable enough living from the gleanings of the foul rubbish of the sewer. It was the only life he had known; the only life he wanted.

Puddler never took a dog to protect him from the packs of rats, as some of the other toshers did: its barking could draw attention to his silent progress through the sewage. And he always closed his lantern when he approached a street grating so he could slip past without causing a curious group to gather, telling the policeman on duty that there was someone moving in the sewer below.

So he would go along, raking the mud below with his hoe, picking in the crevices of the brickwork with the hook, occasionally discovering clusters of small articles that had been lodged in the sewer holes formed in the crumbling brick. He took almost everything he found: scraps of metal, iron, nails, coins – some rusted into a mass ... spoons, ladles, knives and forks. By plunging his hand into the muck up to the elbow he could bring up shillings, sixpences, and half-crowns. He told Ben, almost with a sort of pride, he had twice found half-sovereigns, probably washed down from a cesspool or house drain where they had been lost. He had once found some ladies' jewellery: that had been a good day.

As for Joe Bartle's watch, Puddler had had a feeling about that particular day. There had been some rain after the long summer drought: a heavy downpour had cleared some of the accumulated rubbish. He had decided to work an area he had entered rarely before, because the gangs were too numerous at Snow's Fields, his usual entry point. So he had worked his way carefully from the shore outlet towards Mint Square, where the sewers were noisome with numerous pockets of gas.

Not much of a life, hey?

Shortly after he penetrated the main sewer slushing through the thick sewage, he had heard the dull booming ahead and had quickly stepped into a side sewer, crouching down as the rush of water from the sluice swept past him on its headlong dash to the river. Then he crept forward again, lifting his dark lantern ahead of him, probing with his iron-hoed pole.

The opening of the sluice had moved a fair amount of sludge but the location was not promising: a side cavern in which thick slime had accumulated and where a faint light filtered down from the main grating in Kent Street. He was edging forward, one eye on the grating above with his bull's eye lantern covered, when his pole struck something, soft and yielding. Puddler stopped, edged forward carefully, up to his thighs in filthy mud and groped with his hand for the thing he had struck. He felt the roughness of cloth, an arm ... then a man's head.

Now Puddler was used to finding the occasional corpse in the sewers: sometimes garrotted and stripped, occasional suicides near the river entrance. But this one was fresh, fully clothed, it seemed, and suggested better pickings than usual. Gripping the arm tightly Puddler walked carefully backwards, dragging the body deeper into the sewer, away from the street grating above. It moved sluggishly but easily enough as the sludge gave out sucking sounds and rushes of fetid air reached his nostrils.

In the darker recesses of the sewer Puddler unstrapped his dark lantern from his chest and lifted it high, opening the shutter. Leaning against the ledge at his back he gripped at the collar and heaved. There was a sluggish, reluctant swirling in the mud and the head appeared, hair plastered down, mouth choked black with muck, the face unrecognizable as human in the filth that encrusted it. Puddler laid aside his pole, propping the lantern on its hook, and then he knelt in the mud up to his chest, while his fingers searched through the clothing, the pockets, the vest. He found a handkerchief, keys, some coins and pushed them into the tattered canvas bag on his back. There was a ring on the left hand: it slipped off easily enough where the hand had been gnawed at by rats. His groping fingers found a snuff box in the side pocket and it followed the coins. There was a watch chain, and he eagerly followed it until he encountered the watch itself. It was a hunter: he knew that if he was lucky, it would be gold and that would fetch a pretty penny.

There was little else. He groped and searched blindly, turning the heavy body over and over in the thick mud, but at last, reluctantly, he gave up. It was time to strip the body, because the jacket, shirt and trousers, boots, all could be sold. It was a difficult job, turning the inert body over and over in the cloying filth but at last it was done and there was a satisfying weight in the bag on his back, and the canvas apron at his waist. He picked up his pole, disengaged the lantern. Then he went on his way, stepping aside from the man's body as it sank in the thick slime, to head back down towards the outlet. In a moment he had all but forgotten about the man as he wandered on through the tunnels, picking up the odd piece of old metal, bones, a length of rope.

It had been a good day. He was sure of it. He retraced his steps under the rattle and thunder of the London streets, back to the riverside, and the miasmic air of the Thames. When he emerged, the light was dying and fires glimmered along the landings and in the camps on Jacob's Island.

Ben Gully sighed softly after Puddler finished his account. 'So is that it?'

Puddler was silent for a little while, staring at Gully and the threat of the hand fearfully. At last, he shook his head in despair. 'That's it, Mr Gully. But I don't like getting involved in things like this. It's not my way. You got to understand, I go me own road, I don't interfere with others, I don't arsk questions, I just pick up what I find...'

'The body was under Kent Street, you say.'

Puddler nodded eagerly, stroking his throat with tender, caressing fingers. 'That's right. Under Kent Street. But that ain't necessarily where he started, of course. Could have been washed down. There's a powerful current just there, running from the north side of the street ... a main junction–'

'We'll have to tell the police,' I interrupted.

Puddler let out a wail. 'Mister Gully, I can't be pulled up before no police! I swear I didn't do nothing to the–'

'Shut up,' Gully snapped. 'Your name won't be passed on.' He glanced at me. 'The polis, informin' them ... I'll leave that to you, sir. You can tell them you acted on information received, without disclosing the part played by our young friend here.' He grinned wolfishly at the boy on the bed. 'Because he's going to help us further.'

Puddler moaned lightly. 'I don't want to get involved in no peeler business.'

'He's going to take me into the sewers,' Ben Gully said pleasantly. 'And he's going to show me just where he found the body from which he took this watch. And he's going to give me the benefit of all his considerable experience ... and show me where the body might first have been dumped into the sewer.' He glanced at me. 'And then we'll see what's what.'

I need hardly tell you I was happy enough to leave that particular task to Ben Gully.

Chapter Five

1

So Joe Bartle was dead. And by the looks of it, murdered. Ben Gully confirmed the likelihood with me next day after he'd been down into the sewers with Puddler: from Bartle's head injuries it looked as though he'd been beaten to death.

The missing witness at the *Running Rein* hearing would now never be able to tell us why he had failed to turn up at the trial, who had persuaded him into his course of action, or what part he might have played thereafter in the spiriting away of the horse after Baron Alderson demanded that *Running Rein* be produced in court. But it probably had led to his violent murder.

'So you still think Bentinck is behind this?' Ben Gully asked me, doubt in his voice.

'At the Carlton Club he put pressure on me to stop ferreting further,' I insisted. 'Now we know why.'

Ben Gully growled deep in his throat. 'It won't be an easy task, pinning a murder on the Dictator of the Turf. And I'm not as certain as you are, Mr James. When we look at the facts ... well, we know Bartle was at the stables on the Wednesday before trial, then disappeared. There's a report he was at Hampstead Heath for the Porky Clark–Sam Martin fight on the Sunday afternoon. Monday, your case got dismissed 'cos *Running Rein* wasn't to be found.' He shook his head in doubt, breathing hard as his errant eye wandered in his head.

'You say you think Bentinck is behind all this, but we also got to consider whether Lewis Goodman didn't have a hand in the business. And that possibility makes me shiver.'

I'd wondered about that while Ben had rowed me back from Jacob's Island. I'd stayed silent then, while I looked about me: the mist was rising, but wispy tendrils still stubbornly gathered along the side creeks, and the monotonous, mournful sounds of the sirens still wailed along the river as the coal boats drifted past us like silent ghosts and the sound of river steamers came clunking through the mist.

But I'd settled my mind on Lord George.

Now, standing just off Chancery Lane, while bewigged men of law hurried past on their way to one court or another, and pock-pitted creatures peered at us in dirt-encrusted suspicion through the lane's patched and papered windows, I could see that Ben was wondering whether we should persist in our enquiries.

'So what do you suggest, Ben?' I asked at last.

'Leave it, Mr James. It's no longer just about a missing horse. You could be throwing good money after bad.'

Stubborn pride was swelling in my throat. That's always been my trouble, you know. I always hated losing. It made me a successful and aggressive advocate, of course, but it also got me into all sorts of trouble over the years. Like the time I called Gladstone little better than a pimp and he threatened to sue me, oh, yes, quite an exchange of letters that was. But I'd have nailed him if he'd taken me to court, you know, and he knew it ... all those 'fallen women' he took back to his lodgings for prayers for their immortal soul!

And that day with Ben I felt that if I stopped at this point it would be an admission of defeat, Bentinck and Goodman and Fitzroy Kelly and even that old blunderer Baron Alderson would be the winners in all this. 'I'm reluctant to give it up now,' I advised Ben. 'I want to find out what happened to that damned horse.'

'And why Bartle had to die too?' Ben queried, eyeing me carefully. 'You've already been warned off pursuing these matters. Best all left alone, Mr James.'

But I could not do that and told him so. Gully shrugged, nodded finally and said with a sigh, 'It's your tin, Mr James. If this is what you want, I'll see what I can do. Give me a few days to make some further enquiries ... and meanwhile, you get a report to the peelers. But keep all names out of it; it'll only make things more difficult if names get used.'

So off he went, stumping past the rickety children playing in the dirt while I made my way, reluctantly I admit, to Bow Street Police Station. There I laid an information. That very evening I watched at a safe distance as a group of policemen gathered at the grating in Kent Street, while a workman clambered down into the sewer. When they finally brought out the corpse I was at the edge of a curious crowd but I did not wait around to take a closer look.

I already knew who it was.

After that it was no real surprise to me a few days later when an unwelcome visitor appeared on the steps of the Old Bailey, when I was leaving after the successful defence of an actress accused of indecency on an omnibus. I'd persuaded the court that she was merely fumbling in her skirts for the price of the ride. I was smiling, and a few guineas richer, when I emerged, but I sobered when I saw the stiff, blue-coated man waiting at the foot of the steps.

Inspector Redfern.

'Good morning, sir,' he said politely

enough, stepping forward and raising a courteous hand to his tall black hat. 'And congratulations.'

He wasn't here to follow my forensic career. I frowned. 'What can I do for you, Inspector? I'm rather busy: I have to appear at the Exchequer Court in a little while and–'

'If you have no objection I'll walk along with you, Mr James,' Redfern announced breezily, glancing around him at the busy street. 'It's difficult to be heard here.' In those days, you see, the street outside the Old Bailey was surfaced with wood blocks ... the idea was that this would allow proceedings in court to be more audible since wood made less road noise than cobbles. But this day a huge iron cylinder was being painfully hauled along by eight sturdy navigators, tamping down the gravel beaten into crevices of the under-layers of the road and the clanging din was indescribable. So I would be forced to suffer the companionship of a peeler while I walked to the Exchequer Court.

Hardly enamoured of being seen in such company, gruffly, I replied, 'Well, perhaps if we took coffee...'

There was a dilapidated eighteenth-century coffee house nearby, one not usually frequented by my colleagues at the Bar. I led Redfern there. We made our way through the narrow doorway into the dark-panelled interior and once seated it was not long before he came to the point. We had located ourselves in a quiet corner of the coffee house, seated on a knife-scarred oak bench. I ordered coffee from a stoop-backed servant, aware it was likely to be nothing better than coffee essence which, I tell you, my boy, had a distinctly odd taste. Like pigswill-flavoured mud. When it arrived, Redfern seemed to enjoy it.

He had removed his tall varnished hat but his blue coat still marked him out as one of Sir Robert Peel's men. Two men seated nearby glanced our way, drained their mugs quickly, and left. Redfern favoured me with a grimace that passed for a smile. 'They'll be up to no good, I'll be bound.' He glanced around, eyeing the other denizens of the coffee house. 'First time I've visited this location. Not my beat, you see...'

'You wanted to talk to me,' I muttered, anxious to keep our meeting as brief as possible.

Redfern showed his yellowing teeth in a mirthless grimace, and nodded. 'I thought you might be interested to know that no further proceedings are to be taken with regard to that young jumper ... the woman we pulled out of the river the other day. Coroner's inquest quickly over; no formal identification. The name you provided,

Harriet, well, as I guessed it didn't take us very far.'

'So she'll be buried–'

'At public expense,' he assured me, as though I had been offering to pay. 'So you can forget all about that sad affair. All over and done. But now ... well, there's this other one.'

I knew what he was alluding to but affected ignorance. He would have read the record at Bow Street: he would know it was I who had placed the information regarding the dead man in the sewer. He stared gloomily at my raised eyebrows. 'It seems you're beginning to make a habit of helping us with our official enquiries.'

'I'm not certain I know what you are referring to.'

'I refer to the body found under Kent Street.'

I remained silent, glowering at my coffee.

After a short pause, Redfern went on, 'I happened to read the report this morning. It mentioned your name as the party who had laid the information. That made me curious. So I thought I would have a word with you, sir. Find out if there is anything else you can tell us about this unidentified corpse.'

'I explained at Bow Street that a client of mine told me...'

'So the dead man wasn't someone you knew personally, then?' Redfern's suspicious eyes bored into mine. 'Like the deceased young lady?'

I had drawn the line at naming Bartle. Giving the body a name could have led to unforeseen complications. I shook my head emphatically. 'No. I filed an information. I knew nothing more about the unfortunate individual.'

'Yes...' Redfern murmured, almost to himself. 'Beaten to death. But I am curious. How did you come by the knowledge that there was a dead man in the sewer?'

I took a deep, wavering breath. 'Inspector Redfern, I must be frank with you. I am not in a position to explain how this information came to me. You must realize that mine is a profession which brings me into contact with all levels of society from aristocrats to vagabonds. Persons from all walks of life come to my chambers. But no matter who these people might be, if they become clients, I am sworn to secrecy in regard to what they tell me. I am able to disclose nothing of what is said, or occurs, between me and a client. It is my sacred duty – recognized by the courts – to disclose nothing. It is like the secrecy of the confessional.'

He eyed me disbelievingly, seeing little of the priest in me. 'You are telling me that a client of yours merely *happened* to mention there was a body in the sewer under Kent

Street but that's all you can disclose to me about the matter?'

'That is so.'

'Even if the client in question might have been the murderer?'

I raised my jaw loftily, giving my impression of an honest pugilist. 'Of that I can give you an assurance. My informant did not kill this ... unknown person.'

Redfern's saturnine features were scored with doubt. 'And you can say no more?'

'I disclosed the information regarding the whereabouts of the corpse as a matter of public duty,' I said stiffly. 'But for me, the matter then ends there.'

'I see.' Inspector Redfern was silent for a while but his sharp eyes never left my face and once again I gained the impression he knew I was lying, guessed I was concealing something from him. But we both knew there was nothing he could do about it. At last he sighed. 'Well, that must be that. But I was drawn to ask you, sir, because my inspection of the corpse leads me to believe he was not of the gentry. Rather, a working man, coarse hands, and yet not a labourer...'

'So?' I croaked nervously, my mouth dry.

'His clothing had been taken, of course. Toshers, I imagine. Mudlarks.' He eyed me reflectively.

'I would know nothing of that,' I lied.

Redfern shook his head mournfully. 'Well,

sir, the fact is just as we have more of our share of jumpers, as you have seen, so we have a considerable number of deaths in the streets from the violent actions of the lower classes. Of course, there are many crimes we are unable to pursue to a conclusion by discovering the perpetrator, though the success rate of our new detective force is, I may perhaps immodestly state, considerable.' He was silent for a few moments, as though weighing his words carefully. 'And naturally we must deal in priorities. Instructions often come down from the Commissioner to the effect that we should devote more time to certain cases than to others. But...' He paused, and his eyes flicked up to mine, giving away nothing. 'It's the first time in my experience we've been told by our superiors that we should take up *no* further police time in the investigation of the dead man found in the Kent Street sewer.' His eyes bored into mine. 'Now why do you think that should be, Mr James?'

Bentinck.

It had to be. No further investigation. Close down the matter. He had already warned me off this whole business. Now, as a man of considerable influence, he must have dropped a word into the ear of the Commissioner. Only a man of his stature and connections would have been able to derail an investigation in this manner.

'So,' Redfern said, when I made no reply, 'a pauper's funeral for the girl, an unmarked grave for the man in the sewer.' He finished his coffee with every sign of doleful enjoyment. Then he stood up, reached for his hat and looked down at me. 'So, Mr James, your public duty has come to naught.'

Not yet, I thought fiercely. Not yet. Bentinck may have turned off the police but he had not got rid of me. There was still one line of enquiry for me and Ben Gully to follow. One we should perhaps have pursued earlier.

Next afternoon, after I met Ben Gully at the *Blue Post* the drive to Epsom was a relief. We emerged from the sweaty streets of the metropolis into the open air of the countryside. Neither of us spoke much during the drive, once I'd told him of my conversation with Redfern. He made no comment upon my suggestion that Bentinck had stymied the peelers by putting pressure on the Commissioner. As we drove past the leafy hedgerows and the rolling countryside about Epsom I relaxed somewhat, only to become preoccupied with other matters.

I was under renewed pressure from my creditors. I had lent what little I had to Lester Grenwood, and since then I'd had a bad run at the tables, apart from the money I'd borrowed, and lost, at the Derby. As we rattled along the country lanes I began making a mental list of acquaintances upon whom I might prevail to sign a note or two, in order that the baying wolves might be kept from my door. My grandfather had gone to Leamington for the waters; Lester Grenwood had vanished into the country, leaving his own trail of debts; I had exhausted the possibilities among one or two middle-aged widows of my acquaintance, and some of my tradesmen creditors were threatening to set up camp at my door. Few such people are gentlemen, you see.

There was always Bulstrode, of course, but he was financing the present operation and I had the feeling I would be well advised to keep him in reserve for the time being. But musing over such matters was boring. Finally, I dismissed thoughts of money, looked about me and enjoyed the drive, and considered the matter of our visit to the stables where Joe Bartle had worked, *Running Rein* had been trained, and from which the colt had been mysteriously abducted.

What was noticeable was that within a few minutes of our arrival at the stables, Cornelius Smith, our erstwhile witness at the Exchequer Court, was sweating.

The conversation with Ben Gully had begun casually enough.

We had arrived at the Epsom stables late in the afternoon and we found Smith, who had appeared for us in the *Running Rein* débâcle, in the stableyard, standing by while a groom rubbed down a sweating horse. As the animal shivered and steamed and stamped on the cobbled yard and Gully began to talk to Smith, I contented myself with observing the stables, the buckets and paraphernalia scatted about the untidy, straw-strewn area, and wondering about the general air of desuetude about the stables. There were few people about: two young lads desultorily mucking out a stable, a scattering of discontented chickens strutting in one corner, a steaming mound of evil-smelling manure and an arrogant, confident rat preening its whiskers in the sunshine against the far wall. I gave Gully my attention only when he moved away from the usual civilities and told Smith he was continuing the enquiries about the disappearance of *Running Rein* because the principals in the matter were still not satisfied, and the whole issue might be reopened.

My insouciance seemed to have unsettled Smith somewhat: he had been watching me from the corner of his eye as I stood casually by, but now that Gully had reached the reason for our visit to Epsom, Smith rolled his wall eye and adopted a surly tone.

'I already done all I could to help, gents. I don't like them courtrooms, but I came along, didn't I? I gave my testimony, I was straight with his lordship and there's nuthin' more I can say, reelly...'

Gully sighed, a bit theatrically I thought, and rummaged in his ample pockets for some tobacco. He looked about him, then leant his broad shoulder against the stable door. As he lit his pipe he eyed Cornelius Smith silently; Smith avoided his glance and paid closer attention to the sweating animal beside him. I said nothing as Gully puffed at his pipe contentedly for a little while, but never taking his eyes off the stableman. Smith shrugged an uneasy shoulder, barked snappishly at the groom and was clearly ill at ease under Gully's scrutiny. At last, he glared at Gully and muttered, 'Wot else is it you want from me, Mr Gully?'

When Gully made no immediate reply Smith shot a nervous glance in my direction. For some reason my presence unsettled him, but I've found that to be the case often in the courtroom. It was never just my situation as an advocate: there's always been something about my pugilistic appearance that has worried men, even though, I am forced to admit, it seems also to have attracted women. Now, I looked at Smith, my glance slowly travelling from the top of his head to his stained boots and he shivered. His bow-legged stance was wary, and after a nervy silence he suddenly swore, snatched the curry comb from the groom, shouldered the youngster aside with a curse and began to apply himself vigorously to the flanks of the nag standing in the yard.

We watched him in silence for a while, then Gully wrinkled his nose and said, almost casually, 'Tell me, Smith, these men who took *Running Rein* that day: you didn't know them, you say.'

'Like I said in court, they was strangers,' Smith muttered hoarsely.

'Strangers, yes,' Gully remarked ruminatively. 'But horse-stealers like them, what's your general experience?'

'Dunno what you mean,' Smith replied carefully.

'Come on, you've been in this business a long time. You must have come across coopers like them before now. Who *are* these people, in the main?'

'Horse-stealers, you mean?' Smith wiped a sleeve across his sweating brow. He leaned one elbow on the flank of the horse, frowned, shrugged his narrow shoulders. 'A low, unprincipled class of men, if you arsk me, Mr Gully. Horse-coopers like them, they're usually wandering gypsies, or tinkers.'

'So you're saying the men who took *Running Rein* ... they were of that kind?' Gully persisted.

Cornelius Smith was too fly to be caught out that simply. Warily, he shook his head. 'No, I can't say that. Never seen them afore.

They didn't look rough, if you know what I mean. But then, maybe they was rigged up, of course, to look better than they was but though they *could* have been horse-coopers, I couldn't have sworn to that.'

I watched him closely. He shot another nervous glance in my direction and I guessed the reason for his reticence: he knew that if I had been allowed to question him closely in court on the matter and had given such evidence it would have raised all kinds of further questions – from me, and from a more suspicious judge on the bench. But by indulging in his own prejudices Baron Alderson had let him off the hook, preferring to attack the Fancy.

Gully drew on his pipe, expelled some satisfied smoke in Smith's direction. 'So you certainly saw these men. You said so in court. And from what you say now, well, they wasn't the swell mob then ... nor gypsies, neither.'

Smith scratched his head, non-committedly. 'I couldn't really say either way, Mr Gully.'

'But they could have been Lord George Bentinck's men, maybe?' Gully mused.

Smith was not being drawn on that. 'I don't know about that,' he replied swiftly. 'I wouldn't know such men if I seed them.'

'And you *did* see them. And would know them again, I guess.' Gully straightened from the stable door, tapped out his pipe and looked piercingly at Smith. 'I'm sure you'd be able to identify them to me if you was to see them again. Sharp character like you.'

The stableowner shuffled uncomfortably. He knew about Gully: he was well aware of his reputation. He could be a hard man. Facing me, an unknown quantity, in court was one thing. Ben Gully was another.

'I saw them ... spoke to them, of course. But I keep telling you Mr Gully, I didn't know them ... they was strangers,' he insisted.

Gully shrugged his shoulders unhappily. 'Pity. But then speaking broadly, using your experience, let's get back to general things... What's the usual practice of these men: these so-called horse-coopers?'

Smith breathed more easily. 'Well, from what I hear ... not that I been involved in such practices, gentlemen ... generally they remove a horse from the park or the stable, shut it up close until the hue and cry dies down, then they trim it up to alter its appearance, take it to some market at a distance, up north maybe, and sell it ... often at an under-price. They don't try to run the nag themselves, up country. They're just after the money, you see.' Smith hesitated uncertainly, concerned that he might already have said too much. 'Leastways, that's what I'm told.'

'They sell the animal on?' Gully wondered.

Smith shrugged. 'Well, yes, so I believe. That's where their profit lies.'

'At market, you say. Smithfield?'

Smith shook his head. 'No, when I say market, I mean they usually stables the animal quietly near the market and then finds a low horse dealer...'

'Londoners?'

Smith grinned conspiratorially. 'There's more than a few in the Old Kent Road, I hear.'

'And you're absolutely sure you don't know these men who took *Running Rein?*'

'No, Mr Gully, that's the honest truth. Look, it's just like I said in court, in front of Mr James here, with me hand on the Book. These lowlife characters, they just told me they come from Mr Wood to collect the horse, and I took 'em at their word, and...' His voice died away, and he brushed even more vigorously at the flanks of the sweating horse he held by the bridle.

'Mmm...' Gully looked quizzically at his empty pipe as though it held some secrets for him, then slowly placed it in the pocket of his waistcoat. He stood up away from the stable wall and shook his head. 'Pity. You acted like any innocent man would have done, I suppose. Now if Joe Bartle had been here, maybe *he'd* have known these horse-coopers. You think so, Smith?'

'Bartle?' Smith squeaked. 'How would he have known them?'

Gully shrugged. 'Well, ain't it possible? Joe Bartle was working here at the stables ... putting in the hours, looking after *Running Rein*. Maybe he'd have seen these suspicious characters hanging around.'

'He didn't say anything to me about it,' Smith replied warily. 'But maybe he could have...'

'And if he *had* seen them, would he have reported the matter to you?'

'I don't know, Mr Gully.'

'You're in charge of the stables, Smith.'

Cornelius Smith paused in his labours, seemed to consider the matter, then nodded his head vigorously. 'Well, yes, that is right, but you got to understand I didn't know Joe Bartle very well. Not a very communicative man. Said little for himself. His business was his own. Hadn't been at the stables long. Mooched around with a face as long as a fiddle, most times...'

'And he didn't speak to the men who came for *Running Rein*?'

Alarm flared in the stableowner's eyes. I could guess at his thoughts: you don't catch Cornelius Smith like that. ''Course not. I already told you clear. The horse was took during the trial. On the Sunday. Joe Bartle didn't show up here at the stables after that

258

Wednesday previous...'

'Ah, yes, I remember.' Gully walked slowly towards the horse as it stood shivering slightly beside Cornelius Smith. He ran a gnarled hand gently along its flank. The twitching horseflesh steamed gently in the afternoon air. Gully stroked its quivering muscles, appreciatively. 'Nice animal ... I hope you'll take good care of it, Mr Smith. Better than you did *Running Rein*.' Gully smiled coldly at the bow-legged little man. 'But as to Joe Bartle. You say he didn't turn up at the stables after the Wednesday. That's a couple of days before the trial began.'

He glanced at me. I nodded. 'Saturday,' I confirmed.

Ben Gully turned back to the nervous stableman. 'So, why was that?'

'Didn't talk to him,' Smith said boldly, 'so how would I know?'

'When you last saw him ... on that Wednesday, perhaps what was he like? What was his demeanour?'

Cornelius Smith leaned against the horse, both arms along its back as he wrinkled his brow and assumed an air of earnest thought about the matter. 'Well, he was always silent, kept to himself, like I said, but that day ... it was the Wednesday, like you said... well, he seemed worse than usual.'

'Worse? How do you mean?'

'Well, you know, it was like something was

worrying him. He had a brow like thunder, as they say. Snapped at the grooms. Was in some kind of temper.'

'So he seemed ... upset.' Gully considered. 'But he gave you no reason for his disappearance. What was it made him leave the stables, do you think?'

'Can't say, Mr Gully.'

'You've no idea why didn't he turn up for work after Wednesday?'

'I honestly don't know, Mr Gully,' Smith replied, staining his tones with innocence.

'It wasn't because he had an argument with you? No fuss about *Running Rein?*'

'No, I swear!' Smith protested.

'No argument with anyone else?'

There was a brief hesitation. 'There wasn't anyone else around that day, apart from the grooms, I mean,' Smith replied earnestly. 'I mean, Bartle looked out of sorts, but there was no quarrel.'

'Mmm.' A light breeze had arisen, ruffling Gully's hair. He looked at me, thoughtfully, and then turned back to Cornelius Smith. 'So I suppose, in a sense, as far as we can tell, you were the last person to see Joe Bartle before he went off ... wherever he went off to.'

Smith shrugged. 'I suppose you can say that.'

'Do you think maybe he disappeared because he didn't want to give evidence in the *Running Rein* trial?'

'I couldn't say, Mr Gully.' An edge of confidence was creeping into Smith's voice. He was feeling more self-assured.

'Perhaps it was because he'd been *told* to make himself scarce,' Gully suggested softly.

Cornelius Smith shrugged his narrow shoulders, carelessly. 'I already told you. I keep telling you. I don't know why he disappeared, Mr Gully.'

'It would hardly be Mr Wood who'd want him to disappear,' Gully mused, almost to himself. 'Bartle was due to give evidence to support Mr Wood ... and confirm Mr Goodman's evidence, of course ... so *they* wouldn't want him out of the way.'

Smith shook his head, indifferently. 'I can't say. Not thought about it.'

'Of course, there's always the thought that perhaps Bartle had decided *not* to support Goodman's story. Now that would have made his presence in the courtroom uncomfortable for Mr Goodman, wouldn't it?'

'I don't really see—'

Gully held up a warning hand. 'Just let me think this through for a moment, Mr Smith. Aloud. There was no quarrel, you say, but Bartle clearly had something on his mind on the Wednesday. Next day he didn't turn up at the stables: he just disappeared, and you made no enquiries about him.'

'No cause to. Employed by the horse

owner, he was. Wasn't my place to arsk around. He's a growed man...'

'But he was a witness in the *Running Rein* hearing and the evidence he would have given, in support of Mr Wood's case has now gone. Disappeared with him.' Gully shook his head thoughtfully. 'Yes, it seems to me that the whole question of Bartle's disappearance has to do with the trial and the later abduction of *Running Rein*. Wouldn't you say so, Smith?'

The stableowner shrugged his shoulders regretfully. 'I don't really have an opinion, Mr Gully.' The curry comb began to work briskly once more.

'I'm beginning to form one, however,' Ben Gully said pleasantly as he returned his pipe to the deep pocket of his chesterfield. 'There's got to be a link between the theft of *Running Rein* and the disappearance of Joe Bartle. And in a sense, *you're* the key to the lock that shuts the truth to us.'

'Me? How is that, Mr Gully?'

Gully glanced at me. 'Mr James, here, he's had some thoughts about the matter. Ever since he found what he did in the sewers under Kent Street.'

It was my time to step forward. I frowned seriously, intervening for the first time. Cornelius Smith froze, staring at me. 'Yes, that's right. In my considered opinion you're the key, Mr Smith, because you were the last person, it seems, to have seen Joseph Bartle alive.'

For a long moment the statement failed to register with Cornelius Smith. He gaped at me, turned to look open-mouthed at Gully, and struggled to form the words. 'You say ... alive? You mean Joe Bartle's *dead?*' He was sweating again. He was panicked.

In questioning Cornelius Smith that day, it was the first time I saw the kind of panic that in later years I was able to induce regularly in the witness box under cross-examinations at the Old Bailey. It brings to one a kind of triumph, a superiority, a confidence that surges through the veins, a belief that further probing can tear a man's will apart, shred his confidence. It's the wash of feeling I had at that moment, I felt I could read Smith's mind: he knew something to his detriment; he was holding something back from us, but he could not imagine how things had come to this. Disappearance. Death. Somewhere along the line he had allowed himself to walk into a trap, and now he could not think straight. 'Joe Bartle's dead?' he said again, stupidly.

'As last week's mutton.' I confirmed. 'And as far as we can determine, you were the last person to see him.'

I folded my arms magisterially. I looked at Gully and nodded.

Gully smiled, and reached into his waistcoat pocket. He took out the watch, glanced at it, shook it and held it to his ear before smiling in satisfaction. 'Still working. Now then Smith, in my experience ... and it is an extensive experience in matters of skulduggery ... a man who owns an expensive watch like this takes a certain pride in its possession. If he loses it, he's likely to report the loss; if he sees it taken by an urchin he raises a hue and cry. But nothing like that seems to have happened in relation to this watch.'

Cornelius Smith was staring at the hunter, a rabbit fascinated by a snake.

'I got sources,' Gully continued. 'We've already followed them up. And they led me to the owner of this piece. He was in the sewer under Kent Street. And the polis have been informed. By Mr James.'

'The peelers?' Cornelius Smith croaked.

'No less,' Gully said gravely. He glanced at me.

'I laid the information myself,' I confirmed. 'But I named no names. I thought it best we should have a little discussion with you first.'

'So the peelers don't yet know who he is.' Ben Gully nodded, as though confirming something in his own mind. 'Never did like peelers. They got this tendency to jump to conclusions. Not least about the blokes who last saw the corpse alive. So, I don't care to offer them assistance. And Mr James and me, well we got our reasons for looking for the truth. So we ask ourselves, who would want to do a job on Bartle ... maybe the horse-coopers, you think, Mr Smith? Or perhaps it was he who was involved with taking the horse. Maybe he had an agreement with these mysterious horse-coopers since the Wednesday that he disappeared from the stables. Maybe later it was they who done him in. Who knows? Who could know, if he was dead?' He watched as the little stableowner's features took on a faint shade of green.

Casually, I nodded, appearing to consider the matter, 'Yes, Gully, I suppose it's possible that Bartle died at the weekend, or maybe later. Or there's the distinct possibility that he died here on the Wednesday, the day on which Mr Smith saw him. Dumped later in the sewer. Who's to say? I don't doubt the police will form a view, however.'

The perspiration was trickling down the back of the stable-owner's neck. I could see the beads staining his grubby shirt collar. 'He can't have died here, Mr James, I don't know nothin' about it! I've said all I know.' He rubbed his sleeve against his nose in a snuffling gesture. 'I told you ... Joe Bartle left here on Wednesday afternoon—'

'So *you* say,' I commented, shrugging.

'But that's the way of it. You can't be suggesting–'

'I'll tell you what *I'm* suggesting, Smith,' Gully interrupted, his tone hardening. 'I don't think you've been entirely honest about all this. I think you're in this business up to your neck. I don't know what happened here, but I think you had a quarrel of some sort with Joe Bartle. Maybe he told you he didn't want to give evidence for Mr Goodman. Maybe told you he was keeping out of the way. I think words were exchanged. I think you took your chance to beat him and then–'

'That's nonsense!' Cornelius Smith dropped his curry comb. His voice rose to a panicked squeak. 'I had no quarrel with Joe Bartle. I hardly knew him.'

'But it seems you were the last to see him alive!' I snapped.

'I didn't even know Joe was dead!' Smith expostulated in panic.

One of the peculiar attributes of Ben Gully was the manner in which he could explode into violence. His tone could be gentle one moment, his appearance casual, and yet the next he could be all menacing muscle. I saw the transformation in that moment. In a swift motion he reached out, grabbed the squirming stable-owner by the shirt front. He thrust his grim, scarred features close to those of the terrified stableman. 'All right, maybe it wasn't a personal quarrel between you and Bartle ... maybe you were *told* to smash his face in! Or maybe you were here when someone else did it. Whatever the truth, there's only you to talk about it. You were last to see him around here. What'll the peelers make of that, Smith? What if they find something here in the stables to incriminate you? Like this watch, for instance?'

'But I never seen that watch before! It was you brought it here!'

'But if we was to *say* we found it here,' Gully pressed.

'A jury would probably believe us rather than you,' I asserted. 'And you know, there are other judges like Baron Alderson who have no love of the Turf, or of Turf men...'

'You'd be hung out to dry,' Gully murmured quietly.

'And in view of my interest in the matter,' I intervened in a grimy tone, 'I would be prepared to act for the prosecution without fee!'

There was a long silence. Spittle drooled from Smith's loose, open mouth. Gully leaned forward, brushed at Smith's shoulder with a gnarled, reassuring hand. 'I think Mr James would find it easy to convince judges like Baron Alderson that you were lying in your teeth, that Bartle had changed his mind about the evidence he was going to give, that you were under instructions to do something about it... And after beating him to death, you kept the watch for yourself, before selling it to some fence in town.'

Cornelius Smith twisted in Gully's firm grip, a panicked rabbit trying to escape the net. 'No, it wasn't like that!'

Sweating profusely, the stableman wriggled desperately, stamped his feet in the cobbled yard. Once again I could read it in his twisted features. He was involved, but he hadn't been paid to deal with issues like this. Entering a ringer in a race was one thing; turning a blind eye to the stealing of a nag was no great matter to him. But getting dragged into a murder enquiry ... that was another matter.

'I think it's time I went to Bow Street again, to add to the information I've already laid, Gully,' I said, gloomily shaking my head. 'There could be a charge of murder, here ... it's out of our hands.'

'You tell me Joe Bartle's been done in, but I had nothing to do with it!' Cornelius Smith almost screamed, shaking his head violently. And then, after the outburst, the life seemed to drain out of him. His head dropped, he was limp in Gully's grasp. His hands were hanging lifelessly by his side.

'If the peelers learn you *were* the last to see him alive,' I pressed ruthlessly.

'No.' There was a short silence. Gully and I waited, while the stableowner sweated with his fear of the man who had paid him against the terror inspired by the thought of a rope around his neck. 'No, there was someone else here that Wednesday afternoon.'

'Who?' Gully asked, almost dreamily.

'Sam McGuire.'

There was something familiar about the name. I stared at Gully, puzzled, raised my eyebrows. Then I recalled it, from my court brief. 'McGuire? You mean the man who trained *Running Rein* in Ireland?'

'That's right.' Smith nodded anxiously, despondency and panic suddenly turning to an eagerness to please. He was emboldened by the possibility of seeing a neck other than his own being stretched in a noose. 'And I saw them here in the stables, that day. There was a quarrel. They was having words, voices raised, down here in the yard. McGuire was here. He was quarrelling with Bartle. So I wasn't the last one to see Joe. It could be him who done for Joe Bartle, later!'

Gully smiled thinly. 'So what *have* you been paid to keep quiet about, Mr Smith? You'd better tell us all about it, my friend. If not murder, what was it?'

Smith shook his head in terror, but the pressure had all been too much for him, and he seemed almost glad to be able to confess to something that would have nothing to do with the death of Joe Bartle. He half-sobbed, his breath rasping in his throat, and he finally told us what we had wanted to hear. 'It was the horse.'

'You helped in the abduction?'

Smith shook his head. 'Not exactly. I was paid to look the other way. When the coopers came. And then, later, after he was put down, I had to help bury him.'

'The horse? You buried him?' I gasped.

'That's right. We buried him. *Running Rein.*'

It was late evening when we reached the location.

Above our heads in the darkness of the overhanging trees an owl screeched, its harsh, lonely call echoing eerily across the narrow valley. We had engaged two men – who according to Gully knew how to keep their mouths shut – and we made our way by the light of a bull's-eye lantern, following Cornelius Smith, picking our path across a small stream, stumbling among hidden rocks in the bushes that covered the floor of the valley. After a little while we emerged on the far slope that led down to the flat pastureland beyond the trees. There we paused, sweating, and the two diggers at the rear hefted their shovels uneasily as they looked about them with nervous glances. They were being paid well enough for this evening's work but they had no love for it:

they could not understand the urgency that had driven their paymasters out under a moonless, sharp sky where the shadows lay deep under the faint starlight and night sounds whispered and rustled about them.

We crossed the field and passed through a wooden gate. The small field was surrounded by dark, silent copses of hawthorn and oak. After a certain hesitancy, our shivering, frightened leader at last called a halt. Smith looked about him, kicking at the turf; he trudged around at the edge of the clearing for a little while, a little bow-legged man dogged with uncertainty, until at last he paused to the right of a small stretch of low bushes. He kicked again with his boot at the loose turf and uttered an exclamation. Then he turned and raised his arm, beckoning us forward.

'Here!' he called. 'It was here, I'm certain.'

Ben Gully stepped forward. He had draped himself in a long black cloak against the night air and a dark hat hid his battered features. He stood beside Cornelius Smith and dug his heel into the turf. He nodded, turned and gestured to the men with the shovels, while I stood back under the trees, a little distance apart, watching the men as they began their work.

I hadn't been sure I wanted to be present at this occasion, but curiosity had drawn me. The scene was macabre. I watched the

men as they dug: they were railway navigators, middle-aged men with bowed backs
and hard muscles who had worked for years
on the canals and the railway cuttings and
who were always prepared to do a dirty job
provided the pay was right. Even so, working in the darkness in this manner was
another matter, in spite of the ale that they
had consumed at the expense of the man in
the cloak, and a certain reluctance had
marked their passage across the clearing,
but once they started they went to it with a
will.

I stood there watching silently. Ben folded
his arms as he hunched there overseeing.
The two navigators thrust their spades into
the turf, swearing occasionally in an Irish
brogue, shoving and stamping with their
heavily booted feet, turning the sod, clearing an area, and grunting as they struck
something other than earth or stone, hawking and spitting noisily as the smell rose to
their nostrils from what lay under the earth.

I heard the owl hooting again, more
distantly now, a call that was challenged by
the faraway screech of a young buzzard in
the trees nearby. Then the valley was quiet
again as the sweating navigators rested on
their shovels, breathing harshly, faintly
staining the air with their beery exhalations.

'Get on with it,' Gully snapped at last,
while Cornelius Smith stood shivering by

his side.

The shovels thudded dully into the earth once more and as the first evidence was exposed they moved sideways, digging in a wider area, turning over the cold black earth as the luminescence appeared, shining and glimmering bone-white under the faint starlight.

'It's here it'll be, bejazus,' one of them grunted suddenly, and stood aside. 'Sure enough, as the man says.'

Ben Gully glanced back to where I stood under the trees, twitched his cloak and leaned forward. He raised the dark lantern, unshuttered the bull's eye and shone it down into the area of disturbed earth. Slowly, I made my way forward until I stood at his elbow. The navigators had stepped aside. Ben and I stared at the thing that lay at our feet: the bones were almost bare, the flesh already half eaten away in the quicklime that had been liberally thrown about the carcass, but there was no doubt in Ben's mind, nor mine, about what the navigators had uncovered.

Ben Gully leaned forward, snatched a shovel from one of the navigators and clattered its blade against bone. He heaved and there was an evil sucking sound as he turned up the half rotted skull of the horse. There was a sour taste in my mouth. Cornelius Smith whimpered slightly at my elbow.

'Didn't I tell you the truth? Didn't I say it was here?'

Ben looked at me as though enquiring what I now wished to do. It was something I had not considered: finding the animal was an end in itself. Disinterment seemed pointless. To know what had happened was enough, for the moment. I drew my own cloak across my lower face, shielding my nose from the smell as I looked down into the grave. Cornelius Smith pointed with a shaking finger, scared at what he had done, along with the horse-coopers who had come to his stable. There was a quaver in his voice, as he spoke, turning to me almost placatingly.

'*Running Rein,*' he said.

'And the man who paid you to organize this?'

Smith's reply rasped nervously in the night air. 'It was Sam McGuire,' he said. 'It was he who organized everything. He came to the stables late Saturday night and told me to hand the colt over to the horse-coopers when they arrived on Sunday. Then I was to help them later, with the interment here in this field. I was just getting paid to help, and keep my mouth shut.' He shivered, looked about him in the silent clearing. 'But no one told me anything about murder...'

Gully looked at me and nodded. As he ordered the navigators to shovel earth back over the half-destroyed corpse I turned away, made my way back to our carriage. So we had half the story now. The final answers would now have to come to us from the colt's trainer.

Sam McGuire.

2

I would never claim to be a courageous man. Foolhardy on occasions, yes. There was that bouncing cannonball in the field outside Salerno, for instance: I outpaced my companions to the shelter of the ruined stone wall on that occasion, I can tell you, even though I've never been built for running. Garibaldi strolled back, insouciant, but he *was* a brave man. Of course I entertained more than a few ladies back in London afterwards with my account of life under fire, and I fear I exaggerated for their benefit, boasting about my exploits in Italy on the campaign that summer of '61. But courageous, never ... except in the courtroom.

So why did I go with Ben Gully a few days following our gruesome discovery? He tried to dissuade me, told me it could be dangerous, but I was all fired up, you see. The fraud over *Running Rein,* the betrayal by Cockburn, the sneers and malevolent threats of Bentinck, the stinging smarts delivered by Baron Alderson, Inspector Redfern's suspicions, they all combined to stoke in me a desire and determination to be in at the kill, so to speak. I wanted to be with Ben when he finally faced McGuire, and got the truth out of him about the whole affair.

The long summer drought had broken and the Long Vacation had begun. That late afternoon, when Gully had agreed we should meet, the sky was sullen and bruised with dark-grey clouds piling up from the west. It had rained for two nights and there had been no need to dampen down the dust in the London streets. Many solicitors had fled the City at end of term and most of my colleagues at the Bar – the successful ones at least – had similarly decamped. I had no briefs to detain me and creditors to avoid so I was not averse to joining Ben in his hunt for the man who could give us the answers we sought.

Bentinck. I was certain it had been Bentinck who had paid Sam McGuire to get rid of the colt once the judge had called for its appearance in court. He had known his reputation was at stake, and he had deemed it better to spirit away the animal rather than face further humiliation in court. But why did Bartle have to die? Had it simply been because he had refused to take part in the plot, or had striven to prevent the abduction? Had Bentinck *planned* for the man to be beaten to death, or had it been unforeseen?

I had to know. I was determined to see things through to the end. And I insisted on accompanying Gully when he told me he had tracked down Sam McGuire to his lair.

There was a hint of further rain in the air when I made my way from my chambers at the Inner Temple, through the Temple Gardens and along towards Charing Cross. Traffic on the river was busy as usual but the low mist that was creeping up the river-banks from Blackfriars obscured some of the shipping and the deep discordant sounds of fog horns formed a mournful echoing backdrop to the clatter and clangs of the Strand.

The hansom cab was waiting under the arch of the bridge: Ben Gully was standing beside it, wrapped in a long, dark, voluminous-pocketed greatcoat. He was bareheaded, but had a scarf drawn high up to his chin. He nodded and raised a gnarled hand as I approached and stepped aside to allow me to enter the cab. The jarvey touched the brim of his hat and, once we were settled inside the hansom, closed the door, flicked his whip and the cab lurched and rattled its way from Charing Cross along the narrow cobbled road away from the city.

'Where are we going?' I asked.

'The docks.'

Ben Gully was silent for a little while, leaning back in his seat and watching the passing traffic as we made our way past Blackfriars and into Thames Street, with the old wharfs perched on the riverside to our right. Then he glanced at me and said, 'Waste of fine horseflesh.'

'What do you mean?'

Gully's eyes were hard. 'I went back to that field. I took a vet name of Spurgeon to take a look at the skull and teeth of the horse we dug up. Just to satisfy my own mind: I don't trust that weasel Smith, scared though he might be. The veterinary surgeon confirmed what Lord George Bentinck suspected all along. The horse that won the Derby was a ringer all right: *Running Rein* was a four year old. Mr Wood was gulled.'

'We all were,' I snapped angrily. 'So how was the fraud practised?'

Gully shrugged. 'The way I've been able to put it together, it seems the fraud started in Ireland with a horse called *Maccabeus*. It was entered in a few races with some success, under this trainer called Sam McGuire. Then Goodman bought it, shipped it across here and masqueraded it as *Running Rein*. It was held back of course, by obliging jockeys, so that its record was not great. But it was a four year old, not a two year old, and so not eligible for the Derby.' He grunted, contemptuously. 'Goodman spread a lot of money around on bets, but he was too fly to enter the animal himself – he sold it to Ernest Wood.'

'Our enthusiastic but gullible corn merchant.' I frowned thoughtfully. 'But where did you get this confirmation of our suspicions?'

Gully grinned maliciously. 'There are ways. I had another long session with Cornelius Smith after you left. Scared the life out of him. I suspected all along he knew more than he was letting on. The thought of being implicated in murder, rather than mere Turf fraud, made him clack like a fox-run hen coop about the nag, but he was still holding back. I had to show him a bit of muscle. He finally told me what he knew about the disappearance of Joe Bartle.'

'So what happened?' I gritted.

Gully shook his head, leaned back in his seat. 'After he'd lost a few teeth he swore he couldn't tell me exactly how it came about, and I think he's telling that straight enough. But his story is that Bartle had got very moody. The stablehand was employed by Wood but must have had an idea about what was going on. Maybe it was the thought of the fraud and his part in it, or the anxiety of a court appearance, maybe not. Smith couldn't tell. Then on the Wednesday Smith saw him talking with McGuire, the Irishman who originally trained *Running Rein,* or *Maccabeus,* or whatever the damned animal was called.'

Gully peered out through the dingy, smeared window of the hansom, noting our progress as we headed for Tower Hill. 'So it's true enough that it was on the Wednesday that Smith last cast his eyes on Bartle, though he heard he turned up that weekend at the Porky Clark fight on the Heath.'

Where he had been involved in some kind of altercation, it seemed. 'That takes us no further forward.'

Gully shrugged. 'Maybe no – but it was the next bit that interested me. Smith finally admitted to me that one of the men who took the horse was Porky Clark.'

'The prize fighter? But what's his part in all this?'

'He's known to be in the pay of Lewis Goodman. So maybe it was Goodman, not Bentinck who ordered the taking of the animal after Baron Alderson demanded it be brought to court. Goodman wouldn't want his fraud to be discovered in court.'

'So was it Clark who persuaded Smith to release the horse?'

'No. He didn't do the talking to Smith. He was just present when the coopers arrived. Looking after his master's interest, I would imagine. No, the removal was achieved by Sam McGuire.'

'At the hearing in the Exchequer Court we were informed that McGuire had returned to Ireland, and was not available as a witness,' I muttered.

'He never did. Though he wasn't around when they buried the horse at Barling's Meadow.'

'I don't understand,' I murmured. 'Porky Clark and Lewis Goodman–'

'I told you,' Gully said with a hint of impatience. 'He's Lewis Goodman's minder. A sporting man, our night-house owner, he likes to go to the prize fights, and likes to have a prizefighter at his back. Slow-witted Porky Clark might be, and too fond of the drink, but he's loyal to Goodman because he gets paid well.'

I was silent for a while. We had found a clear link now between the spiriting away of the horse and Lewis Goodman, but the chances of ever getting Smith or Clark to speak up in court was slim. Clark was loyal; Smith might be scared by Gully, but he was likely to be more scared by Goodman if it ever came to the starting line.

Almost as though he had read my thoughts, Gully said quietly, 'The key is Sam McGuire. He's lying low. He'll know all about the swindle Goodman was perpetrating – but I'll bet my last shilling that he knows what happened to Bartle, and why. And that's where Goodman's web will start to fall apart. A horse racing fraud is one thing: murder is another. So, we need to know what McGuire quarrelled with Bartle about – and why Bartle had to die.'

'To keep him quiet about the fraud?' I pondered.

'Who knows? The important thing is I think it's McGuire who'll be able to tell us. Moreover, maybe he'll be *willing* to tell us.'

'Why?' I asked, puzzled.

Gully was quiet for a little while. He peered out of the cab again, issued some further instructions to the jarvey, and then faced me. 'Because we ain't the only ones looking for him.'

'What do you mean?'

Ben Gully sucked at his teeth thoughtfully. 'The word out on the streets is that Goodman's looking for him too.'

'I don't understand.'

'Neither do I, not yet. Maybe it's to give McGuire the same medicine that was doled out to Joseph Bartle, now deceased.'

'But why?'

'That's what we'll try to find out.'

Thereafter, locked in our own thoughts, we rattled on our way in silence towards Wapping Pier Head.

You'll know the London Dock area as well as any, I suppose, being a man of the sea – you'll be aware of the way it sprawls over St

George in the East, Shadwell and Wapping with its conglomeration of shops and dwellings, narrow streets and low lodging houses, where the dock labourers, sack makers, watermen and whores live packed together in close proximity. Most of the streets boasted a maritime character in those days; the shops were stocked with quadrants and sextants, chronometers and compasses, marine items of all conceivable description, and the cabs and wagons that trundled noisily along their cobbles carried ropes and lines smelling of tar, yellow bins of sulphur or copper ore, and casks of wine. At the corners of the streets were the slopsellers hawking their red and blue flannel shirts, hammocks and well oiled norwesters. And over it all loomed a forest of masts, coloured flags and bunting faded with age and smoke, against a belching line of steam-packet funnels, and the black hulls of massive colliers, tied up at the quayside, their decks lurching and rolling on the tide, twenty feet below the quay from the heavy cargoes in their holds. Changed a lot since then, I suppose, but I've not been down there in a while, so you'll know better.

Anyway, Gully paid off the hansom cab at Tenth Street and led the way into the maelstrom of humanity that whirled around the St George docks. We shouldered our way past gaugers with their long brass-tipped rules, sailors chattering in foreign tongues, butchers, cabbage sellers, piled casks of wine and stacks of cork on the greasy cobbles of the quayside.

We turned down a side alley where the air was pungent with the mingled odours of tobacco and rum, overlaid with the sickening stench of stacked hides. Gully suggested I should wait, standing with my back to the wall, while he entered the warehouse with its long line of lights, oil lamps flickering against the gloom of the sugar-sticky vaults.

I can still remember how, in the distance behind us, at some tavern, the sound of boisterous singing came to me against a jumble of dock sounds: a cooper hammering at casks on the quay, a hurdy gurdy playing for pennies, the rattling of chains flying up from the dark waters of the river, the thunder of empty drums being rolled along the quayside. But my back was cold; I shivered with apprehension. The light was dying about the docks now, and the lamps were being lit, but the fog had advanced up the river, snaking its tendrils through the alleyways and courtyards, and the effect was to cast a gloomy murk about the streets, heavy with the peculiar smell of dry rot.

Gully came back out of the warehouse. He had not told me how he had managed to trace the whereabouts of Sam McGuire but his web of contacts and informers stretched throughout the alleys and docks of old London. I caught a glimpse of a pale-faced urchin who skittered away into the depths of the building. One of Gully's informants, I guessed.

'Right, let's go. Our friend's at home, it seems.' Gully hesitated, stood squarely in front of me, squinted at me in the gathering gloom. 'You *sure* you want to be in on this business, Mr James?'

'I'm sure.'

We went forward. There were women in the streets now, bare-armed and lacking bonnets or caps, and the public houses were opening their doors to bustling sailors seeking grog among a medley of men in greasy sporting jackets, surtouts burst at the elbows, a mockery of gentility with the collars of their paletots worn through to the canvas. Gully turned left into a narrow court: some Irish dock labourers were lolling there, smoking their pipes. They said nothing as we pushed past them, but there was a certain truculence in their bearing as they observed us which made the hairs on the back of my neck rise and tingle. Clothes lines hung across the rubbish-strewn court, festooned with limp, dirty-grey washing and women and men sat at the doorsteps of the narrow houses, smoking and drinking. At the end of the court was an open yard: two costermongers's carts stood at its centre with their shafts up in the air. Beyond the yard was a tall pair of green gates, half open. Gully gestured with his right hand, and led the way to the house beyond.

It had once been a house with a certain grandeur, perhaps a merchant's house overlooking the river, but its small garden was now littered with refuse, and the building itself was in a sad state of disrepair, long since given up to lodging house keepers. I guessed that it would now be a haven for the penurious, the drunk and the vicious. We entered through an open kitchen door. The kitchen itself was full of smoke and the fireplace of the chimney stood out from the brick wall, belching fumes into the room. The floor was unboarded and a wooden seat projected from the wall all around the room. There was one bewhiskered old man in the room: dressed in ancient knee breeches and a soiled red plush waistcoat he was seated on the bench with a bottle of ale in his hand. Gully stared at him, and the man stared back, unflinchingly. Gully put his hand in his pocket and drew out a small heavy bag, tossed it to the man who caught it deftly. He stared at Gully, jerked his head in the direction of the stairs, and without a word rose and left the room.

'Upstairs, but quiet,' Gully warned.

The naked boards creaked and groaned as

we ascended, but from one of the rooms above there was the sound of a man and a woman singing a drunken chorus: it was sufficient to mask the sounds of our progress. Gully paused at the head of the stairs: the corridor was dimly lit by a single oil lamp hanging above the stairwell and there were four doors either side of the corridor. Gully pointed to the last on the left. He had obviously been well primed by his informants.

We walked quietly to the door, Gully leading. He tried the latch: it lifted, but the door did not move. Gully wasted no time on ceremony: he stepped back, drew something from the deep pockets of his coat and with one thunderous kick burst the door off its hinges.

There was a shouted obscenity as Gully threw himself into the room. When I followed a moment later it was to see Gully pinning a struggling man against the wall beside a rumpled bed. Gully had a pistol in his hand. He thrust the muzzle under the man's chin, and in a moment the struggling ceased.

'Hello, Sam,' Gully growled. 'Come down in the world, ain't you? Not the most salubrious surroundings, down here at the docks. But useful for a man on the run.'

Sam McGuire was a short, thickset man with cropped hair and a surly countenance. His skin was tanned but pock-marked and his shoulders were muscular, his chest deep. He would probably have given Gully a run for his money had it not been for the pistol. Now, in the light of the oil lamp hanging from the ceiling he sat tensely on the edge of the bed, his coarse shirt torn, and the dark stubble on his heavy features lending an almost demoniac grimness to his appearance. His broad hands, well used to rubbing down horses, hung between his knees but the thick fingers were curled menacingly, and the muscles of his shoulders were bunched as though he was ready at any moment to hurl himself at Gully, should the opportunity present itself. I leaned against the door jamb, watching, trying to quell the excited thunder in my chest as Gully thrust the muzzle of the horse pistol playfully against McGuire's chin.

McGuire did not lack courage. He found his voice. 'Who are you?' the horse trainer growled. 'What d'ye want with me?'

'The benefit of a little conversation with you, Sam, that's all.'

'What about?' McGuire turned his head, glared at me standing in the doorway. 'If there wasn't two of you—'

'Oh, don't pay mind to the gentleman there, Sam, it's me you got to talk to, and don't think I'm not man enough to put out your lights if you try to cause me any trouble.'

There was a short silence. 'How did you

find me?' McGuire asked at last, in a rasping tone.

Gully sighed theatrically. 'That's the trouble with this world, Sam. There's always a way to solve a problem, if you got the tin. Now you paid well over the odds to get this cosy little berth, didn't you – where you thought you'd be safe from Goodman and Porky Clark? But you couldn't be safe from me, Sam me lad – I got the contacts and connections, and I got the tin.'

'Was it Goodman who sent you?' There was a sudden hint of nervousness in McGuire's voice.

Gully shook his head. 'No, I gather Goody Levy's still hunting around. Thinks you've nipped across to France, maybe. But me, I know you're heading for Ireland and your own folk, soon as the coast is clear.'

'If you're not working for Goodman ... what d'ye want with me?'

'Information.'

There was a long silence. The oil lamp sputtered, casting dancing shadows across our faces. McGuire shook his head. 'I got no information for the likes of you.'

'But what about my little persuader here?' Gully asked pleasantly, stroking the pistol muzzle gently against the man's throat. 'Or maybe you'd prefer we took you along to Goodman, and let him ask you a few questions...'

Sam McGuire sat stiffly, thinking hard. He cast a quick glance at me, standing silently in the doorway, and then abruptly, he asked, 'So what the hell is it you want to know? What's this all about?'

'*Running Rein.*'

McGuire let out an obscene expletive. 'I don't know nothin' about that business.'

Gully shook his head mournfully in mock sympathy. 'Now, that's not so. You're one of the people who knows *all* about that business. But I'll make it easy for you. I'll tell you the way it was. You trained the ringer in Ireland. You brought him over here for Goodman. You helped gull the corn merchant into buying the horse, describing it as a two year old. And then you helped train him up at Malton, until he was entered for the Derby, taken down to Epsom and left under the eye of Joe Bartle.'

McGuire made no reply, but he stared fixedly at Gully with subdued fury in his eyes.

'Now we know most of what happened after that,' Gully went on, 'but we don't know *why*. After the nag won the Derby, Bentinck and Peel turned nasty and the matter ended up in court. When the case turned badly against Mr Wood, and the judge ordered production of the horse all hell broke loose. Goodman knew he was in trouble, and maybe Bentinck wasn't too happy either. So when Baron Alderson demanded the horse be brought to court someone sent you down to Epsom to take the horse away from Smith–'

'That's a damned lie!'

'Not the way Smith tells it,' Gully replied sweetly. 'He says you arranged for the horse coopers and Porky Clark to come down for the horse, and he got paid by you to keep quiet.'

'Then he should have kept his mouth shut.'

'Thing is, who paid *you* to do the job? Since you had Porky in tow, I suppose it could have been Goodman. But Porky was always slow, easily led ... and why would Goodman be looking for you now? And you lying low?'

I had my own theory. I spoke for the first time. 'It was Lord George Bentinck, wasn't it? He provided the cash, you did the deed.'

Gully glared at me, little pleased by my intervention, but after a moment he allowed himself to go along with my suggestion. 'And you took poor simple Porky along with you, for muscle. Which will be how Goodman learned it was you. Porky couldn't have kept his mouth shut, not with Goody Levy breathing on him. Ah, but things changed, didn't they, Sam? It wasn't just taking Bentinck's money, grabbing the horse and putting it down, burying him in quicklime

291

at Barling's Meadow—'

McGuire raised his head angrily, about to say something, but curbed his tongue.

'You got nothing to say?' Gully went on. 'All right. As I was saying, it wasn't just putting down *Running Rein* – it was the matter of Joe Bartle, wasn't it? It spooked friend Cornelius Smith, and that's why he talked to me. And maybe it spooked you too, and made you cut and run.'

'I don't know what you're talking about,' McGuire growled sullenly.

Gully shook his head. 'I think you do. What was it? Why did the stableman have to die? Did Bartle get religion? Did he want to be released from his part in the fraud? Why was he unwilling to go to court? Or maybe, was he going to blow the whistle for other reasons?'

'I got nothing to tell you,' McGuire snarled defiantly.

Ben stroked the muzzle of the horse pistol against McGuire's throat. 'But I think you *are* going to tell me. Because if you don't one of two things is going to happen. Either I turn you over to Goodman – and you won't enjoy that – or I haul you down to the police office, and sing a little song. It goes like this. Joe Bartle had a quarrel with Sam McGuire. Joe Bartle went missing. Joe Bartle turned up with his head bashed in, down a sewer. And Sam McGuire goes into hiding in the docks.'

'I never laid a hand on Bartle. You're bluffing me – you're talking nonsense.'

'The facts are there, Sam, all there. I think there's enough even to get you dancing in the air at Newgate. The police don't take kindly to truculent individuals like you. You want to rot there in Newgate, Sam, until they decide to hang you?'

'I didn't do nothing!'

'Persuade me.' Gully leaned forward confidentially. 'Tell me what the quarrel was all about – between you and Joe Bartle.'

McGuire grunted and shook his heavy head. 'There wasn't a real quarrel. His work was falling away. He ... he had things on his mind, like. And he said he was leaving the stable.'

'Because he didn't want to give evidence at the trial?' I demanded.

McGuire's eyes flickered in my direction. 'I don't know about that.'

'You've got to know about it, Sam,' Gully insisted coldly. 'Because we have a theory, my friend over there and me. We think maybe you had a quarrel because he didn't want to turn up at the trial, and under Goodman's orders you beat him to death–'

'I never!'

'–or,' Gully warned, shoving the pistol muzzle more firmly against McGuire's chin, 'or it was Goodman who put Porky Clark to the business, when he heard from you that Bartle was refusing to give evidence. Maybe Porky was just supposed to persuade Bartle, but knowing the way his slow mind works, things got out of hand, it was almost accidental, like–'

McGuire growled deep in his chest. 'Last time I saw Bartle he was all right. He was at the prize fight on Sunday, at Hampstead Heath, but I didn't speak to him. I don't know what happened to him after that.'

'I think you do, McGuire. You know Goodman arranged it ... because of Bartle's back-tracking–'

'I didn't even know Bartle was dead till now!' McGuire flared.

'You're lying!'

'No.' A sudden paroxysm of fear and fury seized Sam McGuire, sufficient to disregard the weapon in Ben Gully's hand. With a violent heave he threw himself away from Gully, brushing aside the horse pistol. Involuntarily, Gully pulled the trigger and there was a flash and a roar. Next moment Gully was crashing backwards to the floorboards and I found himself thrust violently aside as Sam McGuire dashed from the room.

'Gully, you all right?'

Cursing violently, Ben Gully struggled to his feet, pushed me aside and thrust the horse pistol back into the pocket of his coat.

'Get after him, dammit. We can't lose him now!'

A costermonger was trundling his empty cart into the yard to join the others when we burst out in pursuit of McGuire. The Irish labourers were no longer lolling against the wall, and one of them seemed inclined to step in Gully's way until he saw the expression on his face. I was hard put to it to keep up with Gully as he plunged into the streets, twisting away between sailors in canvas trousers, women in tawdry shawls, and big-whiskered dock labourers. I caught the occasional glimpse of McGuire rushing ahead of us, spilling casks and drawing curses as he plunged headlong through the crowded narrow streets, and Gully clearly kept him in sight, cursing violently as he ran. But after a while it was only the signs of disturbance that I saw ahead of us, the parting of the crowds, men standing in public house doorways, laughing drunkenly and pointing the way. As I told you, I was never built for running.

At last I emerged from the rabbit warren of dark, ill-lit streets, panting hard, some distance behind Gully. I saw him stopped on the dockside itself.

Ben Gully was standing, chest heaving, some twenty yards away, staring along the quay with its jumble of rope and casks and hawsers and casual wanderers. The coal backers and the dock labourers would have been paid off at four in the afternoon and were now busy in the taverns drinking their way to temporary oblivion before they started another hard day. There were several colliers tied up at the quay, some with their decks riding high now their cargoes had been discharged, but there was considerable movement about the hold of one of them as a crew of ballast heavers climbed aboard from one of the Trinity lighters that had shipped ballast alongside from the dredging engines in the Pool.

I walked forward, breathing hard, to stand beside Gully. 'Have we lost him?'

Gully shook his head and sniffed the air like a questing dog. 'No. He's here on the quay. I saw him slip across...' He moved quietly towards the edge of the dock, peering down at the ladders that led to the decks of the colliers below, and then slowly he began to pace along the rough stone of the quayside, manoeuvring between casks and drums, stepping over coils of rope, pushing aside half-drunken lumpers smelling of the timber they had handled. I followed him, watching, looking about, but there was no sign of the fugitive. I was beginning to regret my decision to accompany Gully: I was never much a man of action, my figure was against it, and nights at the gambling tables did little for my physical stamina.

The fog was thicker now, lying heavy on the river so it was no longer possible to see the small tenders tied alongside the colliers. The ballast heavers had started work with pieces of old sail tied around and halfway up their legs as protection against the gravel, and we became aware of the rhythmic, crashing sound of the gravel being thrown up onto the board stage on the partition beams of the lighter, from which it was transferred by two shovellers into the porthole at the side of the collier. Gully moved on quietly, stepping like a cat, surprisingly light on his feet for such a heavy man, and his head was held low as though pointing for his prey. Stray lights from taverns in the side streets illuminated his progress fitfully, but the curling fog obliterated most of the scene while the tall masts of the ships moored to our left faded and vanished creakingly into the thick, smoky air.

'Gully, do you think there's any point—'

Even as I spoke there was a sudden clattering and Gully leapt forward. An empty wine cask came rolling at his legs; he hurdled it and then was in close pursuit of McGuire, materializing from behind a stack of drums and casks. I struggled hard to keep up, following them, and I saw Gully reach out, grabbing McGuire's shoulder, causing them both to fall, crashing down heavily and rolling on the damp stone of the quay, fetching up hard against the wall at the end of the quay. There was a brief struggle on the ground before McGuire staggered to his feet, aimed a kick at Gully's head, which was deflected by an arm, and then he was off again, but staggering now, winded and breathing harshly, heading back towards me. Gully lurched to his feet and set off once more in pursuit, as McGuire staggered along the quayside, cannoning into me, thrusting me aside as I vainly tried to grab him, hold him until Gully could arrive. I was no match for a desperate villain: a powerful, flailing blow to my chest sent me to my knees. Gully shouted hoarsely as McGuire ran away from us down the quayside, seeking the safety of the enveloping fog.

Then out of the mist came a group of coal-heavers. They had been paid off, they were half drunk, and they had linked arms in a roistering group. Gully cried out in desperation, 'A guinea if you stop that man!'

It was doubtful if they heard him; it was doubtful if they would have tried to prevent McGuire escaping for they would have sympathy for a running man. But the shout startled McGuire; he swerved, hesitated, glanced around him for an escape route and saw the lighter tied up beside the empty collier. He ran back towards the ballast heavers.

The deck of the collier was riding high beside the lighter, and McGuire ran for it desperately. He jumped down to the lighter deck and then leapt up onto the staging from which the two ballast heavers were working. One of them stopped, startled, swearing in surprise. Almost instinctively he raised the blade of his shovel, swinging it; the flat of the blade caught McGuire on the upper arm. The fugitive cried out in pain but Gully was launching himself down on the deck of the lighter, grabbing at him. McGuire ran along the staging board and leapt for the gunwales of the collier above his head. His fingers took firm purchase; he was a strong man and he dragged himself slowly upwards. Gully cursed behind him, and reached for his legs, trying to pull him back down towards the staging of the tender. There was a long moment when McGuire hung there, kicking violently, before Gully was forced to release him.

The ballast heavers were shouting angrily as McGuire tried to haul himself onto the deck above them but he was weakening, his strength failing him after the struggle with Gully and his flight through the streets. He hung there for several seconds, dangling helplessly, out of Gully's reach but unable to summon up enough strength to drag himself onto the deck of the collier.

I heard Gully yelling a curse. McGuire was

going nowhere: there was no escape route for him on the collier. Then slowly a surge in the black water pushed the tide of the river and it swung the lighter gently out of position. A sudden gap yawned up between the collier and the ballast heavers. They stopped work, waiting until the port hole was accessible again, staring and shouting, swearing at the man dangling six feet above their heads. Gully saw the danger. 'Swing back to the lighter, man – you're not going to make it!'

McGuire laughed almost hysterically, and swore, but his muscles were straining and the gunwales were slippery. His fingers were losing purchase, and he was unable to support the weight of his body, dangling with feet desperately seeking support from the dark, coal-streaked sides of the collier. He glanced downwards, his muscles cracking with the strain, and a grimace of despair twisted his features as he realized Gully was right: he swung his legs to the left and as his hands finally slipped from their grasp on the gunwales, he tried to launch himself sideways, to regain the stage of the lighter. But the river swell had widened the gap, and it was a gap he could not bridge. As his hands slipped he fell, down between the great wall of the collier's hull and the side of the moored lighter.

I heard the violent splash and the cry and,

standing helplessly beside Gully, I peered over the edge of the quay, down to the dark water swirling between the two vessels. McGuire was somewhere down there, flailing in the dark water. Then I realized in horror that the tide was swinging the collier again, slowly, in a long crushing movement against the lighter. We heard the grinding of the hulls, became aware of a sharp scream cut off in the foggy murk, and then the ballast heavers were shocked from their blaspheming into silence.

We all stood there for a little while, as the noise and bustle of the docks swirled around us and a small crowd of curious, chattering half-drunken labourers and sailors gathered about us, but from the dark waters below there was only the occasional gurgle, and slapping sounds as the river lapped against the hulls of collier and lighter.

For a moment I had a vision of another time, of poor Harriet, dragged up from the mud of the river. I wondered where the body of Sam McGuire would finally emerge. I turned, looked at Gully. His features were dark, set grimly. After a few moments his wandering eye swung to mine. His voice had a croaking, depressed tone, as he put into words what I was already thinking.

'That's it, Mr James,' he said. 'The game's over.'

The long, hot summer was over. We had experienced late storms when the skies had turned black and gusts of rain had sheeted down the streets, thunderous, lightning-laden clouds, and startling rainbows appearing over the rooftops. A black man was admitted as a member of the Middle Temple, and barristers began writing openly for the newspapers. The new county courts were now doing much business and my colleagues complained that there were fewer briefs coming their way. And when the coat of the Solicitor General was stolen from the robing room at Lincoln's Inn it was stated bitterly that there was no longer any respect for the old traditions.

But some things continued in the old ways. The open garden area of Leicester Square was still a repository for dead cats, dogs, and dustbins. Drinking houses near the White House restaurant were still the favoured locations of the scum of Europe: Parisian plotters, Italian bomb-makers, forgers, coiners and the army of French, Belgian and German whores. You could still obtain a chop and kidney supper for 1s 4d, and a pint of claret for 1s 6d. And the *Law Times* inveighed against the highly indecorous practice of one member of the Bar who had demonstrated a lack of taste in sitting down in a public house with a policeman and a witness.

And London could still put on a spectacle for the masses.

I always enjoyed pomp and circumstance.

That autumn the procession to open the New Royal Exchange left Buckingham Palace at eleven in the morning to drive along Pall Mall, the Strand, Fleet Street and Cheapside. It was due to reach the Exchange at midday. The streets had been gaily decorated and the sun shone brightly. There were seven state carriages clattering along with the Queen's carriage drawn by the famous eight cream-coloured horses. The Queen wore a diamond tiara and a white ermine mantle and acknowledged the enthusiastic cheers of the crowd with grace and charm, while that pompous uniformed ass Prince Albert sat stiffly at her side, pretending to be a soldier.

The City authorities joined the procession at Temple Bar where the usual ceremony was gone through with the presenting of the keys. My father, as a newly appointed Secondary of the City, took his place in the procession with the other officials. He was clearly proud of his regalia of high buckled shoes, knee breeches and scarlet and gold coat and tricorne hat. He had to march like that to the Exchange. He enjoyed the experience.

The royal party, preceded by the Lord Mayor with his sword of state, then crossed the quadrangle to the ambulatory and went on to Lloyds' Merchants' Room, through the Underwriters' Room to the throne which had been placed in the Reading Room. That's where we all assembled for the Queen to receive the address prepared for the occasion.

Bulstrode was beside himself with happiness. He had accepted the invitation to be present at the official function – my father had arranged that for me – and he'd told all his cronies in Exeter about the honour that was being done him. He had travelled to London by train, dizzy and proud, and could hardly believe that I'd become so friendly as to make use of my family connections in the City to bestow an invitation upon a humble West Country solicitor.

I didn't really have much choice, of course. After the death of Sam McGuire I had been forced to explain to him that our enquiries into the *Running Rein* fiasco were now over: Bentinck was out of reach; we had no evidence against Goodman, we had reached a dead end. Literally, as far as Sam McGuire was concerned.

I explained to him that the money he had handed to me had been expended in a good cause but we had reached a point where we could do no more. Oddly enough, Bulstrode seemed almost relieved about that, and he was not constrained to ask me too closely about precisely how the money he had provided had been spent. He seemed to have forgotten the last paper he'd signed for me, in a drunken stupor. Or perhaps he chose to forget it. He appreciated it when we commiserated with each other, and I was relieved that he was not inclined to add himself to my growing list of pressing creditors. At least, not after I arranged the invitation to the Stock Exchange opening.

After the ceremony was over he expressed his pleasure at the sumptuous *dejeuner* provided in the Underwriters' Room, where places had been laid for over a thousand guests. He joined enthusiastically in the toasts – Her Majesty, Prince Albert, the Royal Family, the Lord Mayor, the City of London – and noted with delight the vivacity with which the Queen joined in the last toast. And all the while his good friend Edwin James was at his elbow, kindly steering him through the protocol, generously urging he take more wine with the chicken, and partridge, and pheasant, and duck, pointing out Lord Clanricarde and Sir Robert Peel, the Archbishop of Canterbury and Lord Wilton, Lord John Russell and the infamous Mr Bright MP.

Lord George Bentinck was also there. At one point our paths crossed and he hesitated, uncertain whether to acknowledge my presence. But he had won, after all, and he was cool enough finally to nod to me condescendingly, with a lift of his elegant eyebrow.

It soured things for me somewhat, but nothing was going to bruise Bulstrode's enjoyment: for him it seemed to be a day of unmitigated happiness, an exhilarating occasion, and when I suggested in the late afternoon that we should take a hired brougham back to Inner Temple Lane, Bulstrode readily agreed. He chattered all the way as we clattered and rumbled back to my chambers. My clerk Villiers was still working there when we arrived, but after I dismissed him I opened a bottle, poured a generous glass of claret for the West Country solicitor. He protested only half-heartedly, before accepting it and settling back in his chair.

We went over the whole sad story for a while. I explained to him there was now no chance that we would ever bring out the truth about the *Running Rein* affair. The horse itself had been put down; the man who might have been forced to tell the truth – McGuire – had been crushed to death at London Docks; and while we might force some admissions out of Cornelius Smith, it was highly unlikely that Porky Clark – who knew as much as anyone about the business – would turn Queen's Evidence against his paymaster, Lewis Goodman. We had come to an impasse. And as for the murder of Joe Bartle, while we could hazard a guess whose hand was behind it, we would never be able to prove it in a court of law.

Bulstrode seemed largely unconcerned; he waved it all aside in a happy, inebriated haze. There were always winners and losers, he opined generously, and on this occasion it seemed we had lost, but no matter. There would be other times – a rogue like Goodman would slip up one of these fine days. And when I poured him some more claret and off-handedly explained that there were still some outstanding expenses to be covered, laid out in our noble endeavour to get at the truth Bulstrode waved his glass grandiosely. 'No problem, my dear Mr James. If you come back to my lodgings with me I'll let you have a bill immediately. It's been a splendid partnership, splendid – and this has been a most splendid and memorable day.'

Satisfactory, at least, was how I saw it, thinking back that evening as I attended the Waverley Dress Ball at Willis's Rooms. Of late I had realized it was futile to continue thrashing over the whole affair in my mind. I had to be philosophical about the whole thing: I was certain Bentinck had arranged the abduction and killing of the colt and that Goodman had arranged the death of Bartle. But how it all linked together ... I had to leave it, set it aside. I had to get on with my life, and my career – there were other matters to turn to: a commission in lunacy at the Court of Chancery in a few days' time, a conspiracy case in Queen's Bench, and a prosecution arising out of a fatal accident at the Blackfriars Bridge steamboat pier.

There was also the matter of a famous actress who was asking me to represent her in a breach of promise case, and the criminal conversation hearing where I drew out the fact that ex-Inspector Field, now turned private detective, had observed the guilty couple by boring a hole in the bedroom wall with a gimlet ... a great sensation in court, and the briefs were rolling in.

Thoughts about Bentinck still smarted, but it was time to put it all behind me.

Also, oddly enough, my creditors had fallen quiet. I was pleased about that, though a little puzzled. Persons of that kind were always dunning for their cash, and there was a considerable amount of my paper in the City, up for payment or renewal.

But that evening I had no cares. The ballroom was crowded with the rank and fashion of the metropolis. There were numerous people I knew and I moved among them, a word here, a joke there, receiving the occasional invitation to a weekend dinner party. It was always my *forte*, you know, invitations from lonely ladies whose husbands were away in the hunting field. I had a way with me, Society was my scene, I was welcomed for my wit, my banter, my unending good humour. Oh, yes. That evening I managed to claim dances with a number of ladies of fashion, who were only too pleased to take my hand while their husbands were elsewhere. They were still intrigued by my sudden fame as a result of my performance at the *Running Rein* trial, and the crim con case.

When the procession formed for the monster quadrille, it was led by the Marchioness of Londonderry. I found myself partner to Lady Adeline de Horsey: I remember she told me a most amusing story about seeing her father with his mistress at the Prince's Theatre – from which she herself had been banned for outrageous conduct.

In the *salon de danse* no fewer than twenty-six sets were danced that evening; in the supper room Scotch reels and country dances were kept up with spirit. I took part in much of the activity, dancing with various ladies, usually married: two of them were arch enough to tease me with a suggested rendezvous. And late in the evening, a little past midnight I first came face to face with a certain Miss Marianne Edge. The name is familiar to you: that's right. The lady who some years later became my first wife.

I thought she was quite attractive. She was wearing a pale blue ball gown whose *décolletage* revealed a creamy neck and bosom. Her eyes seemed to have darkened with excitement and pleasure, and there was a delightful flush to her cheek. The only drawback from my point of view was that she was on the arm of her fiancé, none other than Lieutenant Crosier Hilliard. Someone should have warned her then: in the contemplation of marriage, a large income is immensely preferable to a luxuriant set of whiskers.

But then, as I understood it, she came from a banking family, so money was no problem.

Hilliard made the introductions, somewhat reluctantly, I noted. I planted a kiss on her gloved hand, gallantly, while his own eye wandered about the room. He seemed distracted. I chatted for a while with Miss Edge – the first of many such conversations that were to occur over the years, until we married, when conversations became screaming quarrels – but finally I turned to the gallant hussar.

'So, Hilliard, you seen anything of our friend Grenwood?'

Our mutual friend, and a man who owed

me money.

Hilliard's whiskers quivered and he turned his attention to me, frowning slightly. 'Hadn't you heard?'

'What?'

'Surely you will have heard he's taken himself off to France?'

'Ah...' I hadn't been to my club recently; I hadn't heard the news. 'His debts, I presume. So his father, Lord Havermere, refused to bail him out.'

'That's about the size of it,' Crosier Hilliard muttered uneasily.

'Leaving Lieutenant Hilliard also in the lurch,' Miss Edge added somewhat frostily.

Crosier Hilliard shuffled awkwardly and glanced at his fiancée. 'Come, come, my dear, I'm sure Grenwood will come up trumps in the end.'

'Not unless he returns to the jurisdiction here in England,' she sniffed. 'Oh, you men,' she exclaimed impatiently, glancing at me and shaking her head. 'You protect each other, you dissemble, you won't face up to facts. I know that Grenwood and you, Crosier, were involved in some heavy gambling together. And now Grenwood's fled to France to avoid his debts.' She turned her dark eyes full upon me. 'My father has had a long discussion with me about it, and I'm being told that I should not worry my pretty head about such things. But I have the feeling there is something most discreditable about the whole affair.'

She clearly disapproved of our fleeing friend, and felt that Grenwood was a gambler who drank too much and spent too much time in the West End, maintaining discreditable companions, perhaps like me, and was seen too often in low company.

That was the first time I met her, as I said. And though she attracted me, I should have recognized there and then that Marianne Edge was the kind of woman who could cause trouble to a man. Strong-willed, determined, albeit with plenty of tin behind her. But, years later, when I followed Grenwood's example and fled to France, and she proposed to marry me, well, I suppose it was a question of any port in a storm. And there was also her fortune, of course...

The conversation lagged after her sharply stated comments. After a few more stiff minutes I took my leave and moved away. I caught sight of her in the crowd again later. She was dancing with her fiancé. The gallant hussar, and the banker's daughter. They made a splendid couple. She drove him to drink, eventually.

I called for my cloak at two in the morning and went out into the night air. I decided to walk back to my chambers, rather than take a hansom cab. At that time in the morning, the air was cool and the sky above me was bright with stars. There were people enough about: Catherine Street prostitutes still plying their trade under the gas lamps, boisterous drunks, an assortment of men about town moving from one night house to another. I walked slowly through the Haymarket, ignoring the offers made to me, and proceeded down towards Trafalgar Square and the Strand. I strolled along easily enough, swinging my silver-headed stick, hardly aware of where I was walking. I was thinking about the events of the last few weeks, aware I'd probably never get my money back from Lester Grenwood, or obtain my revenge on Bentinck.

But I thought also of the good things in my life: I was enjoying my celibate state for there were women enough to satisfy my desires without contemplating marriage, unlike poor Hilliard who I suspected was chewing upon more than he'd be able to digest. My briefs were becoming more numerous; after certain discreet but flirtatious conversations at the ball that evening it was clear I would be getting opportunities for Friday to Sunday stays in country houses; there was good companionship to be obtained at White's even if I was blackballed from the Carlton, and there was always the Liberal Party to think about as a stepping stone for my ambitions...

A sudden surge of euphoria came over me,

and I carelessly swung my stick, striking it against iron railings, jarring my wrist. The sudden pain brought me back to an awareness of my surroundings. I was in Savoy Place, only a short walk now from the Temple, and the dimly lit street was quiet, echoing and empty. Even from the river the sounds of traffic were muted, apart from the occasional warning bull horn as late moving barges made their way downstream to Greenwich. But I also felt a prickling on the back of my neck.

I suddenly had the feeling I was not alone. I knew well enough the dangers of the London streets after dark. I had already seen and even defended enough garrotters in the courts, dealt with more than a few bug-hunters, the loafers who hung around street corners and quiet alleyways in the hope of stealing from drunks. I was far from inebriated myself, and I had my sturdy cane: I slid my hand down its length, reversing it so that the heavy knobbed silver grip was available as a clubbing device.

There were two of them, I guessed: one, a light, soft, almost confident, swinging step, the other heavier, a menacing shuffle a little to his rear. I made no attempt to look behind me; I slowed, then turned right, heading towards the river and Temple Gardens. Only when I finally stepped under a gaslight did I turn, looked behind me.

They came out of the darkness of the narrow street. The first man was tall, elegant in his stride, and smartly dressed. As he came up towards me I could see the black gleam of his hat, the flash of silken white at his throat. A moment later I saw the hulking figure of the other man, a few feet behind. For a few seconds I stood there puzzled, and then I recognized the heavy man from his build: I'd seen him often enough, stripped and bloodied at the prize fights. But he hung back now, shoulders hunched almost deferentially, as the first man approached me.

'Good evening, Mr James.'

It was Lewis Goodman.

A cold ball of fear hardened in my chest. Ben Gully had warned me about this man. My lips were dry, as I snapped, 'You've been following me, sir?'

'Merely taking the night air,' Goodman said, slowing as he approached me. Under the gaslight he stopped, and flashed me a confident smile. His cold eyes glittered as he looked me up and down with an irritating condescension. 'But it's well met, for all that. I've been meaning to call on you soon, perhaps at your chambers, to talk about various things but was, well, reluctant to be seen there. We need not discuss the reasons. The fact is, when Porky saw you strolling along past Willis's he came back into my club in The Quadrant and told me. We came out, guessed you were on the way to your chambers, caught up with you ... and here we are.'

I hesitated, turned and Goodman fell into step beside me as I began to walk again towards Temple Place. I was still not relieved: my breathing was tight in my chest, my heart thudding painfully.

'What is it you want with me?' I demanded, gripping my stick tightly.

'Just a word. In the main, to thank you.'

'You've nothing to thank me for.'

Lewis Goodman chuckled: there was genuine pleasure in the sound. 'But I do. For the sterling manner in which you performed at the Exchequer Court, of course – even though the event ended unhappily, it was not because of any failing on your part. You fought most valiantly. But more importantly, I feel I should also thank you for removing from me the necessity of dealing with Mr McGuire.'

I stopped, and stared at him. 'Are you saying–?'

'My dear man, you've been a great help. I was in a certain quandary about McGuire. You see, I have a reputation to maintain, the man had deceived me, and I can't really allow that sort of thing to occur, not without taking retribution. But it was really too much trouble, going about the business of tracing him...' He paused, smiling at me knowingly. 'But it seems you have contacts of your own, Mr James. A certain Ben Gully, I believe ... and as I say, you saved me trouble, and all's well that ends well.'

'I can't say it's ended well for McGuire,' I snarled. 'Or for me.'

'No?' There was a note of mocking surprise in Goodman's voice. 'You should look at both sides of the balance sheet, Mr James. The *Running Rein* business has brought you to the notice of the public, solicitors are beginning to send more briefs to you; you are launched on what I trust will be a glittering career–'

'But I failed to discover – and expose – the truth behind the whole dirty business. Not least the part played in it by you and that damned Lord George Bentinck!' The bile rose in my throat, making me almost incoherent. 'McGuire knew about it – the ringer, you, Bentinck, but now he's dead–'

'Not at *my* hand, Mr James,' Goodman interrupted me softly.

We were both silent for a while as I digested the implications of what he said. But anger still stirred in my veins. 'But what about Joe Bartle?' I demanded hotly, rashly ignoring the menacing hulk of Porky Clark in the darkness. 'Why did you have to kill him?'

There was a short silence. Lewis Goodman

stared at me, then turned his head to glance back to his companion, and laughed softly. He raised his head, looked about him at the starry sky, as though in contemplation. Then he nodded, and his white teeth seemed to flash in light from the gaslight above our heads. 'Ah, well, I suppose you have a certain right in demanding to learn what really happened in all this business. I think probably you've already guessed most of it.'

'So tell me!'

Goodman laughed again 'Well, the colt, you'll know all about that now, since I understand you were there when the animal was exhumed. Yes, *Running Rein* was a ringer, brought over from Ireland. I sold him to the corn merchant, laid some propitious bets, and did quite well out of the business. But Baron Alderson's proposal, that, I admit, was something I had not expected. I mean, bringing a horse into the courtroom!'

'It would have scuppered you, I imagine,' I sneered. 'Having your fraud exposed.'

'Hmm, yes.' Goodman nodded in reflection, seemed suddenly thoughtful. 'It could have been embarrassing, but in the event the matter was taken out of my hands.'

'So it *was* Bentinck!'

Goodman shrugged. 'As you must have guessed, it had to be *one* of us. And it wasn't me.' He paused, nodding. 'A man of great arrogance, and pride, Lord George. He'd pushed for the barring of the colt before the race because of his suspicions – and his general distrust of my involvement. And after the race he pressed Colonel Peel into welshing – not that it was of great consequence to me. I'd spread my betting in convenient ways. Of course, Bentinck thought that Mr Wood, our corn merchant, would be more of a gentleman than to go to court. But he was wrong. And then the hearing did not proceed as he might have wished. Not least, your tactics – they were yours, weren't they? I noted that your leader, Mr Cockburn, was keeping his own head down. Too much to lose, perhaps. I hear he may soon be taking up a judicial appointment.'

I made no comment on my leader's motives in leaving me to the lions. 'And when Baron Alderson demanded production of the colt?'

'Arrogance, pride ... and doubt,' Goodman murmured, almost to himself. 'Lord George was in a dilemma: he had to face the possibility that he might have been wrong about the age of the animal. Or that the veterinarian surgeon might have been suborned. Which I would probably have managed, I admit. It would have done Bentinck's reputation no good to have been ridiculed further in court. You had already done a good job in that respect ... but if he was shown to have been wrong all the time...'

'So he paid Sam McGuire to steal the horse, and get rid of it.'

'A somewhat foolish and reckless idea, but it worked, I suppose, and brought the proceedings to an end. And, oddly enough, although it was Lord George's doing, it served my purposes well enough, too. On the other hand, it was also an act of betrayal by my servant Sam McGuire. I couldn't allow him to escape scot-free after betraying me for Bentinck's tin. That's why I was looking for him, though only half-heartedly, I admit. Not certain what to do about him, you see.'

He paused, glanced back at Porky Clark, hovering behind him. He raised an elegantly gloved hand, beckoned the pugilist forward into the gaslight. Porky Clark stood before us, his head down. His eyes were swollen, I noticed, and there was a large lump on the line of his jaw. He also moved awkwardly, dragging his right leg slightly. They were not injuries he had received in the ring.

'Bentinck suborned McGuire but the stableman drew in my hired man in addition. Foolish.' His cold eyes swept over the hang-dog prizefighter. 'I could make the stupid Learned Pig recognize the error of his ways, betraying me for a fistful of tin. As you see, he has already paid for his part in the business. He'll not let me down again.'

All this failed to clear the whole picture for me. 'But you still wanted to pay back

McGuire. And what did Joe Bartle have to do with it all? Was it McGuire who killed Bartle? And why did Bartle have to die?'

Goodman was silent for a little while. We resumed our walking. The sound of our steps on the cobbled street echoed against darkened doorways. After a moment Goodman chuckled, and shook his head. 'You do scrabble your fingers into all sorts of pies, don't you, young man?' He cocked his handsome head, glanced at me. 'No, it wasn't McGuire who beat Bartle to death.'

'You?' I demanded. 'Was it you, then? Or ... or was it Bentinck, or on his orders?' I was thinking furiously. 'It *must* have been Bentinck's doing! After we found Bartle's body in the sewers I laid an information at Bow Street but it was not proceeded with! Inspector Redfern came to see me, hinted that someone had influenced the Commissioner to step aside from the murder, pursue it less than zealously. Only Bentinck could have been the one who had the power and influence to do that, pulled strings on a marionette–'

'No, not Bentinck,' Goodman interrupted me in a quiet tone. 'That was me.'

'But how–?'

'It's not only members of the aristocracy who can pull strings, Mr James. You've been to my clubs, haunted my night houses. You know the kind of people who go there to gamble, to seek whores, to indulge in some of the most curious practices one might ever see, in privately hired rooms away from the vulgar gaze. One of them is our revered Commissioner. But the fact is, there are always eyes ... behind mirrors, at keyholes, drilled spy holes in ceilings...'

'The Commissioner–'

'Knows when discretion is the better part of valour in the pursuit of his ends.' Casually, Goodman suddenly linked his arm through mine and we strolled forward together, matching steps. 'Yes, it was I who persuaded the Commissioner to put a brake on Inspector Redfern. It required only a gentle hint, an anonymous note... But in any case, Bartle's death, it had nothing to do with the matter of the unfortunate *Running Rein.*'

'I remain to be persuaded of that,' I replied stiffly.

We were close to Temple Court. Goodman was silent for a little while. Then he clucked his tongue gently. 'You're a remarkable man, Mr James, a fine, witty, aggressive advocate. You'll be a capital man with a jury, but sometimes you have, shall we say, an unfortunate predilection to dogma. An idea gets into your head, you form an impression about a man's character – and you can't move away from it, to see the truth.' He glanced at me, a wicked gleam in his eye. 'I promise you, I had nothing to do with the killing of Joe Bartle.'

'I don't believe you.'

'That's of little consequence,' Goodman replied, taking no offence. His dark eyes remained fixed on me, his hand still clamped on my elbow. 'The fact is, Mr Bartle had a sister.'

'So?'

'You'll have heard Bartle was somewhat distracted at the stables on the Wednesday before the trial. When McGuire checked with him on that day, to make sure he would stick to the agreed story at the hearing, he announced he wouldn't be attending. He had other things to do. He was on the look-out for the man who had seduced his sister.'

I stopped dead. I turned, stared at Goodman. He smiled. 'That's right. The unfortunate girl had got herself pregnant. And the ... gentleman, he was disinclined to do anything about it. Bartle was furious. He sought him out, unsuccessfully. Badgered him in the street. Made a nuisance of himself. Finally tracked him down at Hampstead Heath, on the Sunday.' Goodman's fingers tightened on my arm. 'It turned out to be a most unpleasant business. The girl, you see, ended up in the river, I'm told.'

Harriet.

There was a cold stone lying in my chest.

Lewis Goodman smiled. 'No, Bartle's

323

death had nothing to do with me, or Mc-Guire, or even the *Running Rein* business. It was simply what might be described as a *family* matter.'

'What happened?' I demanded hoarsely.

Goodman shrugged diffidently. 'Bartle approached the gentleman in question on the Heath. On Sunday. They had words, there was a scuffle. Bartle was beside himself with rage. I intervened, my friends held Bartle back, and I persuaded the said gentleman to leave with me, go back to London. But within two miles, on a deserted road, our carriage horse went lame. Bartle caught up with us. Further words were exchanged.'

He glanced back over his shoulder to the hulking man behind us. 'Porky and I, we saw it all. Poor Bartle, a strong man, but he stood little chance. Our gentleman friend, much incensed by the diatribe launched at him by Bartle, lost his temper I fear. Clubbed the man to death, there in that lonely road.'

Astonished, I said, 'You stood by and let it happen?'

Goodman's tone changed slightly, hardened. 'It was none of my business, James. And none of yours.'

'The sewer—'

'Porky organised that,' Goodman replied carelessly, 'while I took the gentleman back to The Quadrant for an evening's entertainment.' He paused, chuckled. 'You might ask why I helped the person in question. You must understand me, James. It was not my business, but on the other hand when something like that happens there might come a day when information of that kind might come in useful.'

I stopped, glared at him coldly. 'So Lester Grenwood has made his way to France not just to escape his debts. He wants to avoid your blackmail, also!'

Goodman stared at me, and I became aware of a slow smile stealing across his handsome, shadowed features. 'Well, well, well, Mr James. You surprise me. So you've guessed the identity ... you know more about this business than I suspected. I shall have to keep an eye on you, shan't I?'

There was a certain admiration in his tone that offended me. Porky Clark was still hovering in the background, menacingly, but my rash temper got the better of me. 'You stood by and watched Grenwood beat that poor man to death. What's to prevent me laying an information now, against you, as well as that bastard Grenwood?'

There was a brief silence. On the river a foghorn moaned eerily; the gas lamps at Temple Court flared and I could hear the early morning traffic, wagons and carts bearing produce for the markets, rattling across Waterloo Bridge. I had a sudden vision of a warm, sad-eyed girl, pleading in the Cider Cellars, but the memory was swiftly overlaid by the remembrance of a sodden, dripping corpse being pulled out of the river at Wapping. I laughed bitterly. A mad fury seized me. 'You're so damned confident, Goodman. But you've made a mistake with me. Don't you realize now you've told me the whole story you've put yourself in jeopardy? You've now admitted to me that you entered a criminal conspiracy to defraud; and you've admitted to being an accessory to the murder of Joe Bartle. I could tell this story in court with great fluency—'

'But you won't, will you?' Goodman interrupted in a soft but menacing tone. 'Your word against mine, that's all there is.'

'The word of a gentleman,' I said hotly, 'against a gambling whoreson who'd sell—'

'Ah, *doucement*, Mr James. We won't talk too much about gambling, will we? Tut, tut,' Goodman admonished, gripping my arm tightly. 'And you really should be more careful, speaking that way about your major creditor.'

I was stunned for a moment. 'Creditor? I've borrowed nothing from you! What are you—'

'I've been watching you, Mr James. I have rather admired your determination and perspicacity. In the courtroom, and outside. So I've been asking around...' Goodman smiled gently. 'Have you not noticed that your creditors have fallen away, recently? Have you not asked yourself why?'

'I–'

'It's because I recently decided to buy up all your paper in the market. There really is rather a lot of it, isn't there?' He smiled, wolfishly. 'You really have been chancing your hand at the tables. Chicken hazard, in particular, I believe. But I admire you, and your splendid work at the bar, and who knows, I might need the services of an eminent lawyer some time in the future. My profession is a somewhat, ah ... shall we say, precarious one. Yes, I've bought up your paper, Mr James, but I don't intend calling it in. Not as long as you ... shall we say ... behave sensibly?'

The fury in my chest raged, and I half raised my stick. The figure of Porky Clark moved forward, lurching menacingly in the dimness behind Goodman. Then slowly the rage in my blood cooled. I realized the implications of Goodman's comment. He held my paper: if he called it in at once he could ruin me. I took a deep breath, and was silent.

Goodman stared at me for a long while. Behind him, Porky Clark's breath rasped harshly in the still air as he waited, powerful shoulders hunched, for a word from his master. At last Goodman nodded, almost casually. 'We'll leave it there then – understanding each other.' He turned his head. 'I think we've escorted Mr James far enough, Porky. We'll walk back to the Haymarket, now.'

He touched his hat with his cane, turned and began to stroll back towards Savoy Place. I glared at his receding figure with feelings of rage mingled with impotence.

Suddenly Goodman stopped, looked back and laughed. 'By the way, you'll be hearing from some of my friends soon. Gentlemen in difficulty, one might say. The briefs they bring will help you; they'll be fat, even though you might not care too much for the clientele.' He laughed again, the sound echoing eerily down the dark streets. 'But I'm also a gambling man, Mr James. Never let it be said I will play only if I hold all the high cards. I'll give you a chance to recover some of your financial standing. The truth is I put *two* ringers in the Derby – *Running Rein* and *Lysander*. I did well out of the business. Well, take my advice. Put as much money as you can on *The Trickster*, in the Chester Cup next week.'

The echo of his laughter seemed to ring back at me long after the man had disappeared into the gloom.

And you know, my boy, I was so incensed that I failed to take his advice. I placed no wager on *The Trickster*. Not that it would have cleared all my debts anyway. But it would have helped.

Anyway, that's how it all began. It's a matter of record: my meteoric rise in the courts, on the back of the *Running Rein* case, and the clients that Goodman sent me, rogues and villains all, but prepared to pay well for my services. My swift rise, and my even more meteoric fall some years later. Which, after my American adventures, finally brought me back to England, to this humble lodging house, with that miserable housemaid...

So there it is... But you know, things are never what they seem. You think you have all the answers, and then something occurs to confound you again, wonder whether you really have got to the truth. It was a week later that my clerk Villiers came into my chambers, dumped a pile of law reports on my desk and then stood there, hesitated. 'By the way, Mr James, did you see that report in *The Times* today?'

'What report?'

'The Chester Cup, at Chester. It was won by a horse called *The Trickster.*'

And I'd put no money on it. I scowled. 'So?'

Villiers chuckled. 'Lord George Bentinck was running a horse in the same race. Apparently he started that old song all over again.'

'What song?'

'You know, claiming the race was won unfairly. He shouted that the horse that came in first – *The Trickster* – was a ringer.'

After what Goodman had told me I had little doubt on that score.

'Moreover,' Villiers continued, 'he averred that it bore a more than remarkable resemblance to the horse that won the Derby.'

'What?'

Villiers nodded. 'That's right. You know, sir. *Running Rein.*'

Afterword

I have no reason to doubt most of what my stepfather told me that night in 1881, for a large part of what he recounted can be confirmed from other, published sources. His account certainly clears up a number of mysteries that surrounded the running of the Derby in 1844.

I consider it well to point out however that his story would not have been completely accurate in all its details: many who were his *confidantes* over the years considered him to be a good companion, but one somewhat inclined to boast and exaggerate his exploits. Indeed, I have been informed often enough (even by my mother) that Mr James was above all an amoral rogue, but no more of that.

The events he described to me that evening over several pints of porter had occurred some forty years earlier and no doubt some of his comments were affected by the hazy memory of an elderly man. For instance, the discovery of Harriet's body could not have taken place on the day the Lord Mayor's barge collided with Westminster Bridge since that event occurred in September 1844, not

July. As for Mr James seeing 'Tony' Trollope in the Cider Cellars it is worth noting that Mr Trollope was never known as 'Tony'. However, his account of the *Running Rein* trial may be confirmed by newspaper reports, although oddly enough he is mistaken in stating Sir Fitzroy Kelly was Solicitor General at that time. The post was actually held by Sir Frederick Thesiger, who was later elevated to the position of Lord Chancellor.

He was not inaccurate in stating that while a Member of Parliament he was with Guiseppe Garibaldi on the march to Rome, indeed an engraving of him in Garibaldi's camp appeared in the *Illustrated London News*. Charles Dickens certainly lampooned Mr James in *A Tale of Two Cities;* Lewis Goodman was a well-known villain with important underworld connections, and Mr James assuredly reached later career heights as a Queen's Counsel in his Old Bailey practice. There was also considerable newspaper rumour to the effect that when my stepfather was MP in the Liberal cause for the important seat of Marylebone, his name was known to have been put forward in 1860 to become Solicitor General, only for the appointment to be blocked on the advice of Prince Albert.

And perhaps, in view of his aversion to reading, he can be excused for referring to

Mr Wilkie Collins's sensation novel as *The Moonshine*. A mere slip of the tongue. It was entitled, of course, *The Moonstone*.

But I need to stress that in 1881 Mr James was, after all, an old, forgetful and boastful man looking back over a successful though ultimately scandalous career that many have suggested had been a waste of considerable talent. On the other hand, throughout my long conversations with him I was left with the impression that, wasteful or not, Mr James had really rather enjoyed his life.

Joachim Stocqueler
Master mariner
1881

The publishers hope that this book has given you enjoyable reading. Large Print Books are especially designed to be as easy to see and hold as possible. If you wish a complete list of our books please ask at your local library or write directly to:

Magna Large Print Books
Magna House, Long Preston,
Skipton, North Yorkshire.
BD23 4ND

This Large Print Book, for people
who cannot read normal print,
is published under the auspices of

THE ULVERSCROFT FOUNDATION

... we hope you have enjoyed this book.
Please think for a moment about those
who have worse eyesight than you ...
and are unable to even read or enjoy
Large Print without great difficulty.

You can help them by sending a
donation, large or small, to:

**The Ulverscroft Foundation,
1, The Green, Bradgate Road,
Anstey, Leicestershire, LE7 7FU,
England.**
or request a copy of our brochure for
more details.

The Foundation will use all donations
to assist those people who are visually
impaired and need special attention
with medical research, diagnosis
and treatment.

Thank you very much for your help.